and
Italy

BOOKS BY SUE ROBERTS

My Big Greek Summer
My Very Italian Holiday

You, Me and Italy

SUE ROBERTS

Bookouture

Published by Bookouture in 2019

An imprint of StoryFire Ltd.

Carmelite House
50 Victoria Embankment
London EC4Y 0DZ

www.bookouture.com

ISBN: 978-1-78681-756-3
eBook ISBN: 978-1-78681-755-6

Previously published as *My Summer of Love and Limoncello*

To all the readers of this book.

Prologue

I enter the Daily Discount Store in the city centre and spot a heaving queue at the checkout, with Sally, one of the cashiers, struggling to keep up. I glance at Till 3, which is temporarily out of use.

'Isn't Laura meant to be on the tills today?' I ask Sally, recalling the weekly work rota.

'She is. She went to the toilets ages ago and seems to have gone AWOL,' she huffs, scanning a multipack of Coke from a sullen-looking teenage girl with heavily kohl-rimmed eyes.

'Mike, can you jump on Till Two?' I plead to one of our new recruits, a gangly eighteen-year-old college student, who's stacking boxes of teabags in a nearby aisle.

'Er, yeah, sure. I've only been shown how to use the till once though.' He shrugs.

'You'll be fine. Sally's on the next till if you have any problems.'

Sally plasters a fake smile on her face, while muttering something under her breath about only having one pair of hands.

It's mid June and there's a summer sale on with a lot of already low-priced goods now reduced even further, with paddling pools, glow-in-the-dark Prosecco glasses and unicorn lifesavers flying out of the door at a rate of knots. Store owner Harry, who's also my husband, likes to keep the shop packed to the rafters with bargain goods. He's always one to spot a deal and the storeroom is already piled high with merchandise for the winter season, including Halloween and Christmas. With Mike seemingly handling the till OK, I go in search of Harry.

'Hi, Maisie,' says Jane, one of the staff, her blonde ponytail swinging as she carries a box of glittery bags to the gift-wrapping aisle. 'I thought it was your day off today.'

'It is. I just need to talk to Harry. He's not answering his mobile. Is he about?'

'Umm… not sure. I saw him earlier but I think he might have nipped out.'

I make my way along the store to the offices at the back. He's probably on the phone, trying to secure a deal for a job lot of something or other. He's a master of negotiation, which is why the shop is usually overflowing with stock. Some of it's easier to shift than others, even with a thirty per cent discount. There isn't much demand for neon-coloured false eyelashes around here, unless you're going on one of those 1980s revival weekends.

I walk into his office but he's nowhere to be seen. There's a half-full mug of coffee on his desk, so I figure he can't be far. I smile at a framed photo on his desk, which shows us both laughing and wearing party hats, Harry blowing a hooter at last year's Christmas party.

Turning left, out of the office, I notice a light on in the stockroom. I twist the handle, but find the door locked. Luckily, I'm a keyholder, so I let myself inside. I think I can hear a faint noise so I walk round the corner, passing cardboard boxes full to the brim of stock, until I am face to face with a pair of giant inflatable Santas.

I don't think the noise is coming from them. Not unless I'm losing my mind. I tentatively creep forward, before parting the smiling six-foot Santas and almost passing out.

Because Laura from Till 3 is there with Harry. And it definitely isn't the stock that they are checking out. The colour drains out of my face and my legs turn to jelly. I want to throw up. As my heart cracks in two, I realise that my life is over.

Chapter One

'So you think I'm depressed then?'

I'm sitting in my local doctor's surgery facing Dr Jazeera, a pleasant, round-faced man with a charming smile and a set of alarmingly white teeth. The surgery is decorated with Zen posters and wooden Hindi sculptures. *Let your soul shine with happiness* screams the large purple poster on the cream wall.

'It would seem so.' Dr Jazeera nods.

'But I don't feel depressed.' I have felt a little anxious about everything lately though, which is why I made the doctor's appointment in the first place. The anxiety can sometimes be the beginning of a dark phase – and I really don't want to go there…

'What do you think depression feels like?' Dr Jazeera is trying not to smile, but he just has one of those naturally jolly faces. I imagine it must be quite difficult for him to deliver bad news to a patient without appearing joyful.

I shrug.

'The thing is, Maisie,' he says gently. 'From the answers you have given on the questionnaire I gave you to fill in, it seems that you don't have much enthusiasm for life at the moment.'

'Probably just recent circumstances.' I sigh, thinking about what I've been through in the last two years.

'I've known you long enough to know that you're not quite yourself. I've witnessed your bouts of depression over the years, remember?' Doc smiles gently. 'There's a misconception about depression. It doesn't always involve sitting around in your night-clothes in floods of tears.'

I've done that too, I think to myself.

'It can present as anxiety and a feeling of being a bit detached from the world. Sustained bouts of stress can indeed lead to depression, so you've done the right thing by coming to see me now before things really take hold.'

So it seems I was sensible to make the appointment. My mother died two years ago, eighteen months before my marriage folded. It was the bleakest of times. In a way I was pleased that she hadn't been around to see the breakdown of my marriage as she would have worried about me. She was happy when I married Harry and thought he would 'look after me', taken in by his charming, self-assured exterior. If only she'd seen what really lay behind it. If only I had...

I barely slept after Mum died. I went to stay in my family home with Dad in the nights following her death, and was able to glean some comfort from sleeping in my old bedroom, the sights and smells of my old home so familiar. I couldn't stay there forever though. I was a married woman.

When I returned to my house in Crosby, I felt as though everything was unravelling. Dr Jazeera prescribed some sleeping tablets for me at the time, with a warning that they could only be used on a temporary basis. True to his word I was never given a repeat prescription and that's when I bought a dream catcher. Sounds silly, I know, but when strands of sunlight flickered through the window in the morning it brought me some comfort. It was as if Mum was watching over me.

I pulled my thoughts back to the present. 'So, can you do anything to help me, Doctor?'

'Hopefully, yes. If I could write prescriptions to give all my patients a month's holiday in the sun, that's what I would do. Sunshine has healing properties as well as a healthy amount of Vitamin D. But, as I can't prescribe a sun-drenched holiday for you, I suggest you try some antidepressants for a while.'

'Surely depression can't be cured by a holiday in the sun?'

'Well, of course it depends on the circumstances, but if the depression is stress-related then it could certainly help. A long holiday in the sun can be quite therapeutic. But, as your question-naire seems to indicate high levels of anxiety as well as a general apathy, I certainly think a prescription for some medication is the way forward. Modern antidepressants can help a lot.' Dr Jazeera clicks a printer that whirrs and spits out a green prescription slip. 'And try to find something you enjoy,' he says. 'All work and no play isn't good for anyone.'

Maybe I should emigrate to Australia. There's plenty of sunshine there, although I'm not sure that I could cope with the spiders. And don't they have the highest incidence of skin cancer in the world? There's always a downside.

I think about Dr Jazeera's comments. Could my anxiety be stress-related? I don't particularly *feel* stressed, although perhaps those close to me would disagree. These days I can't seem to tolerate noisy eaters, barking dogs, people loudly blowing their nose, and a plethora of other everyday nuances that ordinarily I would ignore. I went shopping with my friend Emma last week and while I normally find her dithering over which dress to buy amusing, this time it grated on my nerves somewhat. Not that I'd ever let on how I was feeling. I've become very good at plastering a smile on my face and never revealing my innermost thoughts.

'Thanks, Doctor,' I say, as I place the prescription in my bag.

I don't want everyone knowing I'm on medication, so I decide that I'll call in at the chemist's in the town centre tomorrow, rather than at the chemist's in the local shopping parade, where the assistant behind the counter is not exactly the soul of discretion. Last time I was in there she was discussing with a colleague, in a not-so-quiet voice, how a methadone programme had worked wonders on a former addict who had just left the shop.

I don't know why I should feel embarrassed about people knowing I'm taking anti- depressants. Everyone's supposed to talk about how they're feeling these days, aren't they? People are positively encouraged to share their innermost thoughts. No one will judge you… If only that were true. Definitely best to keep things to myself for the moment.

After a hard shift at work, I climb the metal staircase to my flat and flop down onto the sofa. I never expected to be renting a tiny one-bedroomed flat above a sandwich shop, which is all I can afford these days. But I didn't have much choice after Harry and I split up and we ended up losing the house. Apparently the shops had been losing money for a long time and massive rent increases in the city certainly hadn't helped.

My new job is really handy for work as I am employed by Our Daily Bread, the most popular sandwich shop in the area. It's hard to believe that less than a year ago I was living in a fashionable area of Crosby, a mile up the road, in a smart three-bedroomed house. When I looked out of my bedroom window I could glimpse the sparkling sea and the outline of Antony Gormley's iron men on the beach, a set of mysterious-looking bronze sculptures that sit in the water gazing out across the Irish Sea.

These days my window gives a view of Supersavers across the road or 'the ten-o'clock shop' as it's known locally. Even though it's open until 10 p.m., I would never venture out at that time of night as it's the hangout for local teenagers, usually asking older shoppers if they will buy them some beer or cigarettes.

I sigh as I look round the sparsely furnished lounge. I was married to Harry Knight, who at ten years older than me I thought I would be with for the rest of my life. My 'Knight' in shining armour, as I thought of him. He was a self-made businessman, tall, fair-haired and well-groomed, in a slightly flash sort of way. He has twinkling blue eyes *à la* Paul Hollywood and a cosmetically enhanced smile that can light up a room.

I met him when I was at university in Liverpool and worked part-time in one of his shops, of which he had several dotted around the city. He was charming, witty and attentive and when he offered me a job as shop manager in one of his larger stores, all thoughts of finishing university flew out of the window – I was so excited to get on the career ladder.

Plus I was struggling a little with university life, if I'm completely honest. I found myself unable to switch off, thoughts of coursework swirling around my head at bedtime preventing me from sleeping. As the winter progressed and sleep still didn't come, I became a neurotic mess. One bleak January day, sitting on a bench at the Pier Head overlooking the River Mersey, I began to question everything in life. Strange thoughts enveloped me as I began to wonder what it would feel like to slide under the foamy waves of the river and disappear into another world. When I returned home freezing cold later that afternoon, my mother took one look at me and chaperoned me to the doctor's. Dr Jazeera prescribed some medication, just as he had done five years previously, when a surge of teenage hormones left me unable to cope and spending days on end in my bedroom crying. And that's how it is for me. I can tread water for months, even years, before the lurking beast decides it's time to drag me under for a while.

I felt a sense of relief when I left university and started working in the Daily Discount Store. I worked there for six years and loved every minute of it. You never knew what you would be selling as, alongside the usual toys, toiletries and tinned food, new lines of whacky stock would arrive almost daily. With Harry's marketing skills (i.e. literally going out onto the pavement to charm customers inside), people soon parted with their money. Old ladies responded particularly well to Harry's flattery, as did mothers and daughters who he would tell, 'You two must be sisters.' Cheesy as anything, I know, but Harry had the charm to pull it off. Once inside, shoppers bought countless things they didn't need. Heated foot warmers, flashing Santas at Christmas, that sort of thing. He even managed to shift thousands of colour-changing toilet seats.

Just under a year ago, Harry invested nearly all of his capital in a toy that was going to be the 'next big thing'. People would be desperate to get their hands on Demon Dragon, a flying, fire-breathing beast with flashing eyes. Forget Furbies, Hatchimals or every other craze you can think of. Demon Dragon would be the must-have Christmas toy. I had visions of it being like Turbo Man in the Christmas move *Jingle All the Way* when Arnold Schwarzenegger would stop at nothing to get his son the must-have toy.

Except the toy never really caught on and Harry lost every single penny. Customers who did buy the toy returned it in their droves. Apparently, it didn't fly properly, the lights failed to flash and the supposed roaring sound sounded more like 'a squeaking mouse' according to consumer reviews. Harry was furious. He insisted it was a design fault and couldn't accept that Demon Dragon, along with most of his other stock, was a load of old tat.

Not long after that our marriage went down the pan quicker than the 'Heaven Scent' pink lavatory cleaner that he flogged in his discount shops. Although of course it wasn't purely because of our dire financial situation… I still can't bear to think of the day I walked in on him in the storeroom. Especially as I'd been so looking forward to seeing him in person and delivering the good news that I'd managed to get a couple of tickets to see Bryan Adams at the Echo Arena. After discovering Harry cheating, I took my friend Emma with me instead, crying through the second half of the concert when Bryan played some slow songs and loved-up couples gazed adoringly at each other…

I thought about the last time I had really laughed. It was when Harry had fallen down the stairs in our home, having slipped on a

Demon Dragon left there by his nephew Jack. He's always been a bit accident-prone, but his fall down the stairs was such a metaphor for the failed business venture that I laughed about it for days afterwards. I was unaware at the time that the shops were haemorrhaging money, so our financial demise came as something of a shock.

Of course, losing the shops wasn't the only reason for our marriage breakdown. That horrendous chance encounter at the store definitely had a lot to do with it. If Harry would have answered his mobile phone that day I may never have known of his little indiscretion. Having chatted to Jane in the store (the nice blonde with the swingy ponytail) it transpired that most of the women who worked in Harry's shops had to tolerate his relentless flirting. And, of course, Laura from Till Three had actually slept with him. Turns out my loving, successful husband was a two-timing cheat.

I keep thinking of Dr Jazeera's diagnosis. I'm not sure pills will help my current situation. Nothing will. Actually, that sounds really defeatist, doesn't it? Maybe I *am* depressed. It's been a while since I've felt like I had a handle on things and perhaps ending up on skid row and not being able to afford a place of my own has had an impact, especially after losing Mum. She was the person I would always turn to when I felt a bit wobbly.

❧

'It's looking nice here already, isn't it?' said Emma, a few days after I'd moved into my flat. She'd brought some pretty multicoloured cushions to go on my stone-coloured sofa and a pair of bright red mugs from TK Maxx. 'You'll soon have this place like a little palace.' She winked as she bustled off to the small kitchen to make coffee.

Emma is the most positive person you will ever meet. She always looks on the bright side of life, glass half-full and every other cliché you can think of to describe an upbeat personality. I met her – a pretty, petite brunette – at Liverpool University when we were both studying for a business degree. She was horrified when I left in my second year, but eventually conceded that as I was a shop manager I was still carving out a decent career for myself. Emma went on to finish her degree and now has a well-paid job as a business manager at a local high school. It's a pity she couldn't have given Harry some business advice, as he lived life by the seat of his pants and would have preferred a 'cash only' shop, had he not lived in fear of someone dobbing him in to the taxman.

Harry's currently living with his poor mother, seventy-year-old Gladys, who must be thinking that Del Boy has moved in, as her front room is filled with boxes of bootleg booty for Harry to sell at the market. Apparently things are going pretty well for him. I've heard that people travel for miles to grab a bargain at his stall at Great Homer Street Market.

It's Friday night and I've just finished an eight-hour shift at Tesco Express in Liverpool city centre, which I combine with my job downstairs in the sandwich shop. Emma is staying over tonight as her lorry-driver husband is away on a European trip.

'How was your day?' she asks once I've returned to the lounge after having nipped to the bedroom and done a quick change out of my Tesco overalls into a long white T-shirt and black leggings.

'Not too bad,' I say, flopping down onto the sofa again. 'I spotted a shoplifter nicking a box of coffee pods.'

'I don't blame them,' Emma says, laughing. 'The price of those things is extortionate.'

'Are you condoning shoplifting, Emma? You're one of the most upright pillars of the community.'

'Since when?!'

I take a large glug of white wine. 'Mmm, that's nice,' I say, looking at the label on the bottle. 'That's not one of ours, is it?'

'Co-op. Three quid off the original price, so I bought two bottles,' she says with a grin.

'This is why you are my best friend,' I reply, curling my feet up onto the sofa and savouring the delicious apple and floral flavours of the wine.

A few minutes later there's a knock at the front door as our Chinese takeaway is delivered.

'I'm not sure I should be drinking this really, while I'm on medication,' I say, holding my wine glass up and peering at the straw-coloured liquid.

'What medication?' asks Emma, in surprise.

'Antidepressants. I've been on them for three weeks.' I put down my wine glass and pick up my fork. I wrap some noodles from an aromatic chicken chow mein around it and eat them hungrily.

'I didn't know you were depressed,' she says, a look of concern on her face.

'Well, that's just it, I don't think I am. A bit lacking in patience maybe, even a little stressed, but not particularly depressed. I'm still managing to function. The doc was concerned that my anxiety could develop into a low mood, so he prescribed some tablets. He knows my history, so I have to trust him.'

'I wish you'd said something to me,' says Emma, looking slightly hurt.

There was a reason I hadn't told Emma. As I've already mentioned, she is the world's most upbeat person, who would probably have decided to make it her life's mission to restore my happiness, whereas I just wanted to carry on as usual and talk about normal stuff. I was worried she would have tried to drag me out for revitalising spa days, or talked me into going to yoga and bought me copies of self-help books that teach you 'How to be Happy'.

I stop eating and run my fingers through my blonde, shoulder-length hair. It's been almost a year since I've been to a hairdressing salon. I used to be a regular visitor to Toni & Guy in the city when we were in the money, having my buttermilk highlights conditioned and cossetted every couple of months. I enjoyed being handed a latte and a glossy magazine whilst I relaxed in the black and white salon for an hour or two. Now I have appointments with my friend and mobile hairdresser Cheryl, who is coming round tomorrow to cut my hair. Cheryl, who has also added being a nail technician and a make-up artist to her ever-expanding CV, makes me smile every time I see her and I feel so grateful that she moved in next door to me. They say people come into your life at exactly the right time and I'm so lucky to have met Cheryl when I did. She knocked on my door one wet Sunday morning in November and asked me if I fancied going to her mum's house for Sunday lunch. We became instant friends after that. I was welcomed into the bosom of Cheryl's large, chaotic household, with Cheryl's two sisters and two brothers saying Harry must have been mad to screw things up with me. We ate a huge lamb dinner with a mountain of roast potatoes and vegetables, followed by trifle for dessert. Throughout the afternoon we grazed on chocolates from a tin of

Quality Street that Cheryl's mum had bought for Christmas but couldn't resist opening.

Emma finishes her prawn curry and egg fried rice, then tops her glass up with wine. She hovers the bottle over my glass with a concerned look on her face.

'Don't you worry about me, I'm fine,' I say. 'The tablets I'm taking say alcohol in moderation is OK.'

She pours a thimbleful into my wine glass.

'Maybe I was a bit down before, because these last couple of weeks I have felt a little brighter with the medication,' I continue, sinking back into the sofa. 'I think I'd bottled everything up after Harry and I split, which I know isn't healthy, but I'd barely stopped grieving for Mum at the time. And being permanently exhausted doesn't help.'

'Hardly surprising doing two jobs. Can't Harry help you out a bit with the bills?'

'Harry? You're joking aren't you? He's flogging stuff at Great Homer Street Market now, although he assures me he'll soon be back in business. Knowing him he probably will. He always manages to come up smelling of roses.'

'Anyway,' says Emma. 'You're not in work tomorrow so why don't you have a lie-in? I'll bring you breakfast in bed.'

I knew I shouldn't have told her about the tablets. 'You don't have to.'

'But I want to. Let someone spoil you for a change.'

'If you say so,' I reply with a smile.

We chat for another hour while *First Dates* is on the television in the background. It makes me wonder if I'll ever date again. I can't imagine being in another man's embrace as Harry's are the only arms I still long to have round me. If I close my eyes I can see his face, his bright blue eyes crinkling at the corners when he laughs, and I wonder when I will stop yearning for him and instead picture the face of a two-timing cheat.

When eventually it's time for bed, I climb under my duvet and fantasise about a long lie-in tomorrow morning. It's become the highlight of my week. I really do need to get a life, don't I?

Chapter Two

It's almost noon the next day and I'm lounging in bed feeling incredible. I slept like a baby until ten thirty, when Emma knocked on my bedroom door and came in carrying a floral tray with a glass of fresh orange juice, toast with strawberry jam and a bowl of cornflakes. Harry used to bring me breakfast in bed every Sunday morning as the store didn't open until eleven and he was always awake at the crack of dawn. He would climb back in bed with me, clutching the Sunday newspapers, diving out of bed at the last minute to dash to work. So many little things remind me of him. I wish I could turn myself upside down like one of those snow globes he used to sell at the shop and shake all traces of him from my brain.

'Thanks for breakfast in bed,' I say, feeling genuinely grateful to Emma as she gets ready to head for home.

'You're welcome. Right, I'm off now. Joe's back around two o'clock, must go and make myself beautiful,' says Emma, hugging me before she departs.

'You'd better get a move on then,' I tease.

'Cheeky! What are you up to today then?'

'Cheryl's coming around in a bit to cut my hair, then I'm going to visit my dad.'

'How's your dad doing?'

'He seems to be doing alright thanks, keeping himself busy. He's currently planning a couple of DIY jobs around the house.'

'That's good to hear. Well, do give him my love. Look after yourself, Maisie.'

With that she was off, closing the front door and clattering down the metal stairs.

I'm pretty sure Dad's doing quite well these days, although I don't suppose you can ever really know how someone is feeling inside – I should know that more than anyone. Thankfully, he's good at keeping himself busy and his regular games of snooker at the local British Legion give him something to look forward to; he also enjoys tending to his beloved garden.

Mum died of a stroke at the age of sixty-five. She was as fit as a fiddle and no one could have seen it coming. She juiced her own drinks from organic vegetables and regularly walked miles along the coastal path from Crosby to Southport, enjoying every minute of her retirement from her nursing job.

We thought she was on the mend after the first stroke, when she appeared to be recovering in hospital. But then three days after she was sent home, a second stroke killed her. Her former colleagues were bereft when she was wheeled in to the hospital from the ambulance again. The place where she had once worked so tirelessly, looking after her patients, was to become her final resting place.

Much of that time was a bit of a blur, if I'm honest. I somehow got through each day on autopilot, trying to be strong for Dad. Nothing seemed real. You wonder how you will ever get through such times yet, thankfully, the human spirit has an innate ability to survive.

Dad fell apart when Mum died. My parents had such a happy marriage – they were best friends. He thought it unfair that he was still here despite being a heavy smoker and a lover of greasy bacon sandwiches on thick white bread. He moped around in his tartan dressing gown for weeks after Mum's death, sitting in his favourite brown leather armchair looking through a photo album of their happy life together. Occasionally he would go to the local pub, where his friends would buy him a pint of beer and engage him in lively conversation, or allow him to sit in comfortable silence, depending on his mood. I don't think Dad will ever fully recover from losing Mum, although he is the type to just get on with things.

I'm just out of the shower and dressed when the doorbell rings.

I open the door and Cheryl steps into the flat. 'Right, madam, what can I do for you?' she asks, brandishing her hairdressing scissors. 'I've heard the Mohican is back in fashion. Or maybe blue tips?' She is wearing her own dark hair up in plaits today and reminds me of Pocahontas.

'Cut and blow dry, please.'

'You're no fun. How am I ever going to expand my creative skills when no one will let me loose on their hair?' She laughs.

Cheryl's a brilliant hairdresser. OK, I might get a crick in my neck bending over my small kitchen sink, and the ambience of my tiny flat is not exactly luxurious, but the end results are fabulous and cost less than half what I'd paid at a swanky salon. I've always had a head of good thick hair – flaxen as a child and helped along with highlights as it darkened. Despite my change in circumstances, I'm determined to keep up appearances. I'm lucky enough to have a shapely figure and long, lean legs that I seem to have gratefully inherited from Mum. I have slightly almond-shaped grey eyes and, according to Dad, 'a smile that could light up a room'. Dad tells me that I turn heads wherever I go but I never quite believe him.

'Are you going on holiday this year, madam?' jokes Cheryl, as she massages shampoo into my scalp.

'If madam has a lottery win, then maybe it'll be possible.'

We both laugh.

'Who needs a holiday when we've got the beach up the road?' says Cheryl, rinsing my hair in warm water.

'Pity we don't get the good weather,' I reply, glancing out of the kitchen window at a grey cloudy sky that promises rain in mid-June.

'You make your own sunshine in life. Talking of which, there's a beach party themed night at the Angler's Arms tonight.'

'Beach theme? In raincoats and wellies? Think I might give it a miss.'

'You will not. We're going. It will do you good. Besides, a light shower has been forecast for this afternoon, brightening later in the day. Come to my flat around seven, we'll have a few drinks before we go out. One of my customers brought me a bottle of tequila back from her holiday in Mexico.'

'I don't know if I like tequila.' I lean forward as she wraps a towel around my head.

'It will get you into the party mood. You're not getting out of it, Maisie.'

Going out tonight is the last thing I feel like doing really, but I don't suppose I can spend every evening indoors watching TV and doing puzzles. The doctor said I should accept more social invitations, break out of my rut a little. Maybe it's about time I started trying.

I find Dad in his back garden planting some onions. He has a real knack for growing things and I remember helping him pull home-grown potatoes and carrots from the ground when I was growing up. I recall picking runner beans that scaled the white-painted brick walls in the yard, and eating strawberries from a planter that he'd made himself from an old wooden pallet.

Over the years he's transformed the garden into the most beautiful outdoor area in which I could happily sit for hours when the sun shines. It's not the largest of gardens, but it's so well designed it gives a lovely feeling of space and freedom. There's a patio area with a covered gazebo and colourful bushes dotted around the border, including buddleia which attract butterflies. A wooden wishing well sits against the fence and I recall throwing coins into it when I was a child. If I had one wish now, it would be to sit out here and have another cup of tea with my mum.

Harry, used to bring his nephew Jack, now aged eight, here to look at the little windmills and gnomes scattered about the garden. I miss Jack. That's the thing with a break-up. Sometimes you lose other family members too. Although I've stayed in touch with Jack so far, taking him to the park and the beach for an occasional ice cream, I worry it won't last. I hate the thought of us growing apart.

'Hello, love, nice to see you. Your hair looks pretty,' says Dad, putting his green trowel down and coming over to give me a kiss on the cheek.

That's the thing about Dad, he notices details about people. He always has a compliment ready for a new hairstyle or an outfit and he tunes into a change in people's feelings. He noticed that I'd stopped socialising following Mum's death and my break-up with Harry. He encouraged me to go out more, despite going through his own grief, recognising my bouts of anxiety before I was even aware of them myself. 'Don't cut yourself off from your friends,' he'd advised.

'Thanks, Dad,' I say, stroking my new haircut. 'How are you?'

'I'm alright, love. Just doing a bit of gardening before the rain starts,' he says, glancing at the slate-grey clouds above our heads.

'Cheryl's invited me to a beach party tonight at the Angler's Arms. Fancy it?' I ask, although I can't imagine many people turning out tonight if the weather changes.

'Not really my scene that, love, but thanks for asking. I've got a game of snooker at the British Legion club at six o'clock, then there's a Clint Eastwood film on at nine that I want to be home for.'

'You don't know what you're missing. Pina coladas in the rain, you can't beat it!'

꿈

I put the kettle on and sit in the neat lounge with Dad, drinking tea and eating digestive biscuits. The room has changed little over the years, apart from a newish television that is wall mounted. Two long, mismatched sofas face each other, one covered in brown leather, one in a beige-and-red checked fabric. Cream walls are adorned with family photos, including my wedding photograph. It feels a bit strange to see it still hanging there. On a sideboard, there's a gorgeous photo of Mum in a silver frame, her brown hair in soft curls. She's sitting on a picnic blanket on the beach nearby and throwing her head back and laughing. What I wouldn't give to spend another day with her, paddling in the water and eating some lovingly prepared food from a picnic basket.

Outside, the sky has blackened and suddenly the rain begins to fall. Huge drops pelt against the window and within seconds it's like a monsoon. Rain is dancing on the patio outside and after just a few minutes there are pools of water all around the garden.

'Maybe I should have left those onions until tomorrow,' muses Dad, as he eyes the limp plants. 'The forecast said a light shower, which would have bedded the plants in. This looks as if it will wash them away.'

'They'll be fine. Root veg are tough.' *Bit like you*, I think to myself. Gentle and caring on the outside, tough as steel inside. Old school.

When the rain subsides I drain my tea, resisting any more biscuits. After saying goodbye to Dad, I take the fifteen-minute walk back to my flat.

Crossing the terraced street from my family home, I make my way along Coronation Road past the park. All the streets in this area have names with royal connections. Coronation Road, Princes Avenue, Jubilee Drive and so on. I like to imagine horse-drawn carriages carrying members of the royal family down these streets in days gone by, the pavements lined with excited onlookers waving flags.

I pass a private park with black railings, mainly obscured by tall trees, with access restricted to the tenants of a particular street who have their own key – the privileged families in the area. I always thought it was like something from the movie *Notting Hill*. It was Harry's ambition to have a house on Warren Road so that we could be a part of that scene, having private Sunday morning walks and barbecues in fine weather, locking out the outside world. *We never quite achieved that dream though*, I think, feeling a pang in my heart.

Turning a corner, I find myself standing at the end of the street I once lived in with Harry. Princes Avenue is a quiet, tree-lined avenue of red-brick houses. Some have bay-fronted windows, others are flat-fronted, but each house is perfectly tended to with shiny front doors, polished knockers and neat front gardens with driveways.

I could take a detour but I find myself walking past our old Victorian house, glancing at the new curtains in the front lounge. The front door with the canopy above has a new brass knocker and is now painted a glossy black. It's striking against the black and white eaves of the house. Five years we lived in that house. I shouldn't walk this way really. It's like picking a scab and opening up an old wound.

I'm about to cross the road when I hear someone calling my name. It's Hilary from number 20, a few doors up from my old home. She never gave me the time of day when I lived here, apart from trying to impart gossip.

'I thought it was you!' she's exclaiming, like we were old mates. 'What are you doing around here?'

'Just been to see Dad and took a little detour. I couldn't resist taking a look at the old place,' I admit.

'I'm sure there's something funny going on there now. There's people knocking at the door, day and night.' She sniffs.

I happen to know that Jan, the current resident, is an emergency foster carer, so I can imagine there would be late-night knocks at the door.

'Ooh, what do you think that's about?'

'Well,' she says, looking positively excited to have a listening ear. 'Someone said it might have something to do with drugs. Or receiving stolen goods. Whatever it is, it can't be right, can it?'

I consider telling her that it's a house of ill repute, but decide that it wouldn't be fair as the news would spread around the neighbourhood faster than Usain Bolt.

'As a matter of fact, I happen to know that Jan is an emergency foster carer. It probably explains any late-night calls.'

Hilary's face drops like a stone to the ground. 'Well, right, I must go now, lovely to see you again,' she says, visibly disappointed by this revelation.

I shake my head and smile to myself as I walk along. I like to think that Hilary might think twice about judging people in the future. But I doubt it somehow.

Thrusting my hands into my pockets, I turn a corner and a slice of sunlight breaks through a cloud before quickly being obscured by another one drifting by. I'd better get home and rifle through my wardrobe and find something suitable for my night out. I have a couple of jumpsuits from last summer that could work – I hope they still fit. I've been eating rather a lot of chocolate and Chinese takeaways of late…

Chapter Three

The Angler's Arms is packed for beach-party night and, as Cheryl predicted (or the app on her phone told her), the clouds have lifted. There's a clear sky above and it's still light at almost eight thirty in the evening.

In tropical gear, I'm wearing a floral jumpsuit with a yellow and pink print that by some miracle still fits me, and Cheryl is wearing a long white dress with a big turquoise flower clip in her long black hair. She looks every bit the Hawaiian beach babe. My blonde shoulder-length hair is loosely curled and I am wearing a hint of grey eyeshadow that brings out the grey in my eyes.

The pub is pretty full when we arrive and several blokes turn and give us the once over. DJ Dave plays 'Club Tropicana' which gets everyone up on their feet. Fake palm trees are dotted about and the patio area outside is strung with colourful fairy lights and a giant TV screen showing the opening scene of *Baywatch*, where the men are transfixed by a lithe Pamela Anderson running across a beach in slow motion. The next song up is 'We're Going to Ibiza!' by the Vengaboys.

'Ah, this song takes me back,' says Cheryl. 'I had my first snog at a school disco when this was playing.'

'Really? It's hardly a smoochy number, is it?'

'I know. Michael Brady just sort of grabbed me as I was on my way back from the toilets, telling me that I looked nice and he had fancied me for ages. We ended up snogging outside the caretaker's room.'

'How romantic. Was he your boyfriend after that?'

'No, he just ignored me in school the next day. I think his bold move had been fortified by a couple of sneaky cans of beer,' she says, laughing.

There's a buffet inside the pub so after a couple of spins with the older guys doing their 'dad dancing', Cheryl and I head inside for something to eat. The long table is laid out with mini burgers, pork and pineapple kebabs, plates of fragrant rice and a fresh mango salsa. There's also a chocolate fountain with chopped papaya and strawberries for dessert.

'Mmm, this tastes amazing,' I say, sinking my teeth into some succulent pork and fluffy coconut rice.

'No carbs for me,' says Cheryl, piling her plate with salad and salsa, even though she's as slim as a reed. 'Wish I could say "no carbs before Marbs", but I've as much chance of going to the moon as going to Marbella this year.'

'I'm not sure I'd fancy it anyway,' I say. 'Fast cars and swanky yachts aren't really my thing.'

'I'll remember that when I become hairdresser to the stars. I won't be inviting you with me when I nip over to backcomb Beyoncé's thatch.'

'Sounds painful.'

Terry the barman, wearing a colourful Hawaiian-patterned shirt serves us each a pina colada, adding ice from a retro pineapple ice bucket. We take our drinks outside so that Cheryl can have a cigarette.

'I wish I could quit,' she says, taking a long drag.

'Why don't you get one of those electronic cigarettes?'

'You hear different things about them. Some experts say they're no better for you than the real thing. Plus, I'm an all-or-nothing type of girl. I'll quit one day but it's so hard. I've smoked since I was fourteen. I think living in that madhouse drove me to it.'

Cheryl has told me stories of growing up, hating how she always had to share a bedroom with one of her sisters who wasn't averse to helping herself to Cheryl's clothes. She's still close to her family but she couldn't wait to get out and have her own space. I never had such a problem as I'm an only child. I reckon I would have quite liked someone to swap clothes with.

We walk back inside as a group of lads in their twenties stroll into the bar. We end up having a lot of fun enjoying a little harmless attention from the flirty younger guys, the middle-aged men returning to their pints of beer, exhausted from all the dancing.

'Blimey, this is an old one,' I say as the strains of 'Y Viva España', a big hit in the 1970s, fills the bar. Suddenly the older blokes are back on their feet.

I notice a tall, dark-haired man smiling at me from the corner of the bar, but romance is the last thing on my mind. My heart still sinks when I think of Harry. I thought we were forever and some days I find it hard to believe I'm really living alone in a cramped flat – the realisation winds me.

At the end of the evening a fair-haired, slightly-the-worse-for-wear young man asks if he can walk me home. He hasn't said two words to me all evening but obviously fancies his chances of having a quick leg over. He hasn't even bought me a drink. Cheeky sod.

'How old are you, fourteen?' I reply with a giggle. 'I know the way home, thanks. Anyway, I'll be going home with my lover,' I say, planting a kiss onto the lips of a startled Cheryl.

We laugh as we link arms and walk home together under a bright moon. Dad's right. I shouldn't shut myself away. All work and no play makes for a very dull life.

Chapter Four

The next day I eye the heaving queue in Our Daily Bread and sigh. Things didn't get off to the best start as I overslept this morning. Yes, I know, I live upstairs and I really shouldn't be late for work, but for some reason my alarm failed to go off.

It's particularly busy this lunchtime and I'm already looking forward to a coffee and my weekly fix of *Ten-Minute Break* magazine this evening – I've become a little bit addicted to the competitions in it and live in hope that one day I'll scoop a big cash prize, which I would put towards a nice two-bedroomed house close to the park. Oh, and maybe a hot tub…

White-crusty-bloomer woman is here again, as she is every day. Today she's wearing a camel coat with a silver flower brooch on the lapel. She looks every inch the lady, but appearances can be deceptive.

I push a strand of hair that has escaped from my white cap behind my ear. 'Who's next?' I beam, as the usual orderly queue seems to have turned into a bit of a scrum.

'Me!' barks white-bloomer woman. 'Cheese-and-onion mix. No cucumber.'

As if she needs to tell me. She orders a cheese-and-onion mix or a tuna mayo salad, without cucumber, on a white crusty bloomer every single day. And she never says please or thank you. It really winds me up. As my mother always taught me, manners cost nothing.

'Err, I think it's me, love,' says a bald man with a shiny forehead, who clearly doesn't believe in 'ladies first'.

White-bloomer woman gives him an evil stare.

'Right, what can I get you?'

'Egg mayonnaise on a large white roll,' he grunts.

I'm dying to ask, 'What's the magic word?' but I know my boss, Alison, wouldn't like it.

I'm lifting a plastic container of egg mayonnaise out of the fridge when Pat, a co-worker, barges into the fridge door, knocking the egg mayonnaise all over me. It's sitting there all over my chest like a pool of baby vomit.

'Oh god, love, I'm so sorry,' she says, her hand flying to her mouth. 'I didn't see you there. I thought someone had left the fridge door open.'

'No problem.' I smile through gritted teeth as I nip into the back to change my apron. A bit of the egg mayonnaise drips onto the floor and I accidentally step on it and fall, skidding along the floor tiles on my arse, my only saving grace being that it's out of sight of the customers.

After a few minutes I compose myself and inhale deeply. Emma would tell me that it's not the end of the world and that 'these things are sent to try us'.

'Right then,' I say breezily, hastily composing myself. 'Any salad with that?'

'You took your time,' says shiny-forehead bloke, glancing at his watch.

'Sorry about that,' I say through gritted teeth. 'So, do you want any salad?'

He pulls a face as he peers at the salad bar. 'Dunno. Is it all fresh? I usually just have a bit of cress with egg mayo.'

'Couldn't be fresher. I picked it all myself this morning from our salad garden.'

'Really?'

'No, not really, we have nothing but a back yard. And do you really think I'd pick salad to make sandwiches for a load of ungrateful customers?' I huff as my backside begins to smart from the fall. 'I'm on minimum wage, me. Minimum bloody wage,' I rant as I hook my black apron over my head and fling it at my boss, who is standing there open-mouthed.

'So sorry,' she says to the customers, before pushing me into the back of the shop, while Jean, a stout fifty-year-old, carries on serving.

'What the hell's got into you?' demands Alison.

'Some sense, that's what. Clarity. Vision.'

'Well, er, maybe you could have this life-affirming moment a bit later. There's a shop full of hungry customers out there.'

'You serve them,' I say, feeling suddenly empowered as I grab my bag and walk through the shop to the exit.

White-bloomer woman looks me up and down with pursed lips and a loud tut.

'You might want to avoid the white bread in future,' I tell her. 'It might help with your flatulence problem.'

I'd been stood behind her in a queue at the chemist's the previous week, when she'd let out a loud fart. I'm sure everyone thought it was me, as she stared straight ahead with a blank expression on her face. The gossipy pharmacy assistant had flared her nostrils and glared at me.

'Well I never!' snorts bloomer woman.

'No, you're right, you never. Never said a please or a thanks. Not once. Have a nice life! Goodbye.'

I walk next door to the Co-op and buy myself a large bar of chocolate and my *Ten-Minute Break* magazine. That will take my mind off things, if only for a short time. I climb the staircase to my flat, fuming inside. *Why are people so bloody rude?*

A few minutes later, I slot my key into my front door, pick up the post from the mat and drop it on the table before flopping onto the sofa. I exhale deeply and uncurl my balled fists. Then I think to myself, *What the hell have I just done?*

I look at the post on the table and exhale deeply. *Probably more bills.* That's all I seem to get these days, apart from brochures selling things like heated foot warmers or incontinence pads. I think the previous tenant was an old lady.

Sitting in my small but cosy lounge I try to put things into perspective. It was only a part-time job after all and I'm sure I can find something similar. It's just that it was so convenient being literally downstairs. I don't know what got into me. Maybe I'll try and have a chat with Alison later, although I don't think she'll be too impressed with me for leaving her short-staffed during the lunchtime rush.

I brew some coffee in a cafetière, then sit and think for a while about what I want to do with my future. I'll be thirty next year and I've got two part-time jobs that are going nowhere. Well...

only one part-time job now. I'd better get on my laptop and start scouring the job pages for something else, although jobs for people with half a degree are a little thin on the ground. Not for the first time I wonder how things would have turned out if I had stayed at university and actually finished my business degree.

'You could do some in-house courses,' Emma had said recently, in an attempt to motivate me. 'Retail is one of those careers where you don't always need a degree. You can take qualifications on the job.'

I did give this option some thought, but eventually I decided that I don't actually want a career in retail. I can't deal with the rude customers, of which there are many. The customer is *not* always right. The customer is often an ill-mannered oaf and you have to stand there smiling and suck it all up. It was my parents' idea that I should choose a 'sensible' degree, which is why I ended up studying business, although I wasn't particularly keen on the idea in the first place. I didn't hate it, but I was never passionate about it either. I just wish there was something that really fired me up, something I could throw myself into. Like Cheryl enjoys her hairdressing.

Back then Harry said he had noticed my promise and I was quickly promoted to store manager at the Bold Street store. I'm sure I was the object of gossip from some of the other shop workers, who had worked there for years and never been offered any advancement of their career. I was twenty-one years old at the time, completely flattered by Harry's attention, and two years later we were married at St Luke's Church in Liverpool city centre, followed by a lavish reception at the Titanic Hotel.

Maybe that choice of hotel was an omen. A sign that my marriage was going to sink.

I shove aside the painful thought and drain my coffee, before turning my attention to the post. I pick up an envelope and turn it over. The postmark is from London and there's a red stamp on the back displaying the *Ten-Minute Break* logo. Wondering what it's about, I tear the envelope open and scan the contents of the letter. The first thing I notice are the huge letters saying 'WINNER' emblazoned in gold across the top of the page. Confused, I read on.

Ten-Minute Break Magazine
Argylle House
50 Broomfield Lane
LW1 STS

Dear Miss Mills,

We have been unable to contact you on the mobile phone number you provided, but are delighted to inform you about the GOOD NEWS in this letter.

Congratulations! You are the lucky competition winner of our Holiday in Tuscany for Two, featured in Issue No. 4356 of *Ten-Minute Break* magazine. We have also thrown in a bonus of £1,000 spending money!

Please contact the telephone number shown above for further details.

Congratulations again!

Jennifer Dunn

Competitions Manager

My hands shaking, I read the letter again, unable to take it all in. I'd had to cancel my phone contract, opting for a cheaper pay-as-you-go, which was why they hadn't been able to contact me by phone. I barely remember entering the competition. It must have been months ago. Then again I've lost count of the competitions I have entered. All these years I've been doing them and I've never won a thing.

Excitement coursing through me, I think about how I could certainly do with a holiday – it was doctor's orders, after all! And I figure there's no point in looking for a second job until I get back. Reading the letter again, a smile spreads slowly across my face.

I've only gone and won a Holiday for Two in Tuscany!

Chapter Five

Clutching the letter in my hand, I practically race round to Dad's house the next morning and breathlessly tell him the news. Dad's in his garden pruning a rose bush in the glorious sunshine.

'A holiday in Tuscany? That's wonderful news. Me and your mother always said we'd visit Italy but we never did get round to it. She loved that Gino D'Acampo and watched his show when he travelled around Italy. I think Sorrento was the place your mother fancied.'

I feel a pang of sadness that they never got to see Sorrento together. 'Do you fancy coming with me, Dad?'

He stops pruning his rose bush and fixes me with his soft blue eyes and I take in his appearance, with his grey moustache that matches his hair. He's a handsome man who wouldn't look out of place in one of the Western movies he enjoys watching. 'Me? No, take one of your friends. Go and have some fun. Besides, I haven't even got a current passport. It ran out after our last holiday in Spain. Your mother preferred going on beach holidays in England after that. She fell in love with Dorset. She really only fancied Italy after seeing a travel show on television and then those cookery shows. I thought about renewing our passports and surprising her with a holiday, but then she took ill…' He trails off.

'Try not to feel bad about that, Dad. Besides, I don't think she would have enjoyed flying. She told me a few years ago that she much preferred travelling by train as she didn't think she could be doing with all the security checks at airports. I just thought this might be your only opportunity to go on holiday abroad again.'

'There's life in the old dog yet, don't worry. Hopefully I've got at least another ten years in me.' Dad smiles.

I certainly hope so. He's seventy years old next year and despite his bacon sandwich indulgence (which he has restricted to weekends, along with the odd cigar instead of a daily packet of cigarettes), he doesn't look his age and is in very good health. I think the garden keeps him fit.

'I didn't mean that, Dad. I just meant the opportunity to go away with someone.'

'It's kind of you to ask but, really, take a friend. Take Cheryl or Emma. Or take them both. Doesn't Emma's husband work away all week?'

'Hmm, yes, he does actually. She'd really love the culture of Tuscany. Cheryl hasn't had a proper holiday in ages, though, so maybe I should ask her. The problem is it's only a holiday for two.'

'Well, whatever you decide I'm sure you'll enjoy it. It will do you the world of good. It's just what you need, love.'

He's right, and I start wondering if both my friends could go. Emma could certainly afford to pay for herself, as her job at the school pays well and her husband earns good money as a European lorry driver. Or would she be offended as she's been my friend for a lot longer than Cheryl?

As it's such a lovely day I decide to go for a walk along Crosby Beach to clear my head and mull it over. There are quite a few dog walkers out and a fluffy Cockapoo escapes from its owner and bounds towards me.

I quite like dogs but I'm a little nervous around them, especially when they bark. I've only ever owned a tabby cat called Freda, which disappeared one day from the old house. I don't like to fear the worst about her disappearance and instead imagine her happily ensconced in a new home and being spoilt with dinners of fresh salmon and tuna. Freda always enjoyed the finer things in life.

The dog stops, sniffs my feet then thankfully sprints off again in the direction of its owner who is in hot pursuit, shouting, 'Sorry!'

I walk along a quieter stretch of beach, lined by sand dunes and high rises, the shimmering sea and an outline of Blackpool Tower stretching out before me. The Iron Men of Crosby Beach are interspersed along the sands, some standing in the sea facing outwards. It's quite something to behold and it's a popular tourist attraction. There are 100 of them altogether, occasionally adorned with seaweed scarves or actual football scarves. I think they look slightly sinister after the daylight fades and the water reaches their knees. But I never tire of looking at them and watching the ebb and flow of the tide, with huge waves from the wild Irish Sea rolling in to the shore.

Harry and I had so many walks along this shore and it was the place where we shared our first proper kiss. It was late summer, the days growing shorter as autumn approached, and a warm orange sun was beginning to set on the horizon. When he took me in his arms I felt like the luckiest girl in the world.

I push aside thoughts of Harry and carry on walking until I reach the marina. The yacht club has a restaurant and several diners are seated on the outdoor decking area. Smart yacht-club members sporting expensive hairstyles and stylish clothes sip glasses of wine.

I pass the restaurant and head towards a smaller wooden beach kiosk, emblazoned with a red and yellow banner advertising ice cream. There are wooden tables and benches outside and I'm ordering a cappuccino when I hear a familiar voice.

'Auntie Maisie!'

I look up to see Gladys, Harry's mum, and her grandson Jack, who is running towards me. He wraps his arms round me in a hug.

'Jack! Hi! How are you?' I ask, giving him a squeeze.

'Full of energy,' says Gladys, laughing. 'I'm shattered. He's been in the park.' She gestures to the wooden adventure playground, just behind us, facing the water. 'That was after he'd been swimming at the leisure centre. We've just come here for an ice cream and a coffee, then his mum's collecting him at half past two when she's finished work.'

'I'll get them,' I say getting to my feet. 'Jack, do you want an ice cream or a milkshake?'

'Could I have a monster shake, please?'

I glance at Gladys.

'All that sugar, he'll be bouncing off the walls. But then he has used a lot of energy. Go on then. He'll be with his mum in an hour.' She says with a laugh. 'And can I have a cappuccino, like yours please, love?'

A few minutes later a waitress brings out two coffees and a monster shake, which is essentially cookies, ice cream and everything chocolatey crammed into a large jam jar with a striped wafer straw poking out of it. As Jack tucks into it, and Gladys and I sip our coffees, I tell her about the holiday win.

'That's great news! I'm really pleased for you,' Gladys says, with a huge grin. 'It's been a while since you've had a holiday, hasn't it, love?'

I recall my last holiday to Spain with Harry, which wasn't the relaxing break I'd envisaged. Many an evening I'd been in bed before midnight, reading a few chapters of my book, while he'd stayed out partying with holidaymakers he'd befriended. It was then that I started to realise we were like chalk and cheese, although I still loved him – and would never have found it in me to end things between us.

'I haven't been abroad in years,' says Gladys, looking out across the sand to where families and couples with their dogs are enjoying the beautiful afternoon. 'I don't mind it here in the UK though. Tenby in Wales was always our choice of holiday when Ted was alive. When the sun shone it was like being in the Mediterranean with all those pretty, pastel-coloured houses. A little piece of paradise,' she recalls with a sigh. 'But, as I say, you deserve a holiday more than anyone after what you've been through recently.'

'I suppose so. I know how lucky I am to live near the beach here, but it's the sunshine I'm looking forward to,' I say, imagining the hot sun caressing my skin as I sip a cool drink and forget about everything. Gladys and I finish our coffees and chat for a while longer, then I stand up to leave.

'Well, it's been lovely running into you,' says Gladys. 'You must come over soon, Maisie. Just because my son is a bloody fool, it doesn't mean we can't still be friends, does it?'

'Of course not. And I will come over, or maybe we could meet somewhere for a coffee.'

I don't want to risk running into Harry. I know Gladys would like nothing more than for us to get back together, but I don't think it's on the agenda. We've been separated for a while now, and when I last saw him, Harry mentioned divorce…

For now, I don't want to think about all that. I just want to feel like my old self again. Get my spark back.

As I walk back along the beach, with the sun on my face, suddenly I'm really looking forward to my holiday in Italy!

❦

Cheryl waves the competition letter above her head and gives a loud 'woo hoo!'. 'You lucky thing! Who are you going to take with you then?' she asks, pouring Emma and me a glass of rosé wine, before putting the bottle on the table in my lounge. It's a lovely Zinfandel with strawberry and cherry notes. I'm getting quite good at identifying the flavours without looking at the labels. It's surprising the knowledge you pick up working in a supermarket, stocking the drinks aisle.

'Well, that's the thing,' I say, leaning back on the small sofa. 'I'd love both you and Emma to come. It means we'd have to split the cost for the third person, though. Just the flights, I think, as the apartment in the farmhouse actually sleeps four.'

'That's if the apartment owner isn't an arse about it. They might charge per person,' says Cheryl.

'I never thought of that. Maybe I'll send them an e-mail and ask.'

Suddenly Emma claps her hands together. 'I've just realised. I think I've got loads of unused air miles. I could probably get flights for free!'

'Brilliant. Sounds like we're on…' I can hear the words coming out of my mouth, yet for some strange reason I'm no longer feeling the jolt of excitement I should be feeling. Suddenly I wonder whether it may all be too much of an effort.

Emma turns to look at me as though she is staring right into my soul. 'You may not be in the mood to go right now, Maisie, but this is exactly what you need. Break out of your rut. Didn't the doctor say the same thing?'

'He did and I do feel a little brighter, really. I just feel a little panicked at the thought of preparing for a holiday.' It's true. I suddenly feel overwhelmed. *Have I even got enough summer clothes to wear?*

'I know,' Emma says gently. 'But I'll help you. I'll even pack your case, if you like. Believe me, you really need a holiday. Sunshine, Chianti, fabulous food. What better tonic could there be?'

'Suppose so. Do you really think I need it?'

Cheryl and Emma cast a glance at each other.

'Well, yes,' says Emma. 'You've been stressed for a while now. You can't listen to me sneeze without rolling your eyes. And walking out of a job because people didn't say please or thanks – that's not like you. Usually a glass of wine and a good bitch would fix that.'

It's true. Maybe I have been a bit of a nightmare to be around… I suddenly feel so ashamed. 'Oh boy,' I say, exhaling deeply. 'I'm sorry if I've offended you both. Not so sorry about those rude customers though. Perhaps you're right, Emma. Maybe a holiday is exactly what I need.'

'So we're on then?' asks Cheryl, with an excited glint in her eyes.

'We're on. I'd better go and dust off my suitcase. Tuscany here we come!'

Chapter Six

We leave Manchester in grey drizzle and soon enough we are taking our seats on the plane of a budget airline with orange seats. Thankfully, the owner of the apartment at the farmhouse in Tuscany was fine about all three of us sharing at no extra cost.

'Don't you just love jetting off in the rain, knowing you'll soon be sitting round a pool sipping a cocktail,' says Cheryl, sighing with anticipation.

'Too right. Summer in the UK will probably be the usual washout.'

The flight attendant does a safety demonstration and before long we are airborne. I'm sitting in a window seat near the wing, glancing out at fluffy clouds and dreaming of Italian food, when I think I can hear a knocking sound.

After a few minutes, I turn to Emma. 'Can you hear that?'

'Hear what?'

'A sort of knocking sound. I hope there's nothing wrong with the engine.'

Emma leans over and presses her ear towards the window. 'I can't hear anything unusual. I think it's just engine thrust. We haven't been up very long.'

I can definitely hear a knocking sound and suddenly I'm fearing the worst. As I envisage an emergency evacuation of the plane, I wish I'd paid more attention to the safety demonstration. We're not even over water yet, which would give us a better chance of survival. I feel slightly panicky and I can feel my palms beginning to sweat. I've always been a bit of a nervous flyer and I once went through the flight from hell coming home from a holiday in Spain. We hit severe weather and the oxygen masks dropped down as the plane rocked like a boat, drinks spilling everywhere. I cried with relief when we landed.

'Are you alright?' asks Emma, noting my anxious expression.

'I think so. It's just the noise. Maybe it's nothing. I just need to concentrate on my breathing,' I say inhaling deeply. I really should make the effort to go back to the yoga class that I once enjoyed. Sometimes I don't have the enthusiasm to attend the very things that will help me.

A member of the cabin crew in a tight, navy-blue pencil skirt and a multicoloured blouse is trundling the drinks trolley towards us.

'Here, have a gin, settle your nerves,' says Emma, gesturing to the flight attendant with a twenty-pound note.

'No, thanks, it will only make me feel worse. I'll just have some water.'

After a little while, my deep breathing seems to have done the trick. Once my nerves have settled, the rest of the flight passes uneventfully and we arrive at Pisa Airport to a sultry twenty-eight degrees. We head straight to the baggage carousel, which churns our cases out surprisingly quickly. At Arrivals, there's a balding, middle-aged Italian man with a broad smile, holding up a card with my name on it. Emma is carefully placing our passports, flight documents and European Health Insurance cards into the side compartment of her flight bag, as Cheryl decides to grab us all takeaway coffees from a nearby outlet.

I can't blame Emma for wanting to look after our documents – I don't think she trusts me to look after my own paperwork. This probably stems from a holiday to a caravan park we had as teenagers, when I lost our club entertainment passes and a purse containing a hundred quid. We lived on beans on toast and a bottle of cheap vodka for the remainder of that holiday – not that it stopped us from having fun.

I'm dragged away from my thoughts of the past by the sound of a security guard shouting, 'Stop!' He's giving chase to a younger, scruffy-looking man, who barges into another bloke, causing him to drop his bag, before careering into me and sending my trolley into a wheelspin. The guy whose bag has been sent flying retrieves it quickly, before dashing off into the crowd and almost knocking Cheryl over as she returns with our coffees.

The security guard returns empty-handed with a thunderous look on his face.

'Shoplifter,' the taxi driver informs us, as he leads us to his car and loads our cases into the boot.

'How dramatic! So where's this farmhouse then?' asks Cheryl, as she applies some lip gloss in the back of the taxi.

'A little village called San Marco, not far away from Chianti,' I reply.

'A very pretty village,' says our driver, smiling through his mirror. 'And Villa Marisa is beautiful.'

'It says it's only an hour from Florence,' announces Emma, studying a little pamphlet she has pulled from her shoulder bag. 'I can't wait to visit the museums. Hopefully I'll have a chance to visit Siena too.'

'You will be spoilt for choice of places to visit. The whole of Tuscany is beautiful,' says our driver. 'Whoever called Paris the city of love could never have been to Italy.' He chuckles.

We settle into our journey and are soon traversing the stunning scenery of the Tuscan countryside. Tiny patches of lilac indicate fields of lavender in the distance. Rectangles of emerald-green fields dotted with terracotta-roofed houses are flanked by tall cypress trees. It's all a world away from back home.

Shortly before we arrive at our destination, a large green tractor emerges from a side road causing our driver to brake sharply. The carton of cappuccino in my hand spills all over my cream top. Thankfully it's almost stone cold. I fish some tissues out of my handbag and attempt to clean myself up a little. I look a right sight.

'Idiot!' shouts our driver, raising his fist in the air. The dark-haired farmer toots his horn in response.

'Sorry, ladies, the fool was not looking where he was going.'

'It reminds me of back home,' says Cheryl. 'No one ever looks both ways when they pull out of a side road in our neighbourhood.'

'Drivers on the country roads here are not too bad,' says the driver. 'Apart from careless farmers.'

Ten minutes later, our taxi scrunches across gravel to the front door of Villa Marisa, a picturesque Tuscan farmhouse. The main building is an impressive sight, its cream walls and green-shuttered windows immaculately kept. To the left is a row of single-storey, cream-coloured stone buildings, which are presumably the holiday apartments.

We climb out of the taxi and the driver pulls our cases from the boot. As the taxi pulls away, we are greeted by an attractive woman who has appeared at the door of the farmhouse. She introduces herself as Viola and looks somewhere in her late fifties. She has deep brown eyes and her dark, wavy hair is held up with a clip. A younger woman, with waist-length chocolate-brown hair, crosses the driveway from the apartments and waves. She is strikingly beautiful.

'Maria! As you see, our guests have arrived. Are the rooms ready?' Viola says.

'Yes, Mamma, just,' the young woman replies, smiling.

'Please, please,' urges Viola, gesturing for us to go inside. 'Come through and have a cold drink. My husband will take your cases to your accommodation.'

She calls to her husband, but he appears to have gone AWOL.

'I'm so sorry,' says Viola, shaking her head. 'He is probably with the pigs. Maybe he should stay there,' she mutters, disappearing into the farmhouse.

'Pay no attention to Mamma,' Maria whispers to us. 'My parents always bicker. Papa has probably done something to upset her, although he never means to,' she says, rolling her eyes.

'Did your mother say he might be with the pigs?' I ask, not sure that I heard correctly.

'Yes, this is a working farm. We harvest wheat and olives, as well as keeping pigs. My brother does the farming. But, don't worry, the pigs are half an acre away. You won't have any interesting smells from here!'

Laughing, we thank Maria and enter the farmhouse to a welcome blast of coolness from a ceiling fan above us. The interior is painted a soft yellow, contrasting with the dark wooden furniture. Small terracotta pots of herbs and a vase of colourful wild flowers sit on a window ledge that overlooks the courtyard. The cosy and welcoming room has paintings of the Tuscan countryside hanging on the pale yellow walls and a cat is stretched out on a striped rug near a patio door, catching rays of sunlight.

Viola has set some fresh lemonade, a tomato and basil salad, and an olive focaccia loaf on a table covered with a lace tablecloth. 'Please help yourselves. The olive bread is made with our own olives,' she says proudly, picking up the jug of lemonade and pouring the liquid into three glasses.

'Wow. Thank you. We didn't expect this,' I say, sipping some lemonade. I suddenly realise that I'm hungry. I was too nervous to eat anything on the plane, although Emma and Cheryl managed to devour a cheese-and-ham toastie, a small tube of Pringles and two gin and tonics each.

'You are very welcome. There is also a small welcome pack in your apartment. No one likes to have to go looking for food the second they arrive at a new place.'

'That is so thoughtful, thank you.'

The grey tabby stretches out along the rug, before meowing and heading straight towards me and wrapping itself around my legs.

'She likes you,' notes Viola as she refills our glasses with the tangy, delicious lemonade. 'Cats are very particular about people. They decide who they like.'

Emma, Cheryl and I enjoy slices of olive bread with fragrant, juicy tomatoes, washed down with more lemonade, and then watch as Viola crosses the room to a cupboard and takes a bottle of yellow liquid from a shelf.

She pours a small amount into three shot glasses and hands one to each of us. 'Let me introduce you to limoncello, if you haven't already tried it. It is a liqueur that is usually taken at the end of a meal. Welcome to Tuscany and *salute*!'

'*Salute!*' the three of us say, clinking glasses and smiling broadly.

After we have finished our refreshments, Viola and Maria insist on trundling our cases across the driveway to our accommodation.

'You have this apartment,' Viola says, fishing a key out of her pocket to open the red-painted wooden door. 'There are two honeymooners from Germany next door.'

'I hope the walls are thick!' Cheryl whispers in my ear, and I stifle a smile.

Taking our key and bidding goodbye to Viola and Maria, we step inside the guest accommodation, which is simply furnished and spotless. The walls are solid brick (thankfully) and painted a fresh white. The kitchen has pretty blue cupboards and an oak kitchen table with a small hamper in the centre containing coffee, orange juice, cheese, salami and bread. There are two bedrooms; one is a twin, the other a single. Each have dark wooden beds covered with red bedspreads over crisp white sheets. A lounge area is home to a large green sofa, and a wooden bookcase stands against the back wall, its shelves furnished with an assortment of novels. The scent of fresh lavender permeates the room and I inhale deeply, feeling so pleased to be here – away from everything.

'Right, do you mind if I bagsy the single room?' I ask. 'Just in case I have a bad dream. Sometimes I sleep rather deeply too, I think it's the tablets.'

'You mean you snore? You can definitely have your own room in that case,' teases Cheryl.

'This is just perfect,' says Emma, opening some French doors that give a glimpse of the turquoise pool and the rolling green hills beyond.

'All these books are in Italian,' grumbles Cheryl, turning over a paperback from the bookshelf in the lounge.

'Didn't you bring any books of your own?' asks Emma, who sensibly packed three.

'You can read one of mine, if you like,' I offer. 'Although maybe reading about a serial killer who murders a young woman in a remote farmhouse may not be the best choice,' I muse.

'You shouldn't read stuff like that if you're a bit depressed, Maisie. Books like that affect the mind,' says Emma, tapping her head.

I suppose she's right, but I've always enjoyed a good mystery, devouring Agatha Christie novels when I was younger and being a big fan of murder mysteries on the television. Maybe I should stick to watching re-runs of *Friends*.

'Right,' says Cheryl. 'I'm jumping in the shower, then I'll ask Viola to recommend a good restaurant for tonight.'

'I'm going to unpack and put everything away,' says Emma. 'You could always just check out a local restaurant on TripAdvisor for reviews, Cheryl. For all we know Viola might just recommend her relatives' rubbish restaurant.'

'Don't you sometimes just want to try things with an open mind, choose a restaurant by yourself without having everyone else's opinion on it?' I ask.

'Never,' says Emma, aghast. 'If I'm parting with my hard-earned cash I want to make sure it's for something decent.'

'Well, OK, I'm going to have that shower anyway,' Cheryl says, sighing. 'We can sort out where we're going to eat later.'

I eye my large suitcase in the corner of the room and pull a swimsuit and a beach towel from it. I spied the pool area through the French doors leading to the patio earlier and can't wait to slump down onto a sun lounger and relax. 'I'm going outside for an hour,' I announce. 'The rest of my unpacking can wait.'

Making my way to the pool area, I let out a gasp. The glimmering pool has views of the hills beyond, with patchwork green meadows interspersed with fields of golden sunflowers. To the right of the pool, in the distance, is a large corrugated barn with a green tractor outside and a pen full of pigs. The sun is still fairly strong and I can feel its warm rays on my arms as I head towards the sunbeds.

The swimming pool looks cool and inviting and as it's only four o'clock in the afternoon, I decide to jump in. I tentatively dip my toe in the water and find it's surprisingly lukewarm.

Cheryl and Emma appear in their bikinis a few minutes later, with Cheryl clutching a bottle of Prosecco she purchased from duty-free and three champagne glasses.

I immerse myself fully in the water, feeling the cool liquid cascade over me. Concentrating on my breathing, I do thirty laps of the pool. I'd forgotten how much I enjoy swimming. I used to go regularly after work, when I worked at Harry's store in town, the perfect antidote to a busy day. It made me feel so good afterwards.

Drying myself off, I'm about to soak up the sun when I hear the hum of the tractor. We all sit up and watch as it trundles towards us from across the field, before it stops at a perimeter fence beyond the garden. The driver switches the engine off and jumps down. He's a tall, broad-shouldered young man, with gleaming olive skin, and he's wearing jeans, a black vest and a pair of green wellingtons. He's quite the hunk, I can't help noticing.

'Be still my quivering heart,' whispers Emma, lowering her sunglasses to take a better look.

'It's not my heart that's quivering!' says Cheryl, sitting up and sucking her stomach in.

'Ladies, good afternoon,' the hunk says, sweeping back his dark, untamed hair. 'I hope you had a good journey. My name is Gianni. I am Viola's son.' He extends his hand to each of us. His handshake is firm and his dark brown eyes twinkle as he smiles.

As he shakes my hand, I realise that he's the very same tractor driver with whom we had a near miss in the road. 'You owe me a cappuccino,' I say huffily.

He looks bemused.

'The last one went over my cream top when your tractor almost collided with our taxi. Coffee and cream, quite the combination.'

'You were all in the taxi. I am so sorry! Although maybe your driver, he did not pay attention. I'm sure I saw him fiddling with his knob.'

'I beg your pardon?'

'Knob. Dial. I am sorry. I think he was tuning his radio.'

'Oh… right! Never mind, at least we arrived in one piece.'

Viola appears outside when she hears the sound of her son's voice. 'Gianni. Have you seen your father?'

'No, Mother, not since this morning.'

'When you see him, please tell him I need him here,' she says, before returning to the house.

'So, ladies,' continues Gianni, 'I hope you have a pleasant holiday here at the farmhouse. My mother will do anything for you. It's usually my father she has a problem with,' he says, laughing.

I wonder what his father has done to be in Viola's bad books.

As if reading my mind, Gianni says, 'My father is very charming. He took a female guest to the airport three hours ago and isn't back yet. If I know my father, he will be having a sneaky drink with one of his friends in the village before he returns home. My parents have been married for almost thirty years. They adore each other – but they fight a lot!'

I wonder if Gianni is a charmer like his father…

'Well, it's nice to meet you all. I'm sure I will see you around. *Ciao*,' he says as he fires up his tractor. We all watch him drive off in the direction of the barn.

'Right. I'm going to get dressed now,' I say half an hour later, after lying in the sun. 'I want to take a little walk around the area, check out some restaurants for dinner.'

'I'll come with you,' says Emma, jumping up. 'Are you coming, Cheryl?'

'I think I might just stick around here a little longer.' Cheryl takes a long a sip of her Prosecco. 'There might not be too much of the sun left to enjoy today. Plus you never know who you might meet around here,' she says, gazing into the distance towards the pig barn across the field.

Chapter Seven

A ten-minute stroll downhill, along a cobbled street, passing traditional shuttered houses along the way, takes us into the centre of the village of San Marco. A white church takes centre stage in the square, and we stand for a moment, taking in the shops, quaint coffee houses and a handful of traditional restaurants that surround the square. The smell of fresh bread from a bakery permeates the air and, above the shops, pink and white flowers spill from faded terracotta pots that jostle for space on the balconies of the sandstone houses.

On one balcony, two young girls are playing with an assortment of dolls that are spread out on a blanket. They wave at us as we walk past. Two young men sitting at a table outside a café, their mopeds close by, raise their heads from their mobile phones and say '*Ciao!*' as we walk past.

'Everyone's really friendly around here, aren't they?' says Emma.

I turn round to find the two Italian blokes gazing after us as we meander on. 'I'm sure they are, but Italian men do have a bit of a reputation.'

'I know. Everything's not like it is in the movies though. I'm sure they're perfectly respectable really,' says Emma, beaming.

'You think?'

Emma is charmingly innocent. Even on a girls' night out, she can never tell when a bloke is coming on to her.

Passing Alfredo's, a cosy-looking restaurant with red wooden window frames, we stop to study the menu in the glass case at the front of the restaurant.

'Mmm, this menu looks great. I could eat everything on here,' I say, reading the descriptions of the delicious fish and pasta dishes, not to mention a variety of mouth-watering pizzas. 'Chicken cooked in white wine and finished in a light tarragon cream sauce with a pasta of your choice. Sounds lush.'

'The smoked pancetta in a tomato and mascarpone sauce with tagliatelle appeals to me. But then I love salmon and there are some gorgeous fish dishes here,' notes Emma, as a handsome, middle-aged man with a small beard appears at the doorway.

'Ladies, hello. You are here on holiday?'

'Yes, we arrived today. We're just checking out somewhere for dinner later.'

'Maybe you would like me to reserve you a table here this evening?' he says with a smile. 'Reservation is recommended as we get very busy after eight o'clock.'

I glance at Emma, who shrugs, sighs and agrees.

'OK. That would be nice. There will be three of us, if that's alright. Shall we say eight thirty?'

'*Perfetto!* And for now? Maybe you would like a cold drink?' He gestures to an outside table shaded by a striped umbrella. 'The sun is still hot. By the way, my name is Alfredo, I am the owner.' He lifts our chairs out for us and Emma and I sit down beneath the umbrella, before ordering two beers. Shortly afterwards a smiling young waiter arrives with two chilled bottles of Peroni and a small dish of Italian pretzels.

'What a gorgeous little place,' says Emma, glancing around the cobbled square. Waiters at a grey-stoned restaurant on the far side are setting up outdoor tables with red and white tablecloths, ready for the evening service.

'It really is. I still can't believe I actually won this holiday. I keep expecting someone to inform me that it's all been a mistake and there's a flight waiting to take us home.'

'Well, you deserve it. You work bloody hard,' Emma says.

'So do you. Actually, I'll have to ask the supermarket if I can increase my hours when I get home. Now that I've ditched my job in the sandwich shop.'

'And you have to earn a crust,' jokes Emma.

'I know. Don't want to be short of dough.'

'Well you'd better start thinking.'

'You mean use my loaf?'

'Right, that's it! I can't think of any more bread jokes,' Emma says, giggling.

After finishing our drinks we head back to the farmhouse, spying a cute little bakery with an arched doorway at the edge of the village.

'Let's go in here,' says Emma. 'Get something to tide us over until dinner.'

Stepping inside onto the marble floor of the cool building, we marvel at the glass counter that is full of cakes and pastries. Tiny sponges iced in various pastel colours with cherries on the top look like little enticing jewels. A shelf behind the counter displays an assortment of breads, including crusty plaited loaves, olive focaccias and floury farmhouse loaves sitting alongside each other in rustic baskets. For a split second, the yeasty smell of the freshly baked bread makes me think of my old job at the sandwich shop.

'*Buon pomeriggio*,' says a young assistant with a wide smile. 'What would you like?'

We eye the tempting selection and eventually decide on a *Torta della Nonna*, which translates as Granny's Cake – a pastry case filled with custard and cream, topped with pine nuts and icing sugar. We also buy a panettone in wax paper that should last for a few days.

'I hope you enjoy the cake,' says the assistant, placing our goods into a square paper bag.

We're a few minutes into our walk back to the farmhouse when we hear the toot-toot of a horn. It's the moped guys.

'*Ciao*, ladies. Would you like a lift?' one of them asks.

I have visions of us being murdered and dumped in a lavender field, but Emma is already saying, 'Oh, that's really nice of you. But it's hardly worth it, we'll be there in less than ten minutes. Thanks for asking though.'

'Come on,' says the young man with a dazzling smile. 'Live a little.'

They are probably in their early twenties and I decide that I could disarm them with a few judo moves if they were to try any funny business. I reached brown belt. A long time ago admittedly, but you never forget.

'Sure,' I say, looping my bag across my body.

We hop onto the bikes and I enjoy the brief ride up the hill and past fields, feeling the wind blowing through my hair. A few minutes later, we are being deposited courteously at the front of the farmhouse.

'So, maybe we see you around? You are here on holiday?'

'Yes,' I answer to the young man who gave me a lift.

'Well, enjoy yourselves. There are many attractions in Tuscany,' he says as he eyes me up and down.

'There certainly are,' whispers Emma, as the young men scoot off into the distance.

Chapter Eight

We arrive at the farmhouse to the sight of a balding man lifting his head from under the bonnet of a blue car and dabbing his head with a handkerchief. It's Viola's husband.

'Buongiorno, ladies. I see you took the local transport home.' He smiles. 'I will take you into the village next time, if you like. When I fix my car that is.' He wipes his hands on a rag before shaking our hands warmly. 'My name is Fillipo, the owner. I'm sorry I wasn't here to help with your bags when you arrived.' He bangs the car boot down. 'Right, I think that is enough for one day. It's time for a little drink now. Would you care to join me?' he asks with a broad smile and a twinkle in his eye.

We politely decline his offer as Viola's voice rings out, calling to her husband.

Cheryl is just about to leave the pool area when we wander through to the garden. 'So, did you find somewhere for dinner?' she asks eagerly.

'We did, and the table is booked for eight thirty. I've got this for us to be going on with,' I say, waving the bag of goodies from the bakery.

'Nah, it's almost six o'clock,' replies Cheryl, glancing at her watch. 'I'll just have a few olives,' she says, pulling some from a nearby tree.

'Well, I'm going to have some cake and a coffee. My stomach has rumbled all the way home,' says Emma.

'I was going to walk down and join you, but I ended up having a little snooze,' Cheryl says, stretching her arms over her head. 'It's so gorgeous here. I'd forgotten how much I love the sun. The tanning salons back home just aren't the same.' Her olive skin already has the beginnings of an attractive golden glow.

'Thought you might have been distracted by our farmer,' says Emma.

'No, he never came back, more's the pity,' Cheryl says, pouting.

'Well, he does have a job to do. It's a working farm, I don't suppose he can hang around with the guests all day,' I point out.

'Suppose so. What was San Marco like then?'

'Quaint. A few shops, bars and restaurants, and a church. It's all very pretty. Not to mention friendly locals. We even got a lift up the hill from a couple of guys on mopeds.'

'You never! Can't leave you for five minutes before you go flirting with the locals,' Cheryl says, laughing.

'Says you! Hanging around hoping the hunky farmer would put in an appearance.'

'As if. Anyway, bagsy first in the shower,' says Cheryl, racing towards the French doors.

Back inside, Emma flicks the kettle on before flopping down onto the sofa with her book. She emptied her case before we went out and all her outfits are neatly pressed and hanging in the wardrobe.

'Shame we never got a chance to chat to those blokes for a little longer. The one who gave me a lift was really cute. I wonder how old he was?'

'Emma!' I protest, feeling taken aback. She's a married woman, after all.

'Don't look so shocked,' she says.

'I'm not shocked; surprised maybe. I thought you and Joe were still all loved up.'

'Hmm, hard to be loved up when he's never around. He seems to love being on the road more than being at home.'

'He earns good money, doesn't he? Didn't you tell me he wants to pay the mortgage off early?'

'At what cost though? We spend weekends together like clandestine lovers. You wouldn't think we were husband and wife.'

'Have you told him how you feel?'

'We've talked about it, yes. He doesn't seem to see things my way. He thinks he's doing it all for us. Sometimes I think he just likes the excitement of having a weekend wife.'

'Maybe you could ask him to stop being a tramp and stay local?'

'A tramp?!' Emma laughs.

'Sorry, have I got that wrong?'

'Ha ha, no, the drivers do call it tramping, when they work away from home all week and sleep in their cabs. I don't think Joe's a tramp though. At least I hope not! And don't worry, I'm fine, really. I've got a busy job and great friends like you.' She smiles.

'That's very true. How many mates would take you on holidays to Tuscany?' I say, nudging her gently with my elbow.

She leans in and gives me a hug. 'I know. You're always so kind to everyone. Even when you're not feeling great yourself.'

'Stop it, you'll have me blushing. Right. I suppose I'd better put my things away too,' I say, looking at her neatly arranged belongings.

In the bedroom, I throw back the lid of my hand luggage and a frown crosses my face. *Who the hell does this belong to?*

❧

'Oh great, that's all I need. This is not my hand luggage!' I sigh in exasperation.

Emma strolls into the bedroom and stares into the bag, which contains bottles of wine. 'Who cares? Three bottles of wine! Someone must have been to duty-free and stocked up. Shame to let it go to waste.' She retrieves a bottle and reads the label. 'Shall I go and look for some wine glasses?'

'I'm not sure that we should. It doesn't belong to me.'

'Honestly, Maisie, don't stress. Who's going to worry about three bottles of wine? I hope there's a corkscrew in here.' She's rummaging through a kitchen drawer full of utensils and snags the tip of a fingernail on a cheese grater. 'Brilliant. What a stupid bloody place to put a cheese grater.'

'What, in a drawer full of kitchen equipment? Anyway, don't worry. Cheryl will sort your nails out for you.'

'Did someone mention my name?' asks Cheryl, emerging from the shower, wearing a fluffy white robe and a towel on her head, to find Emma and me staring into the bag. 'Oh, wow! When did you go to duty-free? Or did you bring that with you?'

'It's not mine,' I reply, mildly panicked.

'What do you mean, it's not yours? Whose is it, then?'

'I don't know,' I say, racking my brains as to how a bag full of wine could have come into my possession.

'Well, it obviously happened at the airport. But it's hand luggage, it didn't go into the hold with the big cases, did it? How could it get mixed up?' asks Emma, frowning deeply.

I suddenly remember the incident when a security guard was chasing a man through the airport and my luggage trolley went spinning. 'It must have happened back at the airport. I remember a man crashing into my trolley and dropping his bag. Maybe he picked up the wrong one…'

'Anyway, who cares how you got it? Happy days, is what I say! Let me dry my hair and then we'll crack a bottle open before dinner,' says Cheryl, spraying some heat protector onto her long black hair. 'I can imagine the face on whoever opens your hand luggage to find… uh, what exactly is in your bag, Maisie?' she asks.

'Some books and a load of magazines, including my favourite puzzle magazine. Oh, and a dream catcher. Sometimes I have strange dreams.'

'Don't think that's much of a trade.' She laughs. 'Whoever's got your bag must be fuming.'

'This is not funny, Cheryl.'

'I know. Look, it's simple. Let's phone the airport just to see if anyone's handed your bag in and left any details.'

'OK, yes, that's a good idea. I'll do it now.'

'Right, I'm going to blow-dry my hair,' Cheryl announces.

'I'll jump in the shower next,' says Emma. 'And don't worry. You've done absolutely nothing wrong, Maisie,' she reassures me. 'I'm sure we'll got to the bottom of it.'

Chapter Nine

Half an hour later, on the patio outside, as the sun gently disappears over the horizon, I pour us each a glass of red wine, feeling slightly guilty as I do.

I did phone Pisa Airport and no one had handed my bag in, and the airport staff weren't able to tell me of anyone who had reported some missing hand luggage, so it seems that for now I am stuck with a bag of wine bottles.

'Mmm, this wine tastes pretty good,' says Cheryl. 'I don't normally like red wine, but this's lovely. What a stroke of luck.'

'Lucky for who? I've got nothing to read now,' I tell her. 'And let's hope I don't have any bad dreams. I'll probably wake you up with my screaming, if I do.'

Thoughts of books and bad dreams disappear as I take a sip of the absolutely stunning wine. It's as smooth as velvet and tastes of honey, chocolate and aged oak barrels. It's truly divine and not like anything I've ever tasted before. It's on a whole different level.

When we finish the bottle, Cheryl is all for opening another one, but I have a feeling we have just drunk something very special. 'I may be wrong, but I think this may be a good vintage. It could even be valuable. Sorry, girls, but we're not drinking any more of it. The other bottles are going in the safe.' Thankfully, I'd found a safe tucked into the back of the wardrobe in my bedroom. There was just room inside it for the remaining two bottles of wine as well as any watches or jewellery we might need to lock up.

'Spoilsport,' huffs Cheryl.

'Don't worry. We'll order more wine at the restaurant. Come on, let's make a move.'

As we walk downhill towards the village, it's a still and balmy evening and we are all wearing long, floaty sundresses. We pass the sandstone houses with shuttered windows and inhale the scent of honeysuckle climbing up their walls. Residents are sitting outside their front doors on kitchen chairs, drinking coffee and chatting, catching up on the events of the day. They nod to us as we amble along, feeling thankful that we have chosen pretty, flat sandals rather than high heels, as the stone cobbles gently massage our feet. The lights around the square beckon us towards them like a lighthouse in a dark sea.

When we arrive at the restaurant, Alfredo is chatting to a group of people at a large table. Outside the restaurant, tables and chairs are arranged around a large olive tree threaded with glowing fairy lights. There's a real holiday vibe in the air as diners chat excitedly, the sound of laughter rippling in and around the restaurant.

Seeing us, Alfredo breaks off his conversation and comes over to greet us. 'Ladies, *buona sera*. How good to see you. Please,' he says, extending an arm and guiding us to a table, covered with a red-and-white checked tablecloth, beneath the brightly lit branches of the gnarled olive tree. 'Is this table OK for you?' he asks.

'*Perfetto, grazie,*' I reply, glancing around and admiring our surroundings and the twinkling lights from other restaurants around the square as the darkness slowly draws in.

'Oh, this is really gorgeous,' says Emma, as we take our seats. All around, twinkling lights from other restaurants are lighting up the square as the darkness slowly draws in.

Alfredo disappears inside to fetch menus, before returning a moment later and handing one to each of us. 'So, welcome to my restaurant, ladies. I hope you'll have a pleasant evening. What can I get you to drink?'

'A nice bottle of Valpolicella, if that's OK with everyone?' I suggest. Emma and Cheryl nod enthusiastically. 'And a jug of water, please.'

As Alfredo goes to fetch our drinks, we peruse the menu.

'Oh wow, the food sounds amazing. I don't know what to choose, but whatever I order I always fancy someone else's dish anyway,' says Cheryl, laughing.

'I'm having the salmon linguine,' Emma says, closing her menu.

'That was quick, you've barely looked at the menu,' says Cheryl.

'I picked it out this afternoon when Maisie and I had a glance at the menu outside. I've been looking forward to it ever since.'

Cheryl and I decide on the Tuscan chicken casserole, which is the speciality of the house. We place our order when Alfredo returns with our drinks.

'Would you like to try the wine?' Alfredo pours a small amount in my glass.

I take a mouthful. It tastes of rich blackcurrant with a vanilla finish – delicious. '*Molto bello. Grazie,*' I reply, determined to try and speak a little Italian when I can.

'I'm glad you like it. It's a local wine made from grapes grown at a vineyard only a few miles away.'

I make a mental note to try to visit it.

'I can't believe we're actually here,' says Cheryl, as Alfredo leave us to it. 'A couple of days ago I was up to my eyes in perm lotion. I don't think Mrs Wilson was too impressed when I had to cut her hair early. She wanted it done next week, the day before she goes on her holidays.'

'Couldn't someone else do it?'

'They could, but she only trusts me. She says I knock years off her.' Cheryl laughs.

'Your hairdressing skills and the Botox injections,' I suggest. Moira Wilson is seventy next month and could pass for fifty.

'She denies having Botox, you know. She says it's all down to facial exercises and a good haircut.'

'Yeah, and my name's Madonna.'

We sip our wine and consider our good fortune until the decadent smell of our food wafts towards us. Our young waiter delivers our orders with a flourish and soon Cheryl and I are tucking into Tuscan chicken casserole served in terracotta bowls. The waiter places a basket of fresh, aromatic bread in the middle of the table, along with some olive oil and balsamic vinegar.

'Oh my word, this really is delicious,' I say, devouring the tasty, simple food. The sauce has a rich tomato flavour with a tangy background. Soft, melt-in-the-mouth chicken falls off the bone.

'This doesn't taste like my mum's chicken casserole,' says Cheryl. 'I think they've added balsamic vinegar and anchovies for richness.'

'And slow cooking it makes all the difference,' adds Emma. 'I've made something similar to that at home.'

'Joe must be made up having a cook like you,' I say, in between mouthfuls of the wonderful food.

'He never comments on my cooking. I could give him beans on toast and he wouldn't notice,' she says, shrugging wearily.

'How's your salmon, Emma?' I ask her, wanting to get off the subject of Joe.

Emma closes her eyes and mutters 'mmm' as she places a forkful of salmon in a fragrant sauce wrapped around some linguine into her mouth. 'Just gorgeous. I don't know if it's the ingredients or the ambience, but I don't think I could ever replicate this at home.'

We finish our meals and order tiramisu for dessert – an Italian classic. It turns out to be the best I've ever tasted and not at all like the supermarket ones I've tried, even from the luxury range. I devour the smooth, velvety texture of the cream, the rich shot of espresso balancing the flavour perfectly. As our meal finishes, Alfredo appears with three shots of zesty limoncello liqueur.

'Please have this with my regards. *Salute!*'

'*Salute!*' We all cheer as we chink our tiny glasses together.

'And what happens in Tuscany, stays in Tuscany.' Cheryl winks as we down the refreshing lemony shots.

'So, ladies, what are your plans for tomorrow?' Alfredo asks.

'I've just been thinking about that,' says Emma. 'I'd love to go to Siena, if anyone fancies it.'

'I was hoping to do that in a couple of days. I fancy a pool day tomorrow,' I reply, realising I'm still a little tired. Sometimes my medication makes me feel a little sleepy. Although I guess that's what I'm here for – to relax. 'There's loads of time for sightseeing.'

'Same here,' says Cheryl. 'Prosecco and pool tomorrow. I want to work on my tan.'

'I'm going into Siena tomorrow,' says Alfredo, as he stacks our empty plates onto a tray. 'I have a little business to attend to. I would be happy to give you a lift there.' He fixes his dark blue eyes on Emma. He's probably somewhere in his mid forties and ruggedly handsome in that classic Italian way.

'Really? Are you sure you wouldn't mind? I'm not one for lazing around the pool too much, if I'm honest. There's so much I want to see.'

'Good. I will pick you up at ten o'clock,' he says, before leaving the table.

Cheryl and I exchange knowing glances, which Emma clocks.

'What? I'm getting a lift into Siena, it's no big deal.'

The restaurant has filled up even more over the last hour and the sound of buzzing chat and laughter is ringing around the little square. The illuminated bell tower of the church casts a soft glow over the cobbled square and I feel myself slowly beginning to relax into my surroundings. Warm and sultry air wraps us in a hug and we contentedly soak up the holiday atmosphere. Glancing around I notice several loved-up couples holding hands and I fight a little pang of regret for what might have been with Harry. I force myself to focus on the moment, feeling lucky to be here.

We finish our drinks and are about to leave, when I spot the two guys with the mopeds sitting outside a bar opposite. One of them, wearing tight jeans and a fitted black T-shirt, raises his hand and walks towards us.

'*Ciao*, ladies. Are you having a good time?'

His friend is on a mobile phone and staring straight at me. My stomach flips over. And not in a good way.

I think of the bottles of wine back at the farmhouse. The second man approaches us, still muttering in Italian into his phone, a serious expression on his face. We chat to them for a few minutes, Cheryl flirting with the younger one, and I suddenly wonder if I have their carry-on bag. Maybe my hunch about the wine being valuable was right. The bottles could be worth hundreds of euros. Maybe even thousands. I think it's best if I get this thing over with right away. I take a deep breath.

'Have I got something that you want?' I ask the one who was on the phone. 'Because if I have, I can give it to you back at the farmhouse.'

'Wow! You English ladies are very forward!' His friend looks at him and shrugs his shoulders, a cheeky grin spreading across his face,

Emma realises what I am talking about and pulls me to one side. 'Maisie, what on earth do you think you are doing?'

'They probably know I've got their bag,' I whisper in her ear. 'They were staring at me.'

'That's probably because they fancy you, Maisie. Come on. They're just two young Italian blokes, chancing their arm.'

'Well, whatever… I'm taking that bag back to the airport tomorrow. I should have done it today.'

We say our good nights with the moped guys looking thoroughly confused, and begin the walk back uphill once again. Cheryl and Emma are happily merry and giggle all the way home, with Cheryl teasing Emma about her trip out with her older man tomorrow. But I find that I'm stone cold sober.

'Oh, Maisie, what are you like? "I can give you what you want back at the farmhouse",' mimics Cheryl. 'That poor young bloke's eyes nearly popped out of his head.'

They both collapse with laughter and, despite myself, I laugh along too.

'You need to lighten up, Maisie,' Cheryl says. 'You're worrying yourself over what's probably a couple of mid-priced bottles of wine. That's hardly the Crown Jewels.'

I realise my anxiety is probably making me overthink the whole thing. I bet most people would have drunk the wine by now anyway… Thinking of it, it's probably a very fortunate mix up and a great way to start a holiday.

'Try not to worry so much and relax.' Cheryl and Emma link arms with me as we stroll on.

'I've got a feeling,' says Emma, 'that this is going to be a holiday to remember!'

Chapter Ten

Viola knocks on our front door just after nine o'clock the following morning. She's holding a large jug of fresh lemonade and a bag of olives. She looks as cool as a cucumber in a white cotton dress and with her wavy, dark brown hair loosely pinned up.

'*Buongiorno,*' she chirps. 'Fresh lemonade. And just to say if you are going out today make sure you take plenty of water and a big hat. We have a heatwave starting soon,' she tells us in her heavy Italian accent.

'How thoughtful, thank you, Viola. Don't worry, Cheryl and I are hanging around the pool today. Emma is going to Siena, so I'll let her know.'

'Today is not really a day for sightseeing.' She frowns. 'Later we will have over one hundred degrees.'

I'm about to reply when I spot Gianni crossing the courtyard towards the farmhouse. He waves and says, '*Buongiorno.*' Somehow he looks taller than he did yesterday, and undeniably handsome, with his head of thick black hair and large brown eyes. He's wearing blue jeans, his green wellies, and a short-sleeved T-shirt that accentuates his strong muscles.

'Good morning,' I say, with a smile.

'How are you today? I hope you had a pleasant evening in the village.'

'Oh, it was just wonderful. We ate at Alfredo's. The food was to die for.'

'Ah, I see you have discovered the best restaurant in the village on your first night. You were lucky to get a table.'

'I know. Luckily we reserved it in the afternoon, when we went for a walk to the village.'

'So what are your plans on this beautiful day?' He's maintaining eye contact with those gorgeous brown eyes and for a second I feel a little flustered.

'Chilling around the pool with a book, probably, although I may have a little walk later. The surrounding area is so lovely. Emma's off to Siena shortly.'

'Siena is probably my favourite city. You should definitely see it while you are here.'

'I'll make a note of that. And you have a good day too.'

'Thank you. I have a very busy day ahead of me with lots of meat deliveries. I may also have to call the vet to take a look at one of the pigs that's not eating properly. This doesn't usually happen to a pig, unless there is something wrong. Anyway, I must be off. Enjoy your day.'

'Thanks. I will.'

Gianni strides off to his work, as Fillipo exits the farmhouse and makes his way towards us. Viola gives him a withering look and speaks to him in Italian. He retorts by throwing his hand in the air, then kissing her on the cheek. She bats him away with a tea towel, but there is a smile on her face.

'Hello, ladies, good morning. How are you settling in?' he asks, greeting us the Italian way by kissing us on both cheeks. Fillipo has the kind of gaze that never leaves your eyes and, at around sixty years of age, is still very charismatic.

'Good, thanks. We had a lovely evening in the village last night. It's so beautiful here.'

Cheryl and Emma emerge at the front door. Emma, looking pretty in a knee-length floral dress and a wide-brimmed straw hat, is ready for Alfredo to collect her. I take the opportunity to pass on Viola's warning about the heatwave and give her a bottle of water.

'And, of course, you ladies make this place even more beautiful. Once again I am sorry I was not here yesterday to help you with your luggage. I was a little detained. But now! Anything you need you just shout me, yes?'

'Thanks, we will.' I smile at him.

'OK. Well, *ciao* for now, ladies. Have a wonderful day,' he says, as he departs with a wide grin on his face.

'Blimey, what a charmer,' says Cheryl. 'No wonder Viola is always checking up on him.'

'Talking of charmers…' I say, as a shiny black two-seater sports car crunches its way up the gravel courtyard.

Stepping out of the car, Alfredo is dressed in a white linen shirt and jeans and sporting designer sunglasses. He looks attractive and far younger than his middle years. After he has wished all of us good morning, Emma steps into the passenger seat and Cheryl and I wave her off as the car disappears down the hill.

'So,' says Cheryl, glancing at her watch. 'I'm gonna grab my things and get round the pool. Work on my tan before the sun really gets up.'

'OK, I'll join you shortly. I'm just going inside to give Dad a ring.'

Unsurprisingly, Dad is working in the garden when I phone him. He tells me that he's been experimenting with growing different varieties of tomatoes and has been picking some for a salad lunch. 'So, tell me, how's the holiday going, love?'

'Oh, Dad, it's beautiful here, you'd love it. There are olive and almond trees all around. I could imagine your veg would grow twice the size in this heat. It's a bit of a working farm too. The son here looks after pigs on a piece of land across the field from our accommodation.'

'Sounds lovely. Are you going to go into Florence one day?'

'Yes, and Pisa. Emma is really excited about the history and culture here. Cheryl maybe not so much, although she has agreed to come to Florence and look at the shops. We'll probably go on the open-top bus tour.'

'That's the best way to see a place. Me and your mother did that in London the year before you were born. I remember the first time she saw Buckingham Palace, she was completely bowled over by it. We were lucky enough to see the Changing of the Guard when we hopped off the bus too. There were jostling crowds on a sweltering day but she loved every minute of it,' he recalls with affection in his voice. I suddenly find I have a lump in my throat as I think about Mum. Dad and I chat for a few more minutes before we finish the call, when my mind turns once again to the bottles of wine in the safe. I just can't help worrying about them. I decide to tell Dad all about it.

'What would you do, Dad?' I ask.

'When I was your age? I'm not going to lie I would have drunk them by now!' he chuckles. 'It was a genuine mistake, Maisie, you haven't done anything wrong. I bet the person who they belonged to has bought some more and forgotten all about them by now.'

Perhaps he's right, although I'm not entirely convinced. If that first bottle was anything to go by I still think I am in possession of something rather special…

I decide to go for a little walk to explore the surrounding area, as I'm not quite ready to sit around the pool. After telling Cheryl about my change of plan, I grab my sun hat and a bottle of water and set off. I turn left out of the drive, away from the hill leading to the village, and walk down a road where the low hum of a tractor in a nearby field and the trill of a bird are the only sounds. Soon I am passing some gates leading to a large villa, with cream-coloured walls, green-shuttered windows and an impressive moss-covered fountain in the centre of a sweeping driveway. There's a faded grandeur about the place that gives it a real sense of style.

Strolling on, I pass olive trees along the roadside and catch sight of a splash of yellow from a distant sunflower field. The sky above is painted a cornflower blue with not a cloud in sight. There's a gentleness about this countryside, mixed with an intoxicating smell of lavender, that's revitalising to the soul. It brings a tranquillity that no amount of medication could ever induce.

Continuing my walk, I come across several terracotta-tiled houses set back from the road. A goat in one of the front gardens trots towards the fence to greet me, no doubt hoping for some food. I carry on walking and taking in the stunning scenery, until the sun moves higher in the sky, its heat becoming stronger on my shoulders, and I decide to turn back.

Approaching the farmhouse, I'm lost in a daydream when the tractor that Gianni drives emerges from a narrow farm-access road. He brakes suddenly as I'm about to walk straight out in front of him.

'This is getting to be a little bit of a habit. Good job you don't have a coffee with you today,' he says, raising an eyebrow.

'Gosh, I'm sorry, Gianni. It's so quiet here. You don't really expect to see traffic. Well, not from a field anyway. I was daydreaming, I'm afraid.'

I was thinking about back home, truth be told, hoping Dad's OK and wondering whether Harry is earning enough money on the market stall to make ends meet. Not that I should care about him really.

'We must all have our daydreams.' Gianni smiles. 'Although maybe not along a main road.'

'Sorry,' I say again, feeling like a child who's being admonished.

'Do not worry. So, are you heading back to the pool?'

'Yes, I think I'm going to read for a while and then have a swim. Cheryl is already there working on her tan.'

'Would you like to come and see the pigs first?'

I can't imagine that's a chat-up line that has had much success.

'Please, come,' says Gianni noting my hesitation. 'Afterwards I will drive you across the field to the pool at the villa.' He is already holding his hand out of the tractor to help me up beside him.

I manage to squeeze into the seat beside him and we rumble along towards the barn. Taking a sideways glance, I'm struck at how handsome he looks in profile, with his strong chin and his neat yet masculine straight nose. When we stop, he jumps down to help me climb out. We are greeted by at least a dozen snuffling pigs enclosed in an outdoor pen. Their skin looks almost black.

'What are they?'

'Pigs.'

'Funny. I mean what breed?'

'Tuscan black pigs. They make the finest Tuscan prosciutto. Would you like to try some?'

I'm staring at the pigs, who are snorting and playfully nudging each other. I'm not sure I could sample one of their relatives right at this very moment. 'Maybe another time. When I'm not so close to the living version.'

'You get used to it. I know that they have a good life here. The best.'

The nursery rhyme 'This little piggy went to market' flits through my mind.

After getting up close and personal to the pigs, I decline Gianni's offer of a ride across the field towards the pool area, as it's only a short walk.

'I will see you around,' Gianni says. 'Hopefully not in the road again!' He smiles a broad smile with white, perfect teeth.

❧

Cheryl is sitting upright on her sunbed, watching me as I head towards her. 'Where *have* you been?' she asks.

'I had a good walk around the local area, then bumped into Gianni, who gave me a lift to say hello to his pigs.'

'Oh aye. Has hunky farmer been showing you his salami?'

'Behave! He's a perfect gentleman,' I say, flopping down onto a sunbed beside her.

'If you say so. Anyway, I was thinking… as you know quite a bit about wine, do you fancy a winery tour tomorrow? I've been reading about one in this brochure.' She thrusts a pamphlet into my hand. 'A grand tour of the vineyard and the cellars, followed by wine samples and nibbles at the bar.'

'Sounds good.'

'Shall I see if they have any spaces for tomorrow?' asks Cheryl, fishing her phone out of her bag.

'Go on, then. Book a place for Emma, too.'

'Do you think she might have made have other plans?' asks Cheryl, with a wry smile.

'I'm certain she'll come with us. It will be right up her street. Actually, I'll take a photograph of the wine in the wardrobe and show it to an expert. They should be able to tell us its value.'

'Good thinking.'

Cheryl secures us a place on the wine tour with pick-up at nine thirty tomorrow morning.

'Right, it's getting on for lunchtime. Fancy something to eat? Viola said that if we take a left turn out of the farmhouse there is a small restaurant called Giuseppe's, almost hidden from view about half a mile down a dirt track. The turning is just past a large villa with a fountain in the driveway. She tells me locals use the restaurant more than tourists, but they cook the best casserole in the area and the wine is cheap.'

'Sure,' I say. I only had yoghurt for breakfast and I'll be ready to eat something shortly. 'I walked past that villa less than an hour ago, but I didn't notice the track.'

We stroll along the road, with Cheryl admiring the scenic beauty of the area, a palette of yellows and greens beneath a brilliant blue sky. I suddenly imagine the russet landscape of autumn, with tractors rumbling across fields to collect the harvest. Autumn has always been my favourite season. We pass the grand villa with the fountain in the driveway and I see that the gates are open and there's a large white van outside the villa, with people unpacking chairs from it. We stop to watch as tables and chairs are unloaded and several people are pointing and passing instructions to each other in Italian. The trees in the front are being decorated with soft cream bows and someone else is placing solar lights along the driveway.

A woman in her twenties, with long black hair tied back, sees us watching and smiles. '*Buongiorno*,' she says, before adding, '*Nozze.*'

'Sorry,' I reply immediately. 'We didn't mean to be nosey, we're just curious.'

'No, no! *Nozze*. It means wedding!' The woman laughs.

'Ooh, how lovely. When is it?' asks Cheryl.

'Sunday afternoon. I think the ceremony is at two o'clock.'

'I bet that's going to be gorgeous,' says Cheryl, as we stroll on. 'I can imagine rose-covered arches and all that lovely furniture laid out on the lawn. It will be just a like a scene from one of those romantic movies.' She sighs. 'Imagine preparing the grounds for an outdoor wedding back home, two days before the event? You couldn't guarantee the weather.'

'That's true. Plan a barbecue in a heatwave in England and you're guaranteed rain.'

'I bet there'll be loads of fit men at that wedding. I wonder if we could wangle ourselves an invite?'

'I doubt it. We don't know anyone here.' Then I laugh, thinking to myself that if anyone can charm her way into a party it's Cheryl. Last year she unbelievably managed to gain us both access to the VIP area of a Justin Timberlake concert.

A few yards further on, we spot a simple sign with a wooden arrow that directs us down a track to Giuseppe's and ten minutes later we come across a very rustic-looking house surrounded by golden wheat fields. Half a dozen tables are set for lunch outside on a wooden porch. As we approach we hear the sound of a glass smashing and an angry exchange of words. We glance at each other, debating whether to turn back, when an elderly man appears. He has a huge grin on his face.

'Ladies! Welcome, welcome!' he says. 'Come and have a drink.' He shakes our hands warmly. 'My name is Gennaro.'

We figure a drink can't do any harm, so we order some beers before taking a seat at a simple wooden table. The smell of garlic assaults our senses.

'Something smells good,' I say, as Gennaro appears with two bottles of beer and ice- cold glasses.

'Speciality of the day. Pork stew. Nothing else. Only one thing. Made to perfection.'

'Oooh, yes, please. We'll have two plates of that, please, Gennaro,' enthuses Cheryl.

I didn't think I was hungry enough for anything substantial, but a little while later I am literally eating my words. The delicious peppery pork is served in a dish with a rich tomato sauce and various beans. A large hunk of fresh crusty bread is placed on a plate beside it.

'What is it with the food here? Even the simplest dish tastes amazing,' I say, dipping my bread into the tasty sauce, savouring the tangy tomatoes and enjoying the succulent pork.

'Maybe it's the sunshine. And eating al fresco,' Cheryl replies.

'Who's Al Fresco? I thought we were eating pork.'

'Oh, very funny.' Cheryl groans. 'But, really, when you think about the fancy names they come up with for food in restaurants back home it makes me laugh. They don't need to do that here.' She savours another mouthful of the delicious stew. 'Why don't we play a game. You have to guess the simple food with the poncey title from a French food menu.'

'OK.'

'*Macaronis au fromage.*'

'That's easy. Macaroni cheese.'

'Correct. How about this. *Assiette de charcuterie.*'

'Assorted meats,' I say at once.

'*Très bien*! OK… what is *terrine de pâté de foies poulet*?'

'*Poulet*, er…' I hesitate. 'I think that's chicken. So… chicken liver pâté?'

'Right!' Cheryl cries. 'Finally, aged salami with artisan cheeses on a sourdough base.'

'Easy!' I shout. 'Pizza! Shall we open a restaurant?'

We both laugh.

'I think I could get used to living in a place like this,' I say, as I view the charming surroundings, sated by the wonderful food.

'Could you? It might be a bit quiet for me, beautiful as it is. I'm a city girl at heart. Talking of city, shall we go to Florence in the next day or two? I was thinking of hiring a car as it's pretty cheap over here. I haven't touched my credit card in months, which is a record for me.'

'Hiring a car sounds like a great idea. We'll split the cost three ways, though. Don't be using your credit card.'

We order two more beers, just as four men arrive and take a table on the terrace.

'Things are looking up,' says Cheryl, lowering her sunglasses for a better look.

The owner of the restaurant goes over to greet the men and they begin a rapid conversation in Italian. The four men are all well built and three have dark hair, with the fourth having sandy-coloured hair. They glance over in our direction and smile.

'Where have they come from?' asks Cheryl, when the owner returns to refresh our drinks.

'Funny thing, they just asked me the same about you.' Gennaro laughs. 'They are local farmers working on an estate a few miles away. They make the trip to the restaurant at least once a week for my wife's food,' he states proudly.

When we are about to pay the bill, we discover that our last drinks were paid for by the farmers, who are now drinking beer and laughing loudly. We thank them on the way out.

'No problem,' says one of the hunky, dark-haired men. 'Nice to see two pretty ladies here. Where do you stay?'

The man with the sandy hair is smiling broadly at me. 'You think these two beautiful ladies are going to tell a flirt like you where they are staying?'

'Me? A flirt?' he says, pointing to his chest and laughing.

Despite their jokey demeanour, I can feel my cautious side take over and debate not telling them, but Cheryl has already blurted out, 'Villa Marisa.'

'*Sì, sì*, I know it. Maybe I see you around,' says the farmer, locking eyes with Cheryl.

'You bet. *Ciao*, boys!' she purrs.

I can feel their gaze on us as we walk away along the dirt track, and I feel a little exposed as their laughter rings through the air behind us. Maybe we shouldn't have ventured off the beaten track, although the food was well worth the visit. When the rear of the wedding villa comes into view up ahead I feel quietly relieved.

'I've been thinking about that wine,' I say, when we are almost back on the main road. 'I'm going to ask Gianni where the local police station is and hand it in.'

Cheryl stops in her tracks to face me. 'Are you serious? A couple of bottles of wine? It would go straight home with whoever you handed it in to.'

'I suppose so. But I'm desperate to return it to the owner. I just can't shake the feeling that it might be valuable.'

'Pity it isn't a bag full of cash,' she replies, laughing.

'What would you do if it was?'

'Well, that's easy. I'd keep it and use it to open my own salon. There's an empty shop on Moor Lane that I've had my eye on for a while, but I'll never get the deposit together.'

'Really? I thought you liked being mobile.'

'I do. I always wanted to work for myself. It can be a pain in the winter though. Sometimes it takes a while to get my old car started. Plus, it would make more sense having a salon because I can do nails and make-up too. Never mind. Maybe one day.'

'What would you call it?'

'I'm not sure. Maybe "Curl Up and Dye".'

'Are you serious? Sounds more like a funeral parlour!'

'What about "Fringe Benefits"?'

'Sounds like an insurance policy.'

'What about "Hair by Cheryl".'

'Perfect. No gimmicks. Just great hair.'

'You're a genius! That can be the tagline on my advertisement: "No gimmicks, just great hair".'

Chapter Eleven

Cheryl and I amble back to the farmhouse, chatting easily, and turn into the driveway at the same time as a black sports car, the driver merrily hooting the horn. It's Alfredo and Emma returning from Siena.

'Hi, guys,' Emma calls, waving.

Alfredo gets out of the car and opens the passenger door for Emma, before hurriedly jumping back in, waving goodbye and driving off.

Emma is carrying two carrier bags.

'Have you been shopping?' I ask, stating the obvious.

'Sure have. Cheese mainly, and bread. Oh, and this amazing layered pie from a deli. I figured we needed some food in the fridge. Maybe we can hire a car and do a big supermarket shop one day.'

'Definitely,' I reply. 'We can't afford to eat out for every single meal or our money will run out in no time. How was Siena?'

'Oh, girls, it was gorgeous. All those yellow buildings with terracotta, or should I say Siena-coloured rooftops. It was like walking onto a film set. There are fabulous medieval buildings everywhere. We had lunch on a rooftop restaurant that had a glorious view of the whole city. We must all go there together.'

'We will. We were talking earlier about hiring a car actually. I don't mind driving,' says Cheryl. 'Oh, and tomorrow we've booked you onto a vineyard tour with us, if that's OK with you.'

'Sounds perfect,' replies Emma. 'So what have you two been up to today then?'

We tell Emma all about the delicious lunch and the friendly local farmers who bought us a drink.

'Hardly surprising. You two turn heads wherever you go. I bet they couldn't believe their luck when you rocked up at their local restaurant, So, what we up to tonight?'

We're just thinking about this when, as if reading our thoughts, Viola appears on the driveway. '*Ciao*, ladies, do you have any plans this evening? We are having a little celebration here at the farmhouse for Sophia from the Villa Nina next door. She is getting married in two days' time. She is good friends with my daughter Maria. We have drinks and dinner. It's just a small gathering. There are not many young women in the village to join the celebration and so I think maybe the more the merrier for her special evening.'

'Ooh, do you mean a hen party? I love a hen party,' says Cheryl, grinning.

'*Sì, sì*! A hen's party! Antonio, her fiancé, is going into the village with Gianni and his brothers and some friends. I think maybe the girls don't want to bump into them; the village square is only small.'

We happily accept the invitation.

'I'm going to sunbathe for a couple of hours. I can't wait for this evening, it could be a lot of fun,' says Cheryl.

I think about the last hen party I went to when one of the girls at the shop was getting married. She vomited all over her shoes when she disembarked the mini bus outside her parents' house and hurled her sparkly wedges up into the air in disgust. They landed in the thick foliage of her elderly neighbour's tree in their front garden, where, as far as I'm aware, they remain to this day.

'It could be fun. But maybe the traditions here are not the same as home,' I suggest. I refused to have a hen night as I didn't want to be staring into some oiled-up male stripper's groin. I eventually agreed to have a meal at a Christakis's Greek restaurant in Liverpool, with dancing and plate-smashing, which was surprisingly therapeutic.

⚜

Back in our apartment I flick the kettle on as Emma unpacks her purchases and places them into the fridge. She seems a little quiet.

'Are you OK?' I ask her.

'Fine.' She sighs, then takes her shoes off and curls up on the sofa. 'I had such a lovely day today. It's really invigorating to see other places, isn't it? It's easy to get into a rut at home. I'm so glad I came on this holiday – thank you for inviting me.'

'I know what you mean. I absolutely love it here. It's so different to back home.'

'And being with someone who actually takes an interest in what you have to say is rather a novelty too.' She sighs again.

'Sounds like Alfredo has made quite an impression on you. I thought he was just dropping you in Siena while he had some business to attend to?'

'He did. He left me to explore for a couple of hours then we arranged to meet for lunch, which was amazing. Joe doesn't bother to take me out for dinner any more. Even after being on the road all week, he just likes to flop on the sofa with a takeaway and a bottle of wine. I have to force him to go out. I'm not sure I want to be with a man who has to be persuaded to have a night out with his wife.'

I pass Emma a coffee. 'Oh, Em, I'm so sorry, I didn't realise you were so unhappy.'

'Do you know something? Neither did I. Maybe we just need something to make us realise it. Being here and talking to someone who engages with me and seems genuinely interested in what I have to say… well, it's made me think.'

'Don't most relationships slip into the comfortable zone after a while, though?'

'Not to the point where one of you can't be arsed making any sort of effort.'

'I suppose so. Are you attracted to Alfredo?'

'No, and that's not the point really. I just felt good about myself. Maybe even admired a little, you know, given a little attention. I haven't felt like that in a long time.'

I think about my marriage to Harry. He certainly paid me attention. Little gifts here and there, bunches of flowers for no reason. The problem was I probably wasn't the only recipient of his affections. It hurts like hell when I think about it.

I can see tears threatening to spill over in Emma's eyes, so I put my coffee cup down and wrap her in a hug.

'You'll be just fine.'

'I know I will. I think I'll go and have a little siesta. Shopping in that heat has worn me out.'

I rinse the cups and think about how complicated relationships can be. Still feeling hurt after Harry, I'm quite happy on my own at the moment. Meeting someone new would only open up the possibility of more potential heartache.

Stepping outside onto the driveway, I find Cheryl chatting to Gianni. He turns to face me and smiles broadly. Despite myself, I smile fondly in return. It would appear that one way or another, this place is beginning to have a little bit of an effect on us all.

Chapter Twelve

The hen party at Villa Marisa is shaping up beautifully. Candles inside large glass vases have already been lit along both sides of the swimming pool, their soft glow flickering over the turquoise water. There's a large table, set with cutlery and glasses, at one end of the poolside patio, and fairy lights have been threaded through the branches of a large, ancient olive tree that stands by the perimeter fence. Beyond, the field stretches into the distance.

'This looks amazing,' says Emma, pulling her phone from her bag and taking a selfie of us all against the stunning backdrop. It's another beautiful evening and the sound of chirping cicadas fills the air.

Looking around, we are surprised to find that we are the first to arrive. Viola soon appears from the kitchen, followed by Maria, who looks striking in a long red dress, her waist-length dark hair loosely curled. They are each carrying a huge pot of food. A few seconds later Gianni follows, carrying a crate of wine or Prosecco bottles. He's wearing black trousers and a light blue shirt, looking completely different to his farmer image during the day. He catches my eye and smiles. As he puts the crate down by the table, I stroll over to him.

'How's the sick pig, Gianni?'

'Pregnant. She's off her food but otherwise OK. It's the first time I've seen a sow with morning sickness.' Gianni laughs.

'Really? Are you sure you're not telling porkies?'

'Porkies?'

'Never mind. Anyway, I'm glad it's nothing serious. Enjoy your evening with Antonio and his friends.'

'You too. Maybe I will see you later?' he says over his shoulder, as he walks back to the farmhouse.

'Wow, he scrubs up well,' says Cheryl, joining me. 'Do you think the men will be coming back here after they've been down into the village? It could be a lot of fun.'

'Who knows? It's hardly full of nightlife down there so I wouldn't be surprised if they come back here to finish their evening.'

Over the next half hour, bride-to-be Sophia and seven or eight prettily dressed young women filter into the pool area and take a seat at the large wooden table. Introductions are made and soon we are all tucking into delicious antipasti of various meats, cheeses and tasty olives, all washed down with Prosecco. We dip hunks of crusty bread into a tasty seafood stew called *cacciucco*, topped with fresh mussels, king prawns and juicy octopus rings. Viola tells us that this dish is often served for a special occasion such as this.

'Ooh, this is absolutely delicious, Viola. The sauce is incredible. You must definitely give me the recipe for this one,' says Emma.

'It would be my pleasure. You must make sure to use the freshest fish you can find.'

We chat easily to the guests and Cheryl goes all out schmoozing the bride-to-be, angling for a wedding invite.

It's a stunning and civilised gathering, despite large amounts of bubbly being consumed, and a far cry from the hen parties I've been to back home. Even so, there's an early start tomorrow for the winery tour and I'm considering going to bed, when I hear the raucous sound of male voices and laughter.

'What are they doing back so early?' huffs Sophia. 'It's only a little after eleven o'clock.'

A smiling, slightly-the-worse-for-wear group of men appear at the foot of the table.

'You can't be here. We are still having our hen's party,' says Viola, ushering the males into the farmhouse. 'Fillipo, go and organise a game of poker. Open a bottle of brandy or something.'

The mention of brandy and poker has the men filing obediently into the farmhouse kitchen.

Gathering up a plate of leftover food, Gianni quickly follows the others and Sophia's future husband, Antonio, is blowing kisses at her and mouthing, 'I love you,' as he departs.

'That's very sweet,' notes Emma.

Sophia looks unimpressed. 'Sometimes he's like a little puppy dog. Even on my wedding party he can't stay away,' she says, knocking back a glass of Prosecco.

'It's better than being ignored,' replies Emma, turning to me and whispering, 'Some women are never happy.'

'Those boys look the worse for wear,' Cheryl says, giggling, as a bloke at the end of the line zigzags into the farmhouse. 'It's a good job the wedding is in two days' time and not tomorrow.'

'Pigs!' says one of the diners.

'I wouldn't go that far. The men are a bit drunk maybe, but it is a stag party after all,' I remind them.

'No,' she says, slight panic in her voice. 'I mean *pigs*.'

Sophia is walking across the pool area when somebody shouts her name: '*Sophia! Look out!*'

We all turn to find two black pigs running and snorting their way across the ground at high speed. I swear they even have smiles on their faces. Everything seems to happen in slow motion as the first pig playfully nudges Sophia and sends her sprawling into the swimming pool to the strains of loud gasps. Then both pigs turn round and race happily back through the gate into the field.

'Dear god! Someone must have left the exit gate onto the field open,' says Viola, quickly rushing to close it.

Sophia splutters and curses in the pool, before clambering out looking like a drowned rat. Maria has rushed indoors for a large white towel, which she is now placing around the shivering woman's shoulders.

'Right, I'm going to call it a night now,' says Emma, trying to conceal her giggles. 'Early start in the morning.'

'I'll come with you,' I say, jumping up, grateful that she has made the suggestion because I'm dying for my bed. 'Are you coming, Cheryl?'

'Are you joking? I'm going nowhere,' says Cheryl, topping up her drink. 'Things are just beginning to warm up!'

We say our good nights and thank Viola for her wonderful food, before heading back to our apartment.

'Oh, poor Sophia. I can't believe she was pushed into a pool by a pig! It's a good job she can swim, isn't it?' says Emma.

'I never thought about that. Although I'm sure someone would have saved her bacon.'

'*Groan!* Well, I hope she's able to see the funny side. Fancy a coffee?'

I decline the offer of a hot drink and am soon in my pyjamas under the cool cotton sheets of my bed as Emma bustles about in the kitchen. It's a balmy evening and I have thrown the windows open and am enjoying the gentle breeze blowing around the room. The sound of chatter and occasional laughter ripples gently around the patio not far from my window. The last time I remember hearing similar sounds was one Christmas evening, when my dad, Harry and our next-door neighbour sat outside in the frost-covered garden of our neighbour's old house, smoking cigars. Such bittersweet memories pop into my mind from time to time, but I guess it's something I just have to get used to…

Chapter Thirteen

The next morning a silver people carrier arrives outside to take us to our winery tour. Cheryl stumbled in at goodness-knows-what hour last night and is currently downing a couple of paracetamols with a large glass of water.

'Oh my goodness, girls, you missed all the fun last night. Everyone ended up in the pool after we got started on the limoncello shots! Even Sophia got back in for a bit and was laughing about the rampaging pig. It really lightened her up. Me and Gianni were almost the last to go off to bed. I'm paying for it now, though,' she groans, as she puts on her large shades. 'I'm not sure I can even look at any wine, never mind taste it.'

I imagine Gianni and Cheryl sitting in the moonlight together until the small hours and I wonder, fleetingly, if he walked her to the front door and stole a kiss. She's made no secret of the fact that she finds him attractive.

'I can barely remember going to bed. I have a vague memory of Maria escorting me to my door,' she says, almost as though she's read my mind.

'So, did you get your wedding invitation then?' I ask.

'No, but there's still time.' She grins wickedly.

'Right, has everyone got everything they need?' asks Emma, checking her bag by the open front door. 'I've packed some sunscreen for us all to use later.'

'Whoops. Sun hat!' says Cheryl, heading back inside. 'Viola said it's going to be another scorcher today.'

'In that case grab us all a bottle of water from the fridge,' calls Emma.

A few moments later we fasten our seat belts inside the car, ready to take the thirty-minute drive to the vineyard. We pass through farmland and olive groves and over rolling hills, once again marvelling at our surroundings, until eventually we are pulling up outside a gated building that's home to the Variso Winery. There is a minibus of people disembarking in the car park, some of the women fanning themselves with large, colourful fans.

'I wouldn't fancy being stuck on a coach in this weather,' says Cheryl.

'It's not so bad if it's a short distance, but on a long journey it's a nightmare,' replies Emma. 'We drove for nearly thirty hours on a school trip to Italy once in the middle of June. I'll never forget the smell of cheap perfume and the food from packed lunches.'

We thank our young, slightly sullen-looking driver and make our way to the entrance. A young woman in a black skirt and white shirt is talking into a mouthpiece. 'English tour this way,' she says, gesturing to a path behind a large, cream-coloured building. A crowd of us gather near a tall gate and after a minute or two a handsome young man with gorgeous green eyes and a neatly trimmed beard appears.

'Welcome, ladies and gentlemen, to the home of Variso wine. My name is Frederico and this winery has been in my family for two generations. Today I will guide you on a short tour of the vineyard, then we will move on to take a look at the cellars, with a sample or two along the way. If you have any questions, please feel free to ask. We will finish inside with some locally sourced antipasti and a final drink, as well as the opportunity to purchase something as a souvenir of your visit. I hope you will enjoy the tour. Please… let us begin.'

He slowly opens the tall wooden gate and it's like taking a glimpse into a different world. There are hundreds of vivid green vines in neat rows, bursting with ripe purple grapes. Some workers up ahead, wearing wide-brimmed sun hats, are dropping bunches of the grapes into straw baskets under the cloudless blue sky.

'Holy macaroni, this place is huge. Think of all that wine,' says Emma.

I think of the bottles of wine in the wardrobe back at the villa and realise to my annoyance that I've forgotten to take a photograph of them on my phone. Frederico is just the kind of person who would probably be able to tell instantly if they're a good vintage.

We walk along the vines for a few minutes until our guide stops us. 'So, does anyone know the type of grape we use to make Chianti?'

I raise my hand as if I'm in school. 'Sangiovese grape. I believe Chianti has to contain over seventy per cent or it's not a true Chianti.'

'I'm impressed. I see you have done your homework.' He gives a broad smile.

We stop at the end of a row of vines, where a little table has been set up with some wine and plastic glasses and we are each given a sample.

'Do we spit it out?' asks Emma.

'No, you drink it, of course,' says Frederico, smiling. 'Just savour the taste in your mouth a little before you do so. Try to see if you can pick out any flavours.'

'Mmm, this is nice,' I say. 'I think I can taste plum in this one. It's quite oaky too.'

'Correct. This is a Chianti Riserva, or reserve. It takes over two years to cultivate the grapes for this particular wine.'

Frederico feeds us little nuggets of information as we thread through the vines, sampling juicy grapes as we go. He's a mine of information and punctuates facts and figures with amusing anecdotes, such as the time an elderly gentleman got locked in the cellars overnight after he had nipped to the toilet. He was found the next morning snoring loudly on a bed of hessian grape sacks, having helped himself to a large quantity of a very expensive vintage.

The temperature is climbing steadily as the sun burns brightly and a red-haired lady with a fan is mopping her brow with a tissue. A short while later, Frederico is guiding us inside for a tour of the cellars, to the obvious relief of the redhead. It's like stepping into a cave, as a blast of coolness washes over us in the stone cellar, with wall-to-wall oak barrels dominating the space.

Frederico stops at one of the barrels and pours a little wine into a sample cup. 'Would anyone like to come forward and have a go at identifying the flavours in this one?'

Nobody volunteers, so once again I raise my hand and step forward.

'Ah, lady. May I ask your name?'

'It's Maisie.'

'OK. Maisie, have a little drink. It's slightly different to the previous one you tasted.'

I swirl the wine around my mouth. 'This one tastes more floral. A little dryer, too, I think.'

'Very good. This is a Chianti Classico. It must contain at least eighty per cent Sangiovese grape. And only the red grape. Regular Chianti allows a small percentage of white grape to be used. So,' says Frederico, at the end of the tour. 'We will now take you inside for a final drink in the bar area as well as give you the opportunity to sample the finest selection of Italian cheeses and meats. Please follow me.'

'Good. I'm starving,' says Cheryl, her hangover obviously having disappeared.

'It's your own fault for skipping breakfast. It's the most important meal of the day,' says Emma.

The mention of cheese makes me think of Harry and our cheese and wine evenings. They tended to be on a Sunday evening, when we would nibble cheese and crackers for supper, washed down with a full-bodied red wine. We would then argue over which movie we should watch as we lounged together on our huge sofa.

Shoving aside thoughts of my ex-husband, we walk through a small museum area, stopping to view the displays of old farming machinery and information boards until we reach a metal spiral staircase, which leads us up to the marble bar area on the ground floor.

The bar is set with platters of sliced cheeses and salamis, beside thickly sliced bread and bowls of glistening olives. A smiling lady behind the bar pours a glass of Chianti for each of us, which we enjoy with the antipasti. When we've finished eating, she fills small glasses with a dessert wine and beckons us forward.

'So, go on, Oz Clarke. What's in this wine then?' asks Cheryl.

'Actually, I'm not too familiar with dessert wines, but I think there's a background of apricot in this one,' I say, swirling the amber liquid around my mouth before swallowing it.

'It's called Vin Santo,' says the lady behind the bar. 'It is a traditional Tuscan dessert wine made from a white grape.'

We are about to leave the bar when Frederico asks me if he can have a quick word. 'You are really very good, Maisie. I should offer you a job here on the English tours.'

'A job? No, thanks, I'm here on holiday,' I reply, laughing, unable to gauge whether he is joking or not.

'Actually, I'm only half joking, so if you change your mind I could do with an extra pair of hands. My last English worker left here in rather a hurry. Anyway, think about what I've said. In fact, maybe you would like to come to lunch with me tomorrow and we can talk some more?' He's staring at me with his seductive green eyes and a playful grin on his face. This one could be trouble.

It's Sophia's wedding tomorrow and, as Cheryl seems to have been unable to wangle an invitation for the three of us, I decide to accept his offer.

'*Perfetto*. Please let me have the address of where you are staying and I will collect you at twelve thirty. My brother can cover my absence. He hasn't been pulling his weight enough lately. He owes me.'

I give Frederico the name of the farmhouse and, as we head towards the car, I find myself rather looking forward to lunch with him tomorrow. It's time I loosened up a little. A lunch date with a flirty Italian might be just the tonic I need.

Chapter Fourteen

It's a glorious day for a wedding. There isn't a cloud in the clear, blue sky as I prepare to go for the little walk that has become a bit of a morning ritual for me. Cheryl and Emma are taking it easy back at the farmhouse.

I pause as I reach the Villa Nina, which looks resplendent in preparation for the wedding. The way to the villa is adorned with pots of tall, cream-flowering plants alongside the solar lights that will glow all the way up the sweeping drive to the front door. The trees in the grounds, enhanced with their cream-coloured bows, now also have lights strewn among their branches, ready to be switched on for the evening reception.

I'm about to turn away and walk on when I spot Geni, the bride's mother, step out of the house and begin to walk quickly along the drive towards the gates. I met her briefly on the night she brought Sophia and her friends to the hen party at the farmhouse. On that occasion she was full of smiles, but now, as she approaches the gates, I can see that she has a look of worry etched on her face.

I say, '*Buongiorno,*' as she steps through them, but she just manages to smile stiffly, before turning right and hurrying off in the direction I have just come from. I decide to head back towards the farmhouse with her, hoping all is well. When we get there, Geni bangs on the front door and Viola opens it, wiping her hands on a cotton tea towel. Geni is speaking very quickly in Italian and Viola's brow furrows into a crease.

'Is everything alright?' I ask them.

'We have a problem,' Viola replies. 'Would you believe that the hairdresser who is going to do Sophia's hair for the wedding has been involved in an accident? She is unhurt apart from her wrist, which is broken. The bride and the bridesmaids will never get another hairdresser at such short notice.'

Right on cue, Cheryl opens the door of our apartment. She is carrying her beach towel. 'Good morning, ladies,' she calls, raising a hand and strolling towards us across the driveway.

'Perfect timing,' I say. 'There's a bit of a problem at the wedding today.'

'What sort of a problem?'

'The wedding hairdresser has been involved in an accident. She's broken her wrist.'

Cheryl lowers her sunglasses. 'Was she doing the bridal make-up too?' she asks, turning to Geni.

Geni throws her arms in the air. 'Yes. Yes. The make-up too. We will have to do that also but it will not look as good as professional artist,' she says in her heavy accent. 'I cannot believe this is happening. We have a disaster.' She sniffs and dabs at her eyes with a linen handkerchief.

'Maybe it's not as much of a disaster as you think,' Cheryl says cheerily. 'I am a hairdresser and beautician. Let me get my bag of tricks from the apartment. We can discuss my fee on the way…'

Geni is so grateful that she grabs Cheryl's face and kisses her on the lips. '*Grazie, grazie!*' she repeats over and over again. 'You and your friends must please join us at the wedding.'

Luckily Cheryl never goes anywhere without her make-up case and hairdressing tools. 'Be prepared' is her motto. It certainly seems to have paid dividends this time, as not only has she gone and got herself a job, but she has secured the three of us an invitation to the wedding at two o'clock, which I've just realised I won't be around for. Frederico is collecting me around twelve thirty, so I imagine we won't be back until late afternoon.

'I've managed to get us an invite to the wedding of the year in this village and you're buggering off for lunch? Don't blame you, though. Frederico is pretty hot,' Cheryl admits.

'Well, how was I to know we'd end up with a wedding invite? Besides, I imagine they'll probably be glad that there's one less person to have to cater for. Our invites are a bit last minute.'

'Suppose so. Funny how things work out, though, isn't it? I told you I'd get us an invite,' she says over her shoulder, as she disappears through the front door of the apartment. 'I'm off to tell Emma and get my bag.'

I follow her inside and go into my bedroom to deliberate over what to wear. I wonder what type of restaurant Frederico is taking me to… Finally, I pluck a pair of white linen trousers and a pretty black top from the wardrobe. I sigh, remembering how Harry had stopped noticing what I wore on our nights out. In the early days of our relationship, he would give a little wolf whistle when I walked down the stairs, but latterly, when I asked him if I looked OK, he would simply say, 'You look fine.' Maybe I shouldn't have been surprised that his attention had wandered elsewhere.

As Cheryl passes the bedroom door, she calls out, 'Right, I'm off. I've told Emma. I'll see you later, Maisie. Don't do anything I wouldn't do!' before heading off to Villa Nina to work her magic.

I paint a slick of pink lip gloss over my lips and run a brush through my hair, then stroll outside into the bright sunshine just as a red sports car pulls up in the driveway and the driver jumps out. Frederico is dressed in a black shirt and white jeans. We look like a mirror image of each other and we both burst out laughing. He kisses me on both cheeks, just as Gianni is crossing the courtyard.

'*Ciao*, Gianni, how's things?' Frederico says, smiling.

'*Ciao*, Frederico. Good, thanks,' Gianni replies, without much warmth in his voice, I can't help noticing.

'Maybe I'll just nip inside and change my top,' I say, wondering what the hell I'm going to wear, as it took me long enough to decide on this one. Eventually I select a pale lemon off-the-shoulder top that shows off my nicely developing tan.

'Have a nice day,' says Gianni, as I climb into Frederico's car. 'Maybe I will see you later at the wedding? My mother tells me that you have all been invited.'

'Hopefully, yes,' I reply, feeling slightly disappointed that I'm heading off in the opposite direction. 'I'll certainly be at the party in the evening. You have a good day too.'

Frederico fires up the engine and drives off down the drive. Looking in my wing mirror, I'm surprised to see Gianni standing there, watching us until we disappear from view.

Chapter Fifteen

'I hope you are hungry,' says Frederico, as he drives the sports car along the twisting Tuscan roads. They are flanked by cypress trees, which are becoming wonderfully familiar. 'I have booked us in for the taster menu at the restaurant I've chosen, as I believe it's the best way to sample the delights of Tuscan food.'

'Well, I only ever have a light breakfast, so I'm usually ravenous by lunch. Although, to be honest, I never have too much of an appetite in the hot weather.'

'I like a woman with an appetite,' he says, with a grin on his face. 'The sample menu includes small plates of everything, although by the end you are usually pretty full. So, tell me, are you enjoying your holiday here?'

'Oh, I am. It's just so relaxing. I don't think I could ever get tired of the scenery. You're so lucky to live here.'

'I suppose I take it for granted. Although I'm sure there is nowhere else I would rather live. I went to London last year and although I enjoyed the experience it seemed filthy compared to here.'

'Maybe that could be said of any city,' I say, feeling vaguely protective of my capital city back home.

'Ah, but Florence doesn't feel like that. So much beauty and culture at every turn.'

'You should come to Liverpool if you want beautiful buildings. The waterfront is quite something. Sailors for centuries have commented on how it takes their breath away when they sail into the port and glimpse the Liver Building. The whole waterfront is a UNESCO world heritage site,' I state proudly. 'Not to mention St George's Hall and the two glorious cathedrals.'

'Sound pretty impressive. Maybe I will visit one day. If I find something there that I am interested in.' He turns to gaze at me with his captivating green eyes, just as we're coming to a bend in the road.

'Maybe it's best if you keep your eyes on the road,' I suggest, feeling slightly anxious, as the twisting road ahead is so unfamiliar to me.

'Do not worry. I know these roads like the backs of my hands.'

When we are on a straight bit of road, Frederico puts his foot down and we race along, my hair billowing in the wind. I get the feeling he thinks this will impress me, but all I can think about is how I'm going to give a good impression of a scarecrow when we rock up at the restaurant.

Around half an hour later the road slowly descends into a valley and we pull up outside La Venetia restaurant. A long driveway leads to an imposing, sand-coloured building with a glossy black door. Frederico pulls into a parking space and my eye is caught by an open archway, to the right of the building, which leads to an outdoor dining area. I can just make out black, wrought-iron garden furniture dotted about a gravelled courtyard, and terracotta pots bursting with flashes of red- and mauve-coloured flowers.

I suddenly feel a little under-dressed, even for lunch. 'I may just need a moment or they might not let me in,' I say, as I run a small brush through my hair, before applying another slick of pink lip gloss and a spritz of perfume.

We get out of the car and walk towards the archway, just as a goddess in a mustard shift dress glides across the courtyard, accompanied by her grey-suited partner, making me feel like a frump. 'I spied a small Italian pizza joint on the way here, just off a main road,' I whisper to Frederico. 'Maybe we should turn round and go there?'

Frederico laughs. 'Don't be silly. You look lovely. It's not a showy place, I promise.'

'What about the Amal and George Clooney lookalikes who have just crossed the courtyard?'

Frederico shrugs. 'Some people like to dress up for lunch. It's the Italian way.'

We are welcomed inside and Frederico begins a brief conversation in Italian, before we are shown to a table in a covered terrace area, where there are several other diners. Our table has a thick white tablecloth, with a centrepiece of sunflowers in a clear glass vase. Frederico holds my chair out for me, his arm lightly brushing against me as he takes his own seat.

A blue-eyed waiter, with black curly hair, hands us the tasting menu and I ask for a jug of water, while Frederico orders two glasses of Merlot.

It isn't long before the first course of smoked burrata cheese with an olive and green bean salad arrives. The smokiness of the soft cheese with the saltiness of the olives is absolutely mouth-watering.

'Ooh, this is so tasty. Cheese and green beans. Who'd have thought it?'

'That's what Italian cuisine is all about. Letting the quality of the food speak for itself.' Frederico, having studied the wine list, suggests a bottle of Barolo to accompany the rest of the meal.

The next course to arrive is raw codfish with fresh tomatoes and a melon and lime dressing. I notice that Frederico is watching me as I eat and I suddenly feel a little self- conscious. The cod melts in the mouth and the tomatoes are bursting with flavour. The tangy melon and lime glaze bring all the flavours together beautifully.

'Oh my word, this is all so delicious. I was a bit worried when I saw raw codfish. I don't even like sushi.'

'It is marinated gently so it doesn't have the texture of raw fish,' Frederico tells me. 'Now, tell me a little bit about yourself,' he says, his striking green eyes never leaving mine. 'I recall, from the day of the tour, that you seem to have quite a knowledge of wine. Do you drink a lot of it?'

'Are you suggesting I have a drink problem?' I ask with a laugh. 'And no, not really, since you ask. I've just picked up a little knowledge because of my job.'

'Is there a husband waiting for you when you get home from work?' he probes.

I find myself telling him that we're separated before quickly turning the conversation to my job in the supermarket and how I like to keep myself informed of the things that we sell. I consider telling him about the wine back at the farmhouse, but decide not to. I don't want him thinking I'm some sort of thief, even though it came into my possession quite innocently.

'You must be very committed to your work, to spend time acquiring such knowledge,' Frederico says, his gaze never leaving mine.

I'm sure he usually gets exactly what he wants when he fixes someone with those eyes.

'I just don't like being unable to answer a customer's questions. Probably more to do with anxiety than anything else,' I say, immediately regretting revealing so much about myself. It's been a while since I've opened up, but thankfully he doesn't react.

'Maybe you should think about becoming a wine merchant, selecting the wines for the store. Or you could always work for yourself.'

'I'd never thought about that, but I quite like the sound of it.'

As I mull over the idea, our course of venison, gremolata and sautéed potatoes arrives. The smell assaults my senses as I inhale the heady scent of garlic. The gremolata is a dressing of garlic, parsley and lemon and once again my taste buds are tingling. The venison is melt-in-the-mouth tender with a distinctive earthy, almost musky flavour. I've never tasted anything like it.

'I'm sure I can't eat another thing,' I say pushing my plate away, feeling sated. 'I think I need a lie-down.'

'Now that sounds interesting.' Frederico leans towards me. 'You do know this is a restaurant with rooms?' He nods towards the ceiling, raising his eyebrows.

'Easy, tiger,' I reply, with a laugh.

'Seriously, though, you must find room for the next course. You cannot miss the trio of desserts. They are the star of the show.'

I glance at the dessert menu to discover a mini tiramisu, a panna cotta served with fresh summer berries and a dessert called *Pesche di Prato*. Frederico tells me this is a traditional Tuscan dish of a rounded brioche soaked in a liqueur called alkermes, filled with custard. It is fashioned to resemble a peach.

'I'll just have to make some space then. Why does all this food have to taste so good?' I ask, discreetly opening the top button of my white jeans and wishing I'd just worn a pair of lounge pants. Sod the image.

We chat amiably, Frederico opening up all about his work. He tells me his parents are retired, although his father still likes to oversee things at the winery and regularly pops in. He says his brother lacks the passion for his inheritance, much to the disappointment of his father.

'Luckily for my father, I love the wine trade. I am interested in the whole process from the growing of the grapes to the production of the wine. The winery tours are a lot of fun too. I get to meet lots of interesting people. One of whom is sitting right in front of me.'

I find myself blushing. I've never thought of myself as particularly interesting. I've always led a fairly ordinary sort of life – this holiday is the most exciting thing to happen to me in years.

I 'ooh' and 'ah' all the way through the creamy panna cotta, the richness of the liqueur-soaked *Pesche di Prato*, and the sweet yet sharp tiramisu.

'Ooh, I wish you had booked a room,' I say, flopping back into my chair.

Frederico's eyebrows shoot to the top of his head.

'That way I could head upstairs and make like a beached whale on the top of the bed.'

'You raise my hopes then break my heart,' says Frederico, placing his hand on his chest.

'Behave yourself, we barely know each other,' I reply, throwing a screwed-up paper serviette at him.

'*Signorina*, such behaviour in an establishment of this calibre will not be tolerated.' He flings the serviette back at me and it lands in my wine glass. Frederico grins broadly, showing perfect teeth, and I can see this guy could be someone you could have fun with, no strings attached. But I'm not sure I'm ready for that.

Fifteen minutes later our coffee arrives, although it seems the food fest isn't quite over, as it is served with a plate of panforte, a type of sweet bread made with dried fruit, honey and chocolate. Despite my bulging waistband I can't resist a tiny nibble. As expected, it's utterly delicious. I'm going to have to join weight busters when I get home.

As we leave the restaurant, the waiters shake us warmly by the hand, proud to have shown me some of the finest food in Tuscany.

'*Cibo era, fantastico, grazie,*' I say, hoping that I have correctly told them that the food was fantastic.

When Frederico drops me back at the farmhouse, just after four o'clock, he hugs me tightly and tells me that he will book a room at that restaurant any time I like. As he fixes me with his sparkling green eyes I think about how attractive he is and I imagine Cheryl would be in like a shot.

'I'll bear that in mind. Bye, Frederico. And thank you so much for a wonderful treat.'

Listening to the toot-tooting of his car horn until the car disappears from view, I realise I have had a really good time today.

Although I can't wait to climb under the cool cotton sheets of my bed and have a long snooze, as I'm still stuffed to the gills from all the food. But Cheryl has other ideas.

'What are you doing here? I thought you were at the wedding?' I say in surprise.

'Just nipped over for these,' she says, waving a packet of cigarettes. 'Hardly anyone over there smokes. I was just going to have a sneaky one over here before I go back.'

We go out to the garden and sit on the patio, where Cheryl lights up a cigarette with a rose-gold lighter and takes a long drag.

'So how was the wedding then?'

'Oh, Maisie, it was just gorgeous. Sophia and her husband Antonio looked so happy. It was just as I imagined it would be, too, with an archway covered with jasmine and violets. There were cream satin bows on the chairs and a trio of musicians in the corner. Flower petals were scattered all along the path to where the couple were married. It must have cost a bob or two.'

'Sounds amazing. How did the hair and make-up go?'

'They all looked beautiful, even if I do say so myself. The bride wanted her hair pinned up so I had to send someone into the village to buy some hairgrips, which was the one thing I didn't have. The bridesmaids wanted soft curls, so I used my brand-new curling wand. Sophia looked fantastic. Her make-up really enhanced her natural beauty.'

'And the groom?'

'Nope, the make-up didn't suit him so much. A bit of hair gel was all he needed.' She laughs. 'So, Maisie, how was your lunch date with the hunky Frederico?'

'It wasn't a date! But it was really nice. The restaurant was beautiful and the food was out of this world. I wish I'd just had some *gelato* for dessert though. The trio of puddings finished me off. Frederico certainly knows how to give a girl a good time.'

'Oh yeah, is that why you're so tired?'

'Get your mind out of the gutter. I was talking about the food. But there's no doubt he has an edge to him. I can't deny he's pretty sexy.'

'And you've come back here because…?'

'Because I'm not ready for anything else. It's too soon, Cheryl. Plus I'm shattered.'

'Fair enough. Right. Go and have an hour's nap. But then I'm coming to get you. I can't people-watch with anyone else. There's a woman at the wedding dressed in a leopard-print catsuit and dripping with gold. She's about eighty, if she's a day. She was tearing up the dance floor as I left. Go and get some rest then prepare to party!'

Chapter Sixteen

I glance blearily at the clock, which shows it's six o'clock, as someone is gently shaking my arm. I'm lying fully dressed on top of the bed and Cheryl's face comes slowly into focus.

'Come on, missus. You've had long enough. Up and shower or you'll miss the party. Apparently the evening event is thrown open to the whole village. I've heard there might be some hunky farmers in attendance.'

'Oh right, OK,' I say, stretching my arms out lazily above my head. 'Where's Emma?'

'She's sitting chatting to Alfredo from the restaurant. They looked quite cosy actually.'

'I asked Emma if there was any attraction between them after their day trip to Siena, but she insisted there wasn't. I think she just feels a bit neglected because Joe works away so much.'

'Maybe. Anyway, I don't blame her for being pissed off,' Cheryl says. 'Apparently Joe hasn't rung her in three days and when she's tried to contact him, the call goes to voicemail. I don't know how she puts up with it. I'd have sent him packing by now.'

'Nothing is ever that simple when you love someone,' I tell her, thinking back to the times I believed Harry and forgave him when he stumbled home in the early hours of the morning, saying he had got involved in a game of poker at someone or other's house. You believe the excuses because you want to.

I get up and shower, before getting changed into a long, flowing, pink cotton dress. Then I ask Cheryl to loosely pin my hair up. I apply a little make-up, choosing a bronze- coloured eyeshadow and some nude lipstick.

'Aye, go easy on that make-up. I don't want too much competition from you,' says Cheryl, laughing.

'You won't have. Tom Hardy could walk into the party tonight and I'm not sure I'd even notice.'

'Well, maybe it's time you had a little fun. You know what they say: the best way to get over someone is to get under someone else.'

'Cheryl! That can only ever lead to disaster. You have to let yourself heal first.'

'If you say so, Maisie. So… you're telling me you haven't noticed the way Gianni looks at you?'

'Really? No, actually, I can't say that I have,' I say, feeling genuinely surprised and maybe even a little flattered.

'Well, I have,' Cheryl tells me. 'I've flirted with him since we got here, but not a flicker from him. I thought I was losing my touch until I saw the way he looked at you, then it all made sense.'

'Perish the thought of you losing your touch, eh?' I tease Cheryl. 'And don't think I haven't noticed how handsome Gianni is. It would be impossible not to. I just haven't spent long enough with him to know what he's like as a person.'

'Well, now's your chance,' she says, spritzing me with some perfume. 'Come on, let's get over to that party. Ooh, and can we grab a bottle of that wine from the safe to take with us?' pleads Cheryl. 'It seems such a waste it just languishing there at the back of the wardrobe.'

'No! Not until I've discovered its value,' I snap, a little more sharply than I intended.

'Alright! Keep your hair on! Are you ready then?'

'Yep. Oh… Actually, hang on. Earrings!' Fearing my outfit is a little too plain, I find a pair of drop earrings with a turquoise stone set in the middle. To my annoyance, one of the gemstones has come loose and is almost detached from the earring. 'Oh, that's a shame. These would have set my outfit off nicely.'

'Hang on,' says Cheryl. 'I've got some superglue in my bag. That should do the trick.'

'Why on earth would you carry that about?' I ask, laughing.

'I lost the heel from my shoe once and it was the only thing that fixed it. Since then I've carried it around with me for emergencies.' She pours a pool of glue into the crevice of the earring and places the stone firmly in place. 'There. That will never come loose again.'

⸙

Earring disaster averted, Cheryl and I fall into step as we take the short walk to the Villa Nina next door, the strains of a jaunty song greeting us on the evening breeze. It's still light outside and the sky is slowly becoming streaked with orange and pink. It's a warm, sultry evening and the fragrance of a magnolia bush hits my nostrils as we stroll along.

A marquee has been set up in the grounds and we make our way towards it. The outside space looks stunning, especially the tall pots of cream flowers, and the white fairy lights are beginning to sparkle gently as dusk begins to fall. Groups of people are sitting around on white wrought-iron chairs, chatting and drinking. Men's ties have been loosened and women's heels flung off as everyone relaxes into the evening. Other guests are dancing in the marquee, the flashing disco lights visible through the canvas walls.

A handsome young man with gelled-back hair approaches us as we're about to head in. '*Ciao*, how are you. Are you still enjoying your holiday?'

I give a puzzled expression.

'Ah, I see maybe you don't recognise me without my scooter,' he says, smiling.

'Oh, you're one of the moped guys! Sorry, I don't even know your real name,' I say, feeling embarrassed as I recall our last conversation in the village, when I offered to 'let him have it' back at the farmhouse.

Cheryl lifts two glasses of fizz from a passing waiter and hands one of them to me.

'My name is Luca,' he says, stepping forward and giving us each a kiss on both cheeks.

'Where's your friend?' asks Cheryl.

'Oh, you mean Ralf. I think he is trying to seduce one of the bridesmaids.' Luca laughs. 'He's not having much luck though. I think she only has eyes for Gianni, like most of the women around here.'

I shouldn't be surprised that women find Gianni so attractive, with his tall, dark and handsome good looks and easy manner.

'Excuse me a minute,' says Cheryl as she heads off in the direction of a group of men, who I vaguely recognise as the farmers from the day we went out to lunch at Giuseppe's restaurant.

Luca and I chat for a few more minutes and I discover that he and Ralf are home for the summer holidays from the University of Siena, where they are studying history. Luca tells me he is hoping to visit London and maybe even get a job there over one summer. He would like to go travelling, having been brought up in a very small village.

'I'll leave you guys to it,' I say, after Ralf comes to join Luca and we have been properly introduced. 'Have a good night.'

'You too. Maybe I dance with you later?' asks Luca, a half-smile on his face.

'Maybe.'

Heading off in the direction of Cheryl, I spot Gianni sitting at a table, talking to a woman with long blonde hair. Their heads are close together and she whispers something in his ear, which makes him throw his head back and laugh. *Lucky lady*, I think, surprising myself.

Cheryl beckons me over and I am soon seated with the farmers.

'*Ciao*,' they all say, raising their hands. They are dressed smartly but casually in jeans and short-sleeved shirts. One of them comes and sits beside me. 'So, how long do you stay at Villa Marisa?' he asks.

There's something about the way he is staring at me that makes me feel slightly uncomfortable, but, remembering Cheryl's advice, I do my best to appear friendly. 'A few more days. I could do with a little longer, if I'm honest. It's so beautiful here.'

'You can come and stay with me if you want a longer holiday.' He leans in towards me and I can smell whisky on his breath. 'I hear you English girls know how to have a little fun, yes?'

Yes, but not with you, I think to myself as he eyes me up and down with a lecherous grin. 'I'm just here to relax. Fun isn't really something I'm looking for, to be honest,' I tell him firmly.

I try to attract Cheryl's attention to move into the marquee, but she seems smitten by one of the other farmers. I'm keen to go and find Sophia and her husband Antonio, as I haven't congratulated them yet. Then, suddenly, I hear the sound of a familiar voice speaking my name.

'Emma!' I say, swinging round in my seat. I've never been so happy to see anyone in my life.

'Hi! How was your day with Frederico?'

The farmer next to me mutters something in Italian, before getting up and strolling over to the adjacent table, full of girls, to try his luck there.

'Thanks for that. You just saved my life mentioning Frederico. That bloke was coming on a bit strong. I was about to come and look for you. Where's Alfredo?'

'How should I know?'

'Oh… It's just Cheryl said you were chatting to him earlier.'

'I've spoken to lots of people.' Emma shrugs. 'Alfredo and I chatted mainly about the food. He did the catering for the wedding breakfast.'

'Really? What did you have to eat?'

'Giant ravioli stuffed with ricotta and spinach to start, then grilled sea bream, followed by juicy fillet steak. Chocolate mousse and a cheeseboard to finish. It was absolutely divine.'

'I can imagine. I'm sorry I missed it although I must be honest, the food at the restaurant Frederico took me to was to die for.'

I tell her all about the menu as we stroll along and soon we are entering the marquee, where we are greeted by the sight of a group of women clapping their hands and squealing loudly. Sophia is standing at the front of the group, with her beautiful bridal bouquet in her hands. She is still wearing her silk cream wedding dress, which is a simple, low-necked gown set off with a string of classic pearls. She looks exquisite.

'Are you ready, ladies?'

Sophia hurls the pretty peach-and-cream bouquet high into the air and then it seems to glide slowly down towards the crowd, before one young woman dives towards it, touching it yet somehow managing to miss it. Unexpectedly, the bouquet lurches towards me and I find myself catching it with both hands.

'Suits you,' says Gianni, who has just walked into the tent.

I'm standing holding the bouquet, blushing furiously, when Maria from the farmhouse strolls over.

'Hi, Maisie, are you enjoying yourself?' She is looking stunning in a pale lemon knee- length lace dress.

'I've only just arrived, actually. I went out for lunch this afternoon and needed to have a bit of a lie-down afterwards. The mixture of sunshine and food made me feel really sleepy.'

I pass the bouquet to the young woman who had attempted to catch it and is now standing beside me.

'Thank you so much,' she says.

Continuing my chat with Maria, she hesitates for a minute before asking, 'Forgive me, but I saw you leave with Frederico this afternoon. Do you think you will you be seeing him again?'

'I'm not sure,' I answer honestly.

'I'm sorry for being so inquisitive. I just wanted you to know that Frederico shows interest in lots of women. I believe you would call him a player. I don't think he can commit to just one woman and I should know.'

'You dated him?'

'Yes, for several months. Things never really progressed between us and I realised he would never settle down.' She shrugs. 'I suppose I am just warning you about him, that's all.'

'Thank you for telling me, but I have no real interest in Frederico, or anybody else for that matter. I've been hurt, too, but that's a story for another day.'

The young woman smiles and pats me gently on the arm. 'I hope you will enjoy the rest of the evening,' she says, as she walks away.

So far most of the songs have been in Italian, but suddenly 'I'm Your Man' by Wham! has everybody up on the dance floor.

Luca, the moped guy, sidles up to me and grabs me by the hand. 'Can I have that dance you promised?'

'I never promised,' I reply, but I laugh as he leads me onto the dance floor.

Luca's a fantastic dancer and is soon attracting attention, as people move aside to give him some space. He dances with the ease of a professional, each move more assured than the last. People who had been sitting at tables, chatting, stand up to take a better look. He suddenly does a neat backflip and the crowd begin to clap and whoop. Then he's squatting, flinging his legs out like a Russian Cossack, his repertoire seemingly endless. During the chorus he points at me and sings 'I'm Your Man' as he undoes one of the buttons on his white shirt. It's hysterical. I laugh loudly, thinking that this is the best night out I've had in a long time.

Then, without any warning, Luca lifts me off my feet and twirls me round. My long drop earrings flail around and one of them makes contact with his hair – and it doesn't budge. I realise to my horror that the superglue can't have completely dried and the gemstone has attached itself to Luca's perfectly gelled hair. He bats at his hair in an attempt to dislodge the earring, but only succeeds in covering his face with his fringe. Then, momentarily, he loses his balance before stumbling over and ending up on the floor, with me landing on top of him, my earring still attached to his hair and still threaded through my ear. I turn my head a little, unable to remove the earring from my ear or his hair, to find Gianni standing there with his mouth hanging open.

'Gianni, could you please go and get Cheryl?' I plead. 'She's sitting outside talking to some blokes. And hurry!'

'*Sì, sì,*' he says, rushing off to find her.

The crowd, who fell silent when we first tumbled onto the floor, are now muttering and giggling, some of them openly roaring with laughter. I want the dance floor to open up and swallow me. At least I'm not having a meltdown though. I think I may actually be able to see the funny side, which I'm not sure I could have done without my medication.

'Well, my dance moves usually impress the ladies,' says Luca, as I try to wriggle myself into a less intimate position without pulling at the earring and scalping him. 'But you seem to be really stuck on me.'

'How can you joke at a time like this?'

'I haven't been this close to a good-looking woman in a while.'

Cheryl races into the marquee and bites her lip as she tries not to burst out laughing. 'Oh my days! Stay right there,' she says, as if I'm really going anywhere. 'I've got some nail varnish remover at the apartment. That'll do the trick.'

'Oh my goodness, are you OK?' asks Sophia. 'I was chatting to some guests when I heard an awful lot of laughter from this side of the marquee. I wondered what the source of amusement was.'

'Yes, I'm afraid that was us. I'm OK, thanks, and I'm so sorry that we seem to be the centre of attention. By the way, huge congratulations.'

'*Grazie*. Do not worry. As long as you are OK, that is the main thing. I may have to ask you to shuffle off somewhere soon though when we do our first dance.' Antonio slips an arm round his wife's waist and gazes at her adoringly. He looks like the happiest man in the world.

'Of course,' I say feebly, hoping Cheryl won't take too long.

'Actually, are *you* alright?' I ask Luca, as we lie there on the floor being gawped at like a circus act. 'You broke my fall, but you went down like a ton of bricks.'

'I'm OK. I am young and fit.' He winks. 'Look!' he says, lifting his pelvis from the floor, as he thrusts it up and down.

'Could you please try and stay still?' I hiss. The crowd are laughing even harder as I have no choice but to bob up and down in sync.

Thankfully, at this point Cheryl reappears and, after carefully applying the nail varnish remover, the earring gently falls free, leaving all of Luca's hair intact.

'*Mamma mia*, that was close! I thought my hair would be ruined.' He takes a comb from his pocket and gently teases his fringe back into place. 'I need a drink. Maybe I will go and have a beer with Ralf. Or perhaps something stronger. Can I get you something first?' he asks me.

'No, thanks, Luca. I think I just need to sit down for a few minutes,' I reply, finding a chair and hardly able to believe what has just happened. I'm sure I'll see the funny side soon. Cheryl has gone to rejoin the farmers outside, giggling to herself as she exits the tent.

'Maybe *I* can get you that drink,' says Gianni, as he comes over and sits beside me. He looks handsome in a blue linen jacket over a white shirt and dark jeans. I nod, gratefully, and he heads to the bar with its backdrop of fairy lights. The barmen are all wearing bow ties and waistcoats over white shirts.

A few minutes later, Gianni returns with two drinks in long glasses. Smiling at him and muttering my thanks, I sip the pale yellow contents of the sugar-rimmed glass that Gianni has handed to me.

'What's this?' I ask him.

'It's called a *sgroppino*. A fresh lemon sorbet topped with vodka and Prosecco.'

'Mmm, it's delicious.'

We chat easily for a few minutes, before the lights are dimmed further and the DJ announces the first dance for the bride and groom.

Antonio and Sophia glide onto the dance floor looking radiant and happy. They wrap their arms around each other and sway along to a slow ballad. When they finish their dance, a new song strikes up and they beckon to the guests to join them.

'Shall we?' asks Gianni, as he offers his hand. 'I promise I'll try my best not to end up on the floor with you.' He takes my hand and draws me close to him on the dance floor as we sway to the smoochy number. He smells wonderful – a woody, citrus scent that I can't help inhaling. His body feels toned and I have to resist the urge to wrap my arms round his neck and sink deeper into him. It's been months since I've felt any sort of closeness with a man and it's only now that I realise how much I've missed it.

After the song has finished, Sophia's mother, Geni, announces that the taxi has arrived to take Sophia and Antonio to a hotel. Tomorrow morning they will travel to Santorini for their honeymoon. A crowd gathers and everyone raises their arms to form an arch for the couple to walk through as they wave everyone goodbye. We all follow them to the waiting car and wave them off until they are out of sight at the end of the long drive.

An hour or two later the evening begins to wind down and soon enough the three of us are ready to head back to the farmhouse.

'I am going to stay and have coffee with Geni,' says Viola. Fillipo is sitting at a nearby table drinking brandy and smoking a cigar with a group of older men. He raises his hand and bids us goodnight.

Emma and Cheryl walk on ahead, as Gianni and I stroll behind chatting. I find myself stifling a yawn. 'I'm so sorry, it's been long day. I think maybe I just need a coffee.'

'In that case, would you like to come to my place for a coffee?' Gianni says.

'Sure, why not?' I reply, feeling my pulse quicken and telling myself to be brave and live a little.

When we arrive back at the farmhouse, I tell Cheryl and Emma that I'm going to have coffee with Gianni in the farmhouse. But I am surprised to find that Gianni has his own section of the house in the form of an additional bungalow adjacent to his parents' home. It's beautifully furnished with dark woods and stylish pieces of antique furniture against whitewashed walls. There's a huge, red-patterned rug in front of a log burner.

'Very cosy,' I say, thinking that the place has definitely had the benefit of a woman's touch. I find myself wondering about his love life.

'Thank you. It's a nice place to return to after a hard day's work.'

Gianni brews some coffee and we take cups outside onto a moonlit patio area and sip our espressos. There's a full moon this evening, casting a sheer white light over the flagstones.

'So, would you like to try some of that prosciutto now?' asks Gianni, getting to his feet.

'Go on, then,' I say, realising I'm a little peckish. As he heads inside I consider myself very fortunate to have spent the day dining with two handsome Italians.

Gazing at the white moon against the navy, star-studded sky I experience a feeling of contentment I haven't felt in a long time. They say a change is as good as a rest and this is certainly such a change from my usual environment. Although I very much enjoyed this evening at the party, I was also looking forward to returning to the calm, relative seclusion of the farmhouse. That's always been my way. I enjoy the company of people, but need to spend some time alone to fully recharge. I wonder, fleetingly, who I'd miss if I came to live in a place like this. I realise it's Dad and a feeling of love envelops me, reminding me that my time spent here is a holiday and nothing more.

Gianni appears a few minutes later with a plate of hams, cheeses, olives and crackers. Tucking in, I find the prosciutto is salty and delicious. It's not like anything I've tried before. 'This is really good,' I say, wrapping a piece of salami around an olive. 'Does it have a fennel flavour?'

'Yes, fennel and black pepper are added during the production process. You have a good palate, Maisie.'

Maybe that's why I'm good at identifying wine flavours, I think to myself. *Tomorrow without fail I will try and get some information about the wine stashed in the wardrobe.*

'The olives are home grown too.' Gianni's words break into my thoughts. 'We have them harvested several times a year and turned into our own olive oil.'

'What about the wheat?'

'That is harvested in the autumn. Durum wheat is the main ingredient in dried pasta.'

'No wonder you are always so busy.'

'It's not so bad. The olives take care of themselves, although the wheat fields need looking after. The pigs and the curing of the meats take up most of my time though.'

'Your home is really lovely. You have very good taste,' I say, devouring a sweet soft cheese on a cracker. I think it's burrata, which I sampled earlier today in the restaurant.

'I can't honestly say it is all my own work. Most of it was done by my ex-girlfriend, Juliet. We lived together for three years.'

I'm not sure what to say and find myself asking, 'When did you break up?'

'A year ago. She said I gave more attention to the pigs than I did to her.'

'And did you?'

'With hindsight maybe I did. But you live and learn, don't you?'

'I suppose so. I guess it's all about finding a balance in life.'

'That's easier said than done sometimes. I had to spend many long hours building my business and earning a good reputation. There are many pig farmers in this region so you have to be the best. I like to think have achieved that status now.' Gianni smiles at the thought.

'Do you earn enough money from it? Actually, I'm sorry, I didn't mean to pry. It just seems like such a simple way of life.'

'I don't mind you asking. Many people think farming is a humble profession but I supply some of the finest butchers in Tuscany. I am lucky to have built a good name over the years for my premium prosciutto. I have even supplied royalty, so I actually make a very comfortable living. It's not about the money for me though. I love what I do. But maybe you are right. Perhaps I need a little more balance in my life.'

'It's something I'm working on too I suppose. I've learned a lot about myself these past couple of years.'

'Really? In what way?'

'Well I've realised I need to spend more time with friends and not shut myself away. I never thought that I could live alone either as I suffer with occasional bouts of anxiety and depression. I was so nervous at first, waking up alone in the night, my heart racing thinking I could hear noises in the flat. Although that also happened when I was still married,' I say ruefully.

'I don't understand?'

I find myself telling Gianni all about my marriage and how Harry would sometimes stay out until the early hours of the morning, on occasions not returning until the sun came up. I'm surprised at how I'm opening up to him but he's such a good listener, his eyes never leaving mine as I speak.

'That must have been hard for you,' he says softly.

'At times, yes, but I suppose people go through far worse things than a marriage break-up don't they? I relied too much on Harry, I realise that now. It's rather nice getting to know myself again actually.'

'I'm rather enjoying getting to know you too,' Gianni says gently. 'You intrigue me, Maisie. I haven't been so drawn to someone in a long time.'

I'm trying to keep a lid on my emotions but I find myself feeling both flattered and excited by his words. We talk until the small hours about our families, before Gianni pours us a limoncello each as a nightcap.

'*Salute!* To the future. And your very good health.'

'*Grazie*. Yours too.'

Gianni finishes his drink then stretches his arms above his head and yawns.

'Oh, my goodness. Look at the time.' My watch is showing a little after two thirty in the morning. 'Don't you have an early start tomorrow?'

'I do,' says Gianni. 'But I can have a rest later in the day. It will be worth the tiredness for having spent such a wonderful few hours with you.'

Outside, in the darkness, I find myself blushing. He walks me across the driveway, gently taking my hand in his, and a warm feeling courses through my body. When we stop outside my front door, Gianni studies my face for a few seconds. 'I've really enjoyed spending time with you this evening, Maisie. My heart sank when I saw you leave with Frederico today. I thought you wouldn't make it back here for the evening reception.'

'Really? I'm sure there were plenty of women at the wedding who would have been more than happy to keep you company,' I say, recalling the attractive woman he was chatting to when I first arrived.

'There were other women there? I barely noticed them. There was only one woman I was looking out for.' His breath quickens as he leans in and brushes his lips gently against mine, and to my surprise I find myself kissing him back, inhaling the woody, citrus scent of him once again. It feels like the most natural thing in the world to be kissing Gianni; the perfect end to a memorable evening.

'Good night, Maisie. Sweet dreams,' he breathes into my ear.

The mention of dreams makes me think of my dream catcher, which I realise I haven't had on this holiday, yet I've slept like a log here in Tuscany – this place must be good for me.

Back inside the apartment, I swallow my antidepressant tablet with a glass of water, before creeping silently into my bedroom, careful not to wake my friends. I can almost feel Gianni's presence as I close my eyes and relive that kiss. I recall the moment his lips pressed against mine, his strong arms pulling me close. It felt so right, yet something tells me things may be moving just a little too fast. What do I really know about him? Perhaps he has holiday romances with lots of the women who come to stay here, forgetting about them the minute they leave. I cuddle into my pillow with these thoughts swirling around my head. I must protect my heart. And even if this does end up being a holiday romance, perhaps it's right that it should remain just that...

Chapter Seventeen

The next day I wake to the sight of Cheryl placing a tray with a cup of coffee and a chocolate brioche on my bedside table.

'Good afternoon, Sleeping Beauty.'

'*Afternoon?*' I sit up and grab my phone to check the time. It's just after twelve o'clock. I also notice that I have a missed call from Dad. 'You shouldn't have let me sleep so long,' I say, flinching at the sunlight that is streaming through the window now that Cheryl has drawn the curtain.

'What time did you roll in last night then? Or should I say this morning?'

'I think it must have been getting on for three in the morning.' I sip the delicious, strong coffee and it really hits the spot.

'I saw Gianni earlier, sporting bags under his eyes. You must have worn him out,' she teases.

'Sorry to disappoint you, Cheryl, but we sat up talking, nothing more. Oh, apart from a bit of a kiss at the front door.'

'*A bit of a kiss?* I'd have snogged his face off. What was it like?'

'None of your business. I'm sorry I said anything now,' I say, throwing a pillow at her.

'I told you he fancied you, didn't I? Anyway, get up. I've got a surprise for us outside.'

I grab a robe and follow Cheryl to the front door, to find Emma standing beside a white Fiat in the driveway and chatting to Maria.

'Where did you get this from?' I ask.

'Maria drove me into the next town to collect it from a car hire place,' Cheryl says. 'I've got it for three days. I've been shopping and have stocked the fridge up, too. Would you like a trip to Florence tomorrow? It's a bit late to be going now.'

'Sorry about that,' I say, feeling guilty for sleeping in.

'Don't be daft. You obviously needed the sleep. Besides, it's usually me that stays up until all hours at a party and then stays in bed half the day. So, how do you fancy going to Pisa for dinner later? According to the map it's only a forty-minute drive away.'

'Sounds perfect.' Going back inside, I ring Dad.

'Hello, love, how's the holiday going?'

'Oh, it's brilliant. I'm having a great time. Sorry I missed your call yesterday. Would you believe we were at a local wedding? I'll tell you a funny story about it when I get home.'

'That sounds good. I'm glad you're enjoying yourself, love, it's nice to hear. Actually, I was ringing to ask you if you're doing OK for money? I know you had the prize-winning cash, but that won't last forever.'

'I'm fine, Dad, really. Thank you, though. Anyway, how are you?'

'I'm alright. I bumped into Gladys and young Jack in Crosby village yesterday, coming out of Sainsbury's, so I invited them back here for a drink. I'd forgotten how much Jack enjoys my garden. He picked some strawberries to take home.'

The mention of Jack reminds me of the days when Harry and I would take him to the beach and build sandcastles before taking him for a burger. I must arrange to see him when I get home.

'Ah, that's nice, Dad. What's the weather like there then?'

'Would you believe it's been lovely and sunny these past few days. Seems we are having a bit of a summer after all. I told Gladys she's welcome to call around here any time with Jack.'

'How lovely. I'm sure Gladys will be glad of the company too.' Gladys has been on her own since her husband Ted died five years ago, and I like the sound of them spending some time together. Dad has his friends at the British Legion club, but he doesn't often have visitors to his home.

We finish our conversation, then I head off to the spacious marble bathroom for a long, leisurely shower. I think about the previous evening and Gianni's good-night kiss and find myself wondering what it would be like to spend the whole night with him. I can hardly believe it – this feeling has truly taken me by surprise. It was so lovely to sit outside in the moonlight, chatting easily without a care in the world. But a niggling voice in my head reminds me that this is not real life. This is a holiday. A place of sunshine and wine, an escape from the problems of everyday life.

I'm out of the shower and towelling myself dry when I hear Emma's voice on the other side of the door. She must be on her phone, as she's talking in clipped tones. I have to come out of the bathroom and pass her to get the hairdryer and mouth 'sorry' as I quickly retrieve it from a drawer and head back into the bathroom. I noticed she had a serious expression on her face and I hear her say,

'Well, obviously out of sight is out of mind for you,' so I assume she is talking to Joe. I make a mental note to ask her about it later.

꙳

An hour later we are ready to head off to Pisa.

'Right, how's this for a plan… We grab a coffee when we get there, do the touristy sightseeing thing, then have dinner somewhere there this evening?' suggests Cheryl.

'Sounds good. I don't mind driving us home later if you guys want a glass of wine,' offers Emma, who seems a bit subdued after her conversation with Joe.

'Happy days!' Cheryl laughs.

We take to the road, thankful that the traffic is not too heavy, and soon enough the sight of the Leaning Tower of Pisa comes into view. As we approach the town centre we find that there is a diversion, with the main road cordoned off.

'Oh great, what's going on here then?' says Cheryl.

A nearby policeman informs us that today, being the last Saturday in June, an annual game called the Battle of the Bridge is staged. The city's neighbourhoods are divided into two teams, either side of the river, where they dress up and re-enact a battle. The preparations take all week and the whole town turn out to watch.

The policeman informs us that if we drive out of Pisa a little, we may be able to walk back in if we're 'lucky enough to find a parking space'.

'Oh, would you believe it,' says Cheryl. Yet, unbelievably, several minutes later a guy in a shiny red Alfa Romeo sports car reverses out of a space on a busy side road lined with cars. Cheryl expertly nudges the Fiat into it as a queue quickly forms behind her.

'How lucky was that?' she yelps. 'Right, girls, let's go and grab a cappuccino.'

We head into the Piazza dei Miracoli, the Square of Miracles, and are faced with the leaning tower, which is the bell tower for the adjacent cathedral. There's a large grassy area where groups of people are enjoying picnics, despite signs asking people to stay off the grass.

Everywhere is busy, but we manage to find a café, where, as luck would have it, a young family are leaving an outside table that's shaded by a canopy. We swiftly slide into the vacant seats and a young waitress in a red dress with a white apron over it quickly comes along and clears the table before taking our drinks order.

The café is bustling with tourists of various nationalities, all wearing hats and sunglasses and carrying tote bags with pictures of the tower on the front. We sip our frothy cappuccinos and nibble the almond biscotti biscuits that arrived with the coffee, before purchasing some bottles of water and leaving the café. It's getting on for four o'clock in the afternoon but the temperature is still in the eighties.

We take photos of the tower, each of us taking the compulsory shot of pretending to hold it up. It looks smaller than I imagined it would be. Although maybe if it was really tall it would have toppled over a long time ago.

'I love it here,' says Emma, as we stop at a cart and buy Nutella ice creams. 'There is such an energy about the place.'

'Me too. These buildings are fabulous. I reckon we finish our ice creams and go and have a look around the cathedral,' I suggest, in need of a short respite from the heat.

Stepping inside the cathedral shortly afterwards, we are staggered by its beauty. There are gold artefacts everywhere and paintings of the Madonna and Child. Marble altars are adorned with sculptures of the baby Jesus and the main altar is copper-coloured and shines almost orange as the light floods through the domed glass ceiling above. I think there's something wonderful about the inside of a church – I find churches are places of solace, perfect for reflection. Admiring the beautiful stained-glass windows and richly decorated altars, we take one last look around before heading outside.

Taking a walk along the River Arno, we come across crowds lined up along the riverside. Some of them are settling down with picnics and others are sitting at wooden tables outside cafés, and I can't help noticing there's a feeling of anticipation in the air.

'Oh wow, look at this,' says Emma, grabbing her camera as a group of men dressed in sixteenth-century Spanish battledress march along by the river, led by feather-capped leaders beating drums. An English lady in the crowd tells us that the actual battle will take place on the bridge at ten o'clock this evening, when the opposing sides challenge each other by pushing a cart across the rails of the bridge.

We walk around for about an hour, absorbing the atmosphere in the town, then decide to look for somewhere to eat.

'This should be fun. We were lucky to get a parking space and a table at that café. I think it's going to take a miracle to find a table in a restaurant,' says Cheryl, as her eyes follow the toned backsides of two young Italian men.

'Well, then, maybe we should head back to the Square of Miracles,' says Emma, laughing.

Walking back through the crowds I think I can hear someone call my name. I turn round to find Frederico from the winery with a pretty girl in tow.

'Frederico! Fancy meeting you here,' I say in surprise. 'How are you?'

'I am very good, thanks.' He greets each of us with a kiss on both cheeks, before introducing us to his date, who is called Amelia. 'I take it you have come here for the Battle of the Bridge?'

'Well, we didn't actually know anything about it, we just thought we'd drive to Pisa, have a look round, and then find a place for dinner. I don't think we've got much chance of finding a table anywhere though,' I reply, thinking that our luck must surely have run out.

'It's true. Most of the restaurants will have been booked up for weeks. This is a major event on the calendar. But, do you all like pizza?' he asks.

'We love it. And we haven't actually had one since we've been here, have we, girls?'

Cheryl and Emma shake their heads in reply.

'That's a crime! Follow me,' Frederico says.

We turn down a side street off the main square and walk for about five minutes until we come to an unremarkable-looking building with a grey front door. A sign with small red lettering over the door says simply 'open'. Frederico talks into an intercom and a minute or two later the door is opened by a burly, shaven-headed bloke wearing a black T-shirt and blue jeans.

'I hope this place is OK,' Cheryl whispers in my ear. 'It looks like a strip club from the outside.'

We step inside and are shocked to find ourselves in the most beautiful-looking restaurant. It's traditionally furnished, and has a black and white marble floor and a stunning chandelier suspended from the high ceiling. Diners are sitting at rustic wooden tables with carafes of red wine and pizzas on platters. The smell of oregano and basil in the air is tantalising.

'This is my uncle's place,' says Frederico. 'Have a drink at the bar. My cousin Nico will sort you out with a table as soon as he can. *Ciao* for now.'

Frederico ventures off to enjoy his evening with Amelia, but not before whispering to me that he would love to take me out on another date. Maybe I'll consider it. He really was the most engaging lunch companion. He also tells me that the job offer in the winery is still on the table if I want it, so I guess he was serious about it. I decide I might actually give it some thought. Working in a winery over the summer could be a lot of fun. But could I really leave Dad?

'Maybe going back to miracles square worked,' says Cheryl, as she sits on a bar stool sipping an Aperol spritz, while Emma and I enjoy a moreish pineapple-and-coconut mocktail. We look around us, taking in the atmosphere of the striking dining room, which has a glass dome at the centre of the ceiling. The grey-painted walls are decorated with huge, ornately framed mirrors that give the room an elegant yet relaxed feel. Chunky red candles on the stripped wooden tables suit the décor perfectly.

'I'm starving now. The smell of those pizzas is making me salivate,' says Emma, as a waitress passes by and swiftly deposits a huge pizza onto a nearby table. Emma puts her nose in the air, jokingly inhaling the aroma, as a waiter arrives to show us to our table.

'I see that you are hungry,' he says to Emma, 'which is good because the pizzas here are so delicious, you wouldn't want to leave a single mouthful.'

'Are you paid to say that?'

'No need, *signorina*,' says the charming waiter. 'The pizzas speak for themselves. They are the best in Italy.'

We order a giant pizza split into four, with a section each of Quattro Formaggi, Napoletana, Italian sausage, and garlic chicken with aubergine. We order sides of mozzarella balls and a green salad.

The waiter definitely wasn't exaggerating about the pizzas, as they are truly scrumptious. The flavours of the Mediterranean are right there on the lightest of pizza bases. Every mouthful is simply sensational.

'How the hell can a pizza taste this good?' asks Cheryl, a string of gooey mozzarella stretching from her mouth. She wipes her chin with a red paper napkin. 'This beats Pizza Heaven back home hands down.'

A handsome man in a white shirt and jeans walks over and introduces himself as Nico, Frederico's cousin, and the manager of the restaurant.

'Thanks so much for fitting us in,' I say, smiling at him. 'This is the best pizza we've ever eaten.'

'You are most welcome. Early evening is the best time to arrive. It may have been trickier to fit you in later.'

'How do people even know the restaurant's here though? There's no sign outside,' asks Cheryl.

'Word of mouth, usually. We would be turning literally hundreds of people away if we had a neon sign outside,' Nico says, before excusing himself and disappearing off in the direction of the kitchens.

'What a great position to be in; imagine never having to advertise but still being packed out,' Cheryl says wistfully.

'Well, that could be you one day, Cheryl. People may find they have to wait six months to have a hair appointment with you.'

'Oh, yeah. Nicky Clarke had better watch out!'

The funny thing is, it's not beyond the realms of possibility. A couple of weeks before we left for Italy, I met Cheryl's mentor, Jo, who is an award-winning hairdresser to the Cheshire set. She'd been invited for Sunday lunch with Cheryl and her family at a local pub one weekend when I was there. Jo told me that she'd heaped praise on Cheryl when she was a trainee at one of her salons, but Cheryl would bat it all away with a self-deprecating comment, never fully realising how good she was. I really do hope that Cheryl will have the chance to open her own salon one day. 'I would have offered her a job in a heartbeat but she always insisted she wanted to work for herself,' Jo told me.

We are all stuffed after our feast and decline the offer of the dessert menu, but instead opt for a shot of tangy limoncello.

As we stroll contentedly back through the Square of Miracles, we pass a bustling thoroughfare of stalls alongside the tower walls. They're selling all things touristy and Cheryl stops to buy herself a pair of 'designer' sunglasses and a tin of Italian biscuits, with a picture of the tower on the front, for her mum. I spot some football shirts in boys' sizes and decide to purchase a blue 'Italia' shirt for

Jack. Dad likes to dabble in the kitchen so I buy him an apron with Michelangelo's *David* on the front, which I know will give him a giggle. There are lighters fashioned in the shape of cannons and, with a pang, I can't help thinking that it would be exactly the kind of fun souvenir that Harry would sell on his market stall.

As we amble along, absorbing the atmosphere, the place is buzzing with life, street entertainers and musicians adding to the carnival atmosphere.

'Are either of you two bothered about watching the actual battle?' asks Cheryl.

'Not really,' I say, with a shrug.

'Are you sure? It's just that it only starts at ten so it will be well after midnight before we get back home. I was hoping to get an early start for Florence tomorrow,' Cheryl explains.

'Hark at you being so sensible. Even when you have two chauffeurs at your disposal,' I say.

'Ah, now that is sensible,' says Emma, smiling. 'Florence has so much to see it makes sense to have an early start.'

The three of us stroll back to the car, clutching our bags of souvenirs and savouring our last moments in this enchanting place. Emma opts to do the driving and I sit up front with her as Cheryl sits in the back seat, dozing off.

'Sorry about earlier, when I walked in on your phone call,' I say. 'I don't want to pry, but is everything alright between you and Joe?'

'You're not prying, you're my best friend. And no, not really, since you ask. I didn't want to mention anything today as I didn't want to spoil our afternoon out.'

'I hope you can work things out.'

'Me too, but do you know something? I'm tired of having to wish for a bit of affection. Joe sits there all weekend when he comes home, telling me about his work and the places he's visited, but he never once asks me how my week has been. Sometimes I feel like I'm nothing more than a housemate. We inevitably end up sleeping together after a few drinks. I feel like a friend with benefits,' she says, with a sigh.

'Oh, Em, I'm so sorry. I thought you were still good together. Only you can decide what's right for you. One thing I do know though; you deserve to be happy.'

The lights of an oncoming car illuminate Emma's face and I glimpse a tear silently falling down her cheek. I reach over and squeeze her hand.

'Right. Tomorrow we're going to have the best day ever,' I say, rubbing her arm and thinking what a fool Joe must be. 'I must admit I've wanted to visit Florence ever since I watched the film of Dan Brown's *Inferno*. The city just looks so beautiful.'

'Oh, yes. I think *Angels and Demons* was my favourite in the trilogy though,' says Emma, no doubt grateful for the change of subject. We go on to discuss our favourite Tom Hanks films, my personal favourite being *Sleepless in Seattle*, although *Forrest Gump* comes a close second. Before we know it, we have arrived back at the farmhouse.

As Emma pulls the car to a stop, Cheryl wakes and stretches her arms above her head. 'Blimey, I must be getting old,' she says, laughing. 'Can't take the pace. A few cocktails and I'm in bed before midnight.'

'You were up early this morning,' I remind her.

'That'll be it then. Up early again tomorrow too. After we've been to Florence I'm not moving from the pool for the last few days of our holiday though. There's no way I'm going home without a decent tan.'

'Are you joking? You already look like a local,' I say, eyeing her smooth, mocha- coloured skin. 'Actually, some pool days sounds good. This sightseeing lark is exhausting.'

As we cross the courtyard to our accommodation, I have to pinch myself yet again that I managed to win this holiday. Thinking of my job situation back home, I wonder when I'll be able to afford another break. But when I glimpse a light on in Gianni's home across the pool, all thoughts of home suddenly vanish…

Chapter Eighteen

'I like the name Florence,' says Cheryl, as we prepare for our day out the next morning. 'If I ever have a little girl, I think that's what I'll call her. Not that I can ever see myself having children.'

Cheryl has often talked of how she will never get married and have kids. She says her mother was trapped with five children and never did anything she really enjoyed, so her view of marriage is a little clouded.

'It makes me think of Florence Nightingale,' says Emma. 'Which is nice, because I suppose she was quite an inspirational figure in history. You have to give children's names a lot of thought. There's a kid in my mum's street called Ambrosia. Unfortunately, every time I see her it's not the food of the gods I think of, though, more tinned rice pudding.'

We breakfast on natural yoghurt, sweet nectarines and juicy strawberries, followed by a thick slice of panettone washed down with some delicious, strong coffee.

'Right, I'll just nip to the loo then I'm ready,' says Cheryl.

A few minutes later we are sitting in the car, heading towards Florence. It's another gorgeous morning and we've set off just before nine o'clock, which means we'll be able to make the most of the day. I am in the passenger seat next to Cheryl, and Emma is in the back seat with her nose in a pamphlet.

We drive along the twisty roads, admiring the lines of cypress tress standing to attention between the fields, like soldiers on parade on a patchwork green lawn. The windows are open and I can hear the sound of a church bell chiming in the distance.

'It says here that the best way to see Florence is on foot, as the centre is quite small,' Emma tells us. 'There's still tons to see though. The whole place is a UNESCO World Heritage Site. We need to decide exactly what we want to look at.'

'I suppose Michelangelo's *David* is a must. That's not in the Uffizi Gallery, is it?'

'No, it's in the Accademia Gallery, which is a lot smaller. I agree, that's definitely on our "must see" list.'

'I was thinking maybe we should jump on the sightseeing bus rather than walking,' I say, remembering Dad saying it's the best way to see a place. 'At least that way we can jump on and off wherever we fancy.'

The girls agree it sounds like a good idea.

❧

When we arrive in Florence, it's no surprise to find it bustling with cars and tourists. The traffic is even crazier than it was in Pisa and the sound of car horns tooting fills the air. Coaches full of tourists are crawling along, as motorcycles zip between them. Thankfully, we manage to find a parking space without too much trouble and are soon staring at the wondrous sights all around us. One of the first things I do is find an ATM to get some cash. The nearest one is in the wall of a stunning, grey-stone Renaissance building, which actually houses a hairdressing salon.

'Fancy working here then, Cheryl?' I say, nodding to the glass exterior of the swish- looking salon, wondering how much it would cost for a cut and blow dry.

'And give up cups of tea and gossip in my clients' kitchens? Not a chance.'

We walk on for a while, stopping to get a slushy iced-lemon drink called a *granita* from a street vendor, before finding a stairwell leading onto a section of the walls. Climbing to the top, we discover that the view, across the southern part of Florence, is breathtaking. We spot the magnificent roof of the cathedral, the Duomo, in the distance: a terracotta sphere above a sea of stone-coloured buildings. The adjacent column of Giotto's Campanile, a bell tower sparkling in shades of red, with white and green marble, stretches majestically towards the sky.

'Wow, this is incredible,' I say, putting my camera onto zoom lens and snapping away. Hordes of tourists in the square below are doing the same thing.

A group of four young men, wearing jeans and tight-fitting T-shirts, walks past and Cheryl asks one of them if they would mind taking a photo of us. A handsome guy with a beard removes his designer sunglasses and looks at her with seductive brown eyes.

'Would you like us to get in the photo? Maybe you make your boyfriends back home a little jealous?' he says, laughing.

'I would if I had one,' says Cheryl.

'This can't be true. The men in your home town must be crazy,' he replies, eyeing her up and down.

They take a photo of us girls, then good-naturedly huddle around for a group selfie, the fresh zesty scent of aftershave emanating from them.

'*Ciao*, ladies, have fun!' they say, as they walk off.

'Ooh, how gorgeous were they? Shall we follow them?' asks Cheryl, who I think is only half joking.

We all admire the photo, which makes us look like a group of close friends on holiday.

'Don't worry, I won't put it on Facebook,' I tell Emma. 'Don't want Joe getting the wrong idea, do we?'

Emma shrugs.

After an hour of marvelling at the most stunning buildings, we find a table at an outdoor café and order some iced coffees. Along with the tourists, there are stylish Italian women in loose linen dresses and oversized sunglasses enjoying cold frappes like us. Businessmen in sharp suits sip espressos as they peruse their newspapers.

We finish our drinks then head into a newsagent's next door, where tickets are sold for the open-topped bus tour. The shopkeeper kindly directs us to the nearest pick-up point, telling us that the next bus is due in around ten minutes. When the bright red double-decker bus pulls into the stop, we climb the stairs and are relieved to find that there are quite a few seats available. A tour guide, wearing red shorts and a yellow polo shirt, welcomes us and hands us each a pair of earphones for the commentary during the tour.

We pass the Uffizi Gallery in the Piazza della Signoria and take some photos from the top deck. There's a never-ending queue of visitors waiting to enter the gallery and I think how much I prefer sitting on the bus. As we arrive near the Ponte Vecchio, we decide to disembark and head towards the famous bridge. There are shops dotted all the way along and it's not like anything I've ever seen before. I suddenly think of Southport Pier dotted with its amusement arcades and ice-cream kiosks – we're worlds away from that.

'This is amazing,' says Emma, stopping to admire some Murano glass jewellery in a store window. The jewellery shops jostle for space along the ancient bridge. We enter one selling scarves and gold jewellery and I notice some perfume samples on a stand. Spritzing a cloud of scent onto my wrist, a childhood memory comes flooding back. The scent is lily of the valley – my mum wore it on an almost daily basis.

I swallow down a lump in my throat as I think of Mum. Sometimes I still can't believe she's not alive. I would have so enjoyed going home and telling her all about my adventures in Tuscany. She would have laughed about Cheryl and her stopping to take photographs of Italian hunks. She would love these little stores, too, always being a fan of pottering around gift shops.

Feeling the need to speak to Dad, I tell the girls I'm just stepping outside for a minute. I give him a quick ring and he tells me he's in the village at the local DIY store, shopping for some wood stain. He has oak worktops in the kitchen and he says they could do with a little brightening up. I admire Dad so much. He has tried to fill his days with activities since Mum died, which I know can't be easy. We're just finishing our conversation as Emma and Cheryl emerge from the shop carrying bags of purchases.

'Have you been maxing out your credit card?' I ask Cheryl, who I know isn't exactly flush at the moment.

'I think you're forgetting I got paid a nice little earner for doing Sophia's wedding hair and make-up,' she says, grinning. 'That was an unexpected bonus, so I thought I'd treat myself.' She opens her bag to reveal a gorgeous gold cuff bracelet and some perfume.

'Very nice… Emma, what did you buy?'

'I bought this Murano glass bowl for the lounge,' she says, lifting the bowl from the bag, the iridescent hues of green and blue glinting in the sunlight. 'I think it will complement the new, light blue sofa we've bought recently. It will look good on our dark wooden coffee table too.'

'That's really pretty. You have a real eye for decorative pieces. Right, who's for a *gelato*?' I ask. 'We've hardly tried any.'

We find a stand and buy a raspberry, a lemon and a peach ice cream, each served in a huge waffle cone. Finding a nearby bench to sit on, we enjoy the creamy, fruity ice creams, which are melting fast in the heat. Afterwards, we get up and walk around for a while longer, stopping to admire the striking cathedral with its copper-coloured dome rising majestically into the sky. The colours of the marble on the main façade glint gently in the sunshine. It's so beautiful.

An hour later we decide to find somewhere for lunch, after which we plan to catch the bus to the Galleria dell'Accademia, which houses Michelangelo's statue of David.

Down a side street, we find a rustic-looking restaurant with rough stone walls and a wooden door. There's a heady scent of basil in the air as we enter and we are offered a table near the window. The restaurant is simply furnished with dark wooden tables, its cream-painted walls dotted with photographs of the city. The floor is the star of the show, being set in a blue mosaic with a sunshine fanning out from the centre. Emma and Cheryl order a bottle of white wine to enjoy between them and I opt for fresh lemonade, which arrives in a huge glass with ice.

We dine on the most delicious seafood pasta and for dessert we have *Schiacciata alla Fiorentina*, a Florentine orange cake dusted in icing sugar, which is light as a feather and delicious. We are informed that it's normally only sold around Lent, but the pastry chef here bakes it all year round.

'That was a really good choice of restaurant,' I say, as we stroll outside after lunch. 'And that cake! I'm going to google the recipe and have a go at making that when I get home.'

'Right, let's get going then. There's still so much to see,' says Emma, once again perusing the sightseeing leaflet that she has pulled from her bag. 'After going to see the David statue, I'd like to visit the Piazza della Signoria as I believe Botticelli's *The Birth of Venus* is housed in one of the galleries there.'

'You're such a culture vulture,' teases Cheryl. 'Although there's no denying the beauty of this place.'

Despite the fact that I am trying to watch my money, conscious of losing my job in the sandwich shop, I decide that maybe I will treat myself to a pair of new earrings. My blue ones never quite recovered from the superglue incident. I enter a small jewellery shop on the Ponte Vecchio and, after a good look round, I purchase a pair of white gold earrings set with a small ruby.

Continuing our walk along the bridge, we pass street artists and musicians, and stop to listen to one very gifted violinist, throwing a few euros into his hat as we move on. An artist is seated at an easel, painting a picture of a blue and white boat on the River Arno, perfectly capturing the shaft of sunlight that's shining on the deck. The view across the river is beautiful and it's surprisingly peaceful on the bridge, despite the throng of tourists.

When we arrive at the Galleria dell'Accademia, the queues are not too bad, so we buy some tickets and after twenty minutes we are entering the cool interior, grateful to be out of the searing heat. The David statue is an impressive seventeen-foot-high sculpture displayed in a marble-domed alcove.

'Do you think it was a cold day when David modelled for this?' says Cheryl, staring at the statue's most obvious attribute with a cheeky grin. Without tickets, we are unable to get into the Uffizi Gallery to see *The Birth of Venus*, so once more we head back to the bus.

I know Dad was right to suggest the sightseeing bus, as it really is the best way to see everything. I think of my journey back home on the number 45 into the city centre. There will be no sultry heat beating down on me then, as I make my way to Tesco, more likely the steady drum of rain on the windows.

We hop off the bus a little further on and amble along, taking in more of the sights and sounds, with the sun high in the sky. I can feel the heat on the tops on my feet, of all places, and stop at a bench to spray some sunscreen onto them.

'I burnt my backside once,' says Cheryl, making us laugh. 'I fell asleep on a beach in a thong bikini. I couldn't bloody sit down for a week.'

'Is there anything either of you particularly wants to see?' asks Emma. When we shake our heads, she says, 'Then I wouldn't mind having a look at the Ognissanti. It's a baroque-style church where Botticelli is buried. Also, there is a fresco painting of the Last Supper by Ghirlandaio in the church.'

We head along a main road and look for a place to cross over to the next bus pick-up point. The lanes are crazy busy, with cars and mopeds and buses whizzing in every direction, and it seems as though we will be stuck at the edge of the kerb forever. Zebra crossings don't seem to mean anything here, as cars are practically shunting each other along and horns constantly tooting. It's chaotic but exhilarating.

I think I spy a gap in the traffic and gesture to Cheryl and Emma to cross. I'm making a move, not spotting the motorcyclist who is about to zoom round the corner.

It's as if Emma's muffled voice is in the distance, shouting above the noise in the crowds. I think I can make out her calling, 'Maisie, NO!' And that's the last thing I hear before everything goes black.

Chapter Nineteen

As I run into the foamy waves on the blustery beach, I grip my mum's hand tightly. There's a watery sun in the sky, but a bracing wind has my teeth chattering. We've come to the beach today as it's the perfect weather for flying my kite, but I never imagined paddling in the water. The kite was a gift from my parents for my seventh birthday. It's a Chinese dragon in glorious shades of red, gold and green, which Dad bought from a little shop in Chinatown. It's the best present I've ever had and one of my favourite pastimes is to come to the beach and watch it soar high in the sky, especially on a windy day like today.

'You're shivering,' says Mum, as I jump over an unexpectedly high wave and grip her hand even more tightly. 'I think we'd better get you dry and put your clothes on. Then we'll go and get a nice cup of hot chocolate.'

She smiles at me with her peach-painted lips and I feel a surge of love for her. Then another huge wave surges towards me and I lose my grip on Mum's hand. As the wave recedes it drags me further into the sea. I'm flailing my arms around in an attempt to swim, but I'm being dragged further out to sea.

'Mum!' I call as my head drops into the salty, freezing water.

'Maisie! Hold on, I'm coming!' screams Mum, as she strides towards me, a look of panic on her face.

The sun above seems to shine brighter, its light luring me towards it. I feel tired now, surrendering to this white light in the sky above… Suddenly I feel a pair of arms around my waist as I am scooped from the sea and somehow carried and dragged through the waves to the safety of the shore.

'You're alright, Maisie. I'm here. I will never let anything bad happen to you. I love you…'

❧

I open my eyes and a familiar face with soft grey eyes appears fuzzily in front of me. I wonder whether or not I'm in a different realm. I can feel my eyelids close heavily before I open them again and the face beside me comes into focus. There's familiar grey hair, a moustache and a slightly anxious expression on the face.

'Dad!' I say, glancing around the unfamiliar room. The walls are painted magnolia and the ceiling fan is doing little to ventilate the stuffiness. 'What are you doing here? In fact, where am I?' I ask, attempting to sit up.

'Whoa, take it easy,' says Dad, helping me lie down on my pillow again. 'You're in hospital, love. Welcome back to the land of the living.' He's squeezing me tightly and tears are brimming in his eyes.

I realise with a heavy heart that Mum is no longer here and I have experienced a dream about my childhood.

The doors swing open as a young nurse enters the room and checks a machine that I appear to be wired up to.

'You gave me a right fright,' Dad says, exhaling with relief. 'You've been out for the count for a few days.' He runs his fingers through his hair.

'A few days!' I say, sitting up this time. My head hurts.

There's a huge vase of pink and white flowers on the bedside table beside me. I remember that flowers are not allowed in hospitals back in the UK. Something to do with health and safety, I think… Funny the sort of facts that come back to you at times like this.

'What happened?' I ask, as I gently rub the back of my head.

'You were knocked over by a motorcyclist. You had quite a bang on the head, by all accounts. The doctors put you to sleep for a few days as there was quite a lot of swelling. Thank God you're OK,' he says, his eyes misting over again.

'How are you feeling?' asks the young nurse.

'My head hurts a little, but not too bad actually.'

'Good. Do you remember anything about the accident?'

'Not really. I remember being in Florence, then nothing after that. Where exactly am I now?'

'The Hospital of Santa Maria Nuova. You were brought in by ambulance. Try not to talk for too long.' She smiles warmly. 'A doctor will be in to check you over shortly.' The nurse nods to my father and leaves the room.

'Thanks for the flowers, Dad. They're really beautiful.'

'Oh, they're not from me, love. They're from that Gianni at the farmhouse. He's been here almost every day after work. And there's been another bloke here too. Frederico, I think his name was. Bit of a cheeky chap. He charmed all the nurses here.' Dad laughs, then looks a bit puzzled. 'He said when you woke up to tell you something about he hopes you're soon fit enough for work?'

'Frederico's after seasonal workers at a winery,' I say, not wanting to reveal too much. This accident has thrown any future plans up into the air anyway. 'You say Gianni has been here almost every day?'

'Yes. I met him when I stayed at the farmhouse when I first arrived. I've moved to a hotel near the hospital now, though, so I could be closer to you.'

'Oh, Dad. It must be costing you a fortune. And I didn't think you had a valid passport.'

'I didn't. I went down to the passport office in town and waited for one. It only took a few hours. I think they rushed it through because it was an emergency. And don't you be worrying about the cost of hotels. I've told you, I've got plenty of money. Besides, seeing you here like this makes me realise that money isn't everything.'

'Are you OK, Dad? You must be exhausted.' I know how much he hates being in a hospital – it reminds him too much of Mum's illness, of losing her.

'I'm fine. Even better now that you're awake. I'll sleep better in my bed tonight now.' He smiles.

'Where're Emma and Cheryl? Are they both OK?'

'Ah, now, here's the thing. Cheryl had to go home on the return flight yesterday, as planned. She had some clients booked in. She was in a right state having to leave you, but I assured her I'd look after you. Emma's still here, though. She asked if she could stay on in the apartment for a few more days. She's managed to get a flight booked in a couple of days' time. She'll be thrilled that you're awake.'

I gently put my head back down on the pillow, suddenly feeling overwhelmed with tiredness. I can't believe Gianni has been here nearly every day. He has a lot to do on the farm and yet he's still been making the drive here to see me. And Frederico has been here, too. I've never been so popular!

A different nurse, wearing a light blue trouser-suit uniform, wheels a blood-pressure monitor into the room and attaches a cuff to my arm. '*Buongiorno!* It is good to see you awake. How are you feeling?'

'Not too bad. Bit of a headache.'

'Hardly surprising. Would you like some pain relief?'

'Not at the moment, thank you. I'll let you know if it gets any worse.'

The talk of medication suddenly makes me think about my antidepressants. I inform the nurse and she takes a glance at the medical-record sheet on the clipboard at the foot of the bed. 'I am not usually on this ward, but it looks as though the medicine has been administered while you were asleep. The doctor will talk to you about that when he does his rounds.'

Dad stays for a while longer and I feel myself struggling to keep my eyes open, although he's there every time I look up. 'Go home now, Dad, or should I say back to the hotel. I'm fine, really.'

'I think I might, love. I'll go and have a bite to eat and a nice bath. The hotel is literally across the road. Thank God you're alright. I rang Emma while you were having a little doze, so don't be surprised if you get another visitor shortly.'

Dad kisses me gently and then leaves the room. A short while later, a middle-aged doctor wearing glasses arrives and confirms that my antidepressants have been administered intravenously. I wonder how he knew about them and he tells me that the box of tablets were in my handbag, the contents of which spilled across the road in the accident.

'So, thankfully, your tests don't seem to show any lasting damage and you have managed to escape without any broken bones, which is a miracle. We shall monitor your progress for a while longer, but all being well you will probably be allowed to go home tomorrow. And don't worry if you have the occasional lapse of memory, that's to be expected after a head injury. Things should return to normal in time.'

'Should or will?'

'Almost certainly will. You don't seem to have done any permanent damage. You are lucky. Being young and fit helps.'

I'm allowed to go home. I say the word over and over to myself. *Home.* Where is home? My one-bedroomed flat above the sandwich shop suddenly doesn't feel like a home any more. Maybe I'll go and stay with Dad for a while. Perhaps I could even move back there, although that would feel like my life was going backwards somehow.

The thought of travelling on a plane suddenly makes me feel nauseous. I'm pondering all of this when a hospital worker appears with a trolley, offering bedtime drinks. She is swiftly followed by Emma, who is racing towards me with her arms held out.

'Oh, Maisie,' she says, big fat tears rolling down her cheeks as she hugs me. 'I've just met your dad and he told me you were awake and talking. We thought we'd lost you. You were just lying there on the ground, motionless, with traffic screeching to a halt all around you. I'll never forget that moment. It was the worst moment of my life so far.'

'I'm OK now, Emma. Tired and sore, but otherwise fine,' I say, hugging her back.

She places a box of grapes and a slice of chocolate cake on the bedside table. I also notice she's brought my luggage.

Emma sees me looking at it. 'I brought your things over, Maisie, because I assumed that when you were better, you'd fly home from here. The hospital's a lot closer to the airport. But maybe I've jumped the gun a little. I'm sure you'll want to say a proper goodbye to Gianni.'

I was thinking the exact same thing myself.

'Emma, did you get the wine out of the wardrobe?' I ask, a feeling of panic rising in my chest.

'Yes, it's in your luggage. I must admit I only remembered it as I was about to leave.'

'Thanks, Emma. And is Cheryl OK? Dad says she's gone home.'

'No, she isn't really OK. She was very upset at having to leave you. I told her you wouldn't mind, as you know she has to earn a living. That's the downside of working for yourself, I suppose.'

'Of course I don't mind. I'll give her a ring when I'm feeling a little more myself.'

'I've just given her a quick call to let her know that you're alright. She wept with relief.'

'What happened, Emma? I vaguely remember being on a busy road, but that's it.'

'We were trying to cross that road to get to the sightseeing bus pick-up point. The traffic was crazy, as usual. Anyway, you thought there was a gap in the traffic and gestured for us to cross, but the motorcyclist' – Emma's voice catches in her throat – 'the motorcyclist came from nowhere and crashed into you. You fell and hit your head on the road. It was awful.'

She's crying now as she relives the dreadful moment and I reach out to her. We chat for a while longer, Emma intermittently clutching my hand and saying, 'Thank God you're OK,' before the overwhelming tiredness envelops me again.

'Sorry, Emma, you're not boring me, I promise, but I can't seem to keep my eyes open.'

'Right. I'll get going then. I took over the car hire from Cheryl and I've got the Fiat for two more days until my flight leaves. I'll come and see you tomorrow after lunch.'

Emma fixes my pillows and hugs me one more time before she leaves. I sink my head back into the freshly plumped pillows and eye the milky drink on the bedside table, which I can't seem to summon the energy to drink. It would seem I've had a very lucky escape. I could have been killed that day. My poor old dad has travelled all the way to Italy alone so things must have seemed pretty bad.

The enormity of what happened to me begins to sink in and a wave of emotion takes hold. My shoulders begin to shake as huge tears stream down my face. I realise that I must stop thinking about my past life. I have escaped the clutches of death and been given a second chance. It's time for me to start thinking about tomorrow and what type of life I want to live in the future.

Chapter Twenty

The next morning, I wake to see bright sunlight filtering through the sash window of the hospital room. As I lie there, enjoying the light, a ceiling fan above drones gently. I take in my surroundings, which I was unable to do properly last night, and realise that I am in rather a pleasant room. There is a pink bedspread over crisp white cotton sheets and a few bright floral prints are dotted around the pale-coloured walls. I lean to the right and notice that I have an en-suite bathroom. The gleaming white floor tiles look spotlessly clean.

My phone is plugged into a charger at my bedside and I can only assume Dad did it last night. Dear Dad, he'll probably be over shortly, as I know he's an early riser. The habit of waking early for his job as a train driver is a hard one to break. He told me he'd waited all his life to enjoy a sleep-in, yet, 'Every bloomin' morning I'm wide awake at six o'clock!'

I hear a trolley trundling along outside and a few seconds later the door is opened and in walks a hospital worker.

'Good morning. Would you like coffee this morning?'

I nod. 'Milky, please.'

The small lady in a maroon overall has short dark hair and smiling eyes. 'You are feeling good now, yes?' she asks, as she pours the coffee from a metal jug and adds a long glug of milk.

'A lot better, thanks.' I sit up slowly and realise I do actually feel a lot better, with little sign of a headache, which is a relief.

'I see you every morning asleep.' She smiles. 'I am happy you are awake. Bravo!'

I drink my warm, creamy coffee and glance at my watch to discover it's just before seven o'clock in the morning. The hospital worker tells me breakfast will be around shortly. I've often wondered why hospitals wake you so early for breakfast when sleep is supposedly the best medicine.

Grabbing my phone, I notice two missed calls from a number that hasn't appeared on my screen for a long time. They're from Harry. There are no text messages, just the missed calls. I wonder what he wants? I assume that Dad has informed Gladys of my accident, who must have told Harry. But even so, why is he calling? We haven't spoken in months.

I'm halfway through a breakfast of sweet porridge and peaches when in walks Dad. He looks refreshed after a good night's sleep, I'm glad to see.

'Morning, love. Now that's always a sign of good health, eating properly.' He smiles and plants a kiss on my cheek, before sitting down beside me.

'What did you have for breakfast?' I ask.

'Cornflakes. Oh, and a bit of bread and cheese. There were lots of cakes on the breakfast buffet at the hotel, too. But I couldn't stomach cakes for breakfast.' He pulls a face, then laughs.

'I could, but I'd be the size of a house if I had some every day,' I say.

I finish my breakfast, then tell Dad about the missed calls from Harry.

'Gladys will have told him. I thought about ringing him myself, but I know you haven't been together for a while. Better coming from her.'

'Do you see much of Gladys?'

'I never used to. But since the day I ran into her in the village with young Jack we've met up at the beach café a few times. Jack's brought his kite along when it's been a blowy day. She's good fun is Gladys.' I'm not sure, but I think Dad's avoiding my gaze slightly.

I think to myself that Gladys is the polar opposite of Mum. Mum was strong and resilient, yet gentle and caring – she possessed all the right attributes for a nurse. Gladys is a colourful, quirky character, who smokes and isn't averse to using the odd swear word. Dad's right, though, she is good fun. And she's always been there for me.

'That's nice. I'm happy to see you getting out more,' I say, meaning it.

'So when will you be allowed out, then?' asks Dad, obviously glad to move the conversation on to me.

'I'm waiting for the doctor to do his rounds later, but hopefully tomorrow.'

Our holiday at the farmhouse comes to an end tomorrow and it feels so strange knowing that when I leave hospital I will be going back home to my little flat in Liverpool. I feel disorientated, because I never imagined my holiday would end this way. The last thing I remember was spending a glorious day in Florence with Emma and Cheryl, which should have ended with a shot of limoncello back at our apartment. I feel gutted that the three of us never got the chance to end our holiday properly. I'd like to go back and say goodbye to Gianni, Viola and Maria to thank them for looking after us so well. Especially Gianni… I really do want to see him again.

I am still chatting to Dad when my phone rings. The caller display shows that it's Harry. What on earth does he want? My heart begins to race.

'Just nipping to the loo,' mouths Dad, giving me a minute to take the call.

'Hi, Maisie, how are you?' asks Harry. There's a softness in his voice that I rarely heard.

'Hi, Harry. I'm OK, thanks. Hopefully I'll be getting discharged tomorrow.'

'My mum told me you'd had an accident. It sounded serious. What happened?'

I fill Harry in with as much as I can remember, while secretly feeling happy that he still cares. He sounds relieved that I'm on the mend. I ask him how things are going at the market and he tells me business is booming. I never really had Harry down as the type who would sell stuff outdoors, if I'm honest. There was a time when he would have worried about the rain ruining his designer clothes.

'So, when are you home then?'

That word again.

'I'm not sure. I'll see how I feel. I don't feel much like travelling at this moment in time.'

'Well, if there's anything I can do when you get back, give us a ring. I mean that.'

We end the call with him telling me to 'take care' and I feel pleased that at least we can be civilised to each other now. Who knows, in time we may even become friends. I'm fairly certain now, though, that a romantic reconciliation isn't on the cards.

A couple of hours later, at my insistence, Dad goes for a break and a drink in the hospital restaurant. Soon after he's left the room, the doctor and Emma arrive at the same time.

'You look loads better today,' Emma says, giving me a hug.

'And the good news is that the test results agree,' the doctor tells me.

'So, when can I leave?' I am suddenly desperate to get back to the farmhouse.

'I should probably say tomorrow morning, but as your friend is here…' He hesitates for a moment. 'OK. You can leave today. As long as you take it easy for a while longer. Oh, and you should have someone around who will look after you, keep an eye on you.' With a beaming smile, the doctor turns on his heels and whisks through the door.

A sinking feeling comes over me. Of course there is no one here in Italy to look after me. Maybe I can persuade Dad to stay on here a while longer… He appears a few minutes later and I tell him what the doctor said.

'That's wonderful news,' Dad says, then he turns to Emma. 'Have you booked your flight?' he asks her. When she nods, he says, 'I need to do the same. I only booked a one-way ticket out as I wasn't sure how long I'd be staying.'

'My flight's tomorrow afternoon,' says Emma, fishing her phone from her bag. 'I'll see if there are any more seats available on it.'

'Actually,' I say, hoping to goodness it's possible, 'I don't feel ready to travel home yet. I was hoping to stay on at the farmhouse, maybe for another week. Perhaps you two could travel home together. Unless you fancy staying on for a bit, Dad?'

'Well, I suppose I could,' he says, a look of uncertainty on his face. 'I haven't got much to do apart from a snooker match on Tuesday. I'm in the finals.'

'Then make sure you're there for it,' I reply, suddenly feeling a little selfish. 'I'm fine, really. As the doctor said, I'm young and fit and he would hardly be discharging me if he had any doubts about my health. Besides, it may not even be possible to stay on at the farmhouse. If the apartment is booked out, I may need to find somewhere else. I'll speak to Viola or Gianni as soon as I can.'

At that very moment the door to my room swings open.

'Did someone mention my name?' says Gianni, appearing in the doorway with a giant teddy bear and a huge grin on his face.

Chapter Twenty-One

I hold out my arms for the teddy bear and beam up at Gianni as he hands it to me. 'Oh, thank you so much, Gianni, but what are you doing here at this time of day?' I say, as a warm, fuzzy feeling creeps over my body. The bear is huge and I don't know where to put it.

'I came to see for myself that you are really awake. On my last few visits you were sleeping. When I telephoned the hospital, I had to tell them I was your brother or they would tell me nothing. Oh, and my parents send their good wishes.'

Gianni turns to greet my father and Emma, then picks up the brown teddy and places it on the foot of the bed, before sitting down beside it.

'How are you feeling?'

'A bit better, and the doctor has just told me that I can leave here today. I'm not so sure I'm up for travelling yet, though. He did say that I might suffer some short-term memory lapses. Actually, I was just wondering if it might be possible to stay on at the apartment a little longer, so that I can recuperate. If no one's booked in, of course.'

Gianni rubs his chin thoughtfully. 'It's the height of the summer season now so I'm afraid someone new arrives tomorrow. Both apartments will be hired out. I may have a solution though. There are two bedrooms at my place so you would be welcome to stay with me for a short while.'

Dad and Emma exchange uncertain glances. I know what they will both be thinking without even having to ask. Dad will be feeling relieved that I'll have someone keeping an eye out for me. He has seen Gianni make the visits to the hospital and I know that he has had several chats with him, deeming him to be 'a decent bloke'. I can't expect Dad to disrupt his life for me, especially when it's not really necessary. Emma will be concerned about my welfare and feeling guilty that she's not here to help out, but very thankful for Gianni's offer.

There's a silence between us all as I digest what I have just been offered. Staying in Gianni's house, though, is a whole different scenario…

'Actually, if you prefer it, there are some self-catering apartments a few minutes' walk from the farmhouse,' he says, noticing my hesitation. 'I will make some enquiries, if you like.'

I imagine sitting outside in the sun, reading and healing, and eventually going for little morning walks, like I've been doing ever since I arrived here.

'That would be great, thanks,' I say, decision made. 'Now, does anyone fancy nipping out to buy a proper coffee? The stuff they serve in here is terrible.'

Dad informs us there is a good coffee house a couple of doors away from his hotel, so I put in an order for a large cappuccino and my visitors set off. Once they've gone, I give Cheryl a ring and can barely understand a word she says, as she's sobbing so loudly.

'I'm so glad you're OK,' she says, when she finally composes herself. 'I tried ringing you earlier. I've been worried sick.'

'Sorry about that. My phone was on charge. Listen, Cheryl, I'm fine. Really. All the tests came back OK. I'm a bit bruised and battered, but another week or so and I'm sure I'll be as right as rain.' I tell her about my plan to stay on here a little longer.

'I can't blame you. What a beautiful place to recuperate. I'll miss you, though,' she says in a small voice. 'Who am I going to borrow teabags from now?'

'It's not for long. Anyway, get down to Great Homer Street Market. Dad tells me Harry's selling boxes of discount teabags. You should stock up… Harry phoned me, actually.' I tell her all about our conversation and how he offered to help out if I needed anything when I get back home.

I was expecting her to tell me I should have told him to sod off, but she doesn't. 'How did that make you feel, him contacting you?'

'I'm not sure, to be perfectly honest. I thought it was nice that he cared enough to phone me. He could have just asked Gladys to phone, I suppose.'

'Maybe he's grown up a bit. It's taken him long enough though.'

Perhaps Cheryl is right. We all grow up and life experiences can certainly change our outlook. But can a leopard ever truly change its spots?

❧

Half an hour later everyone returns with drinks and a cream-filled Italian pastry called a *sfogliatella* for me.

'Right,' says Dad. 'There's a room available at the hotel. I nipped in and asked. If you like, you can stay there tonight, while Gianni tries to find something in the village for you from tomorrow. We'll have a nice breakfast together in the morning. You might enjoy those cakes I mentioned.' He laughs. 'Build your strength up.'

'Actually, Dad, I thought I would spend tonight at the farmhouse apartment. You could stay there too.' I am keen to stay at the villa for one last evening with Emma.

'Well, if you're going to do that I might just go home today,' muses Dad. 'I can get the train to the airport from here; the station is not far from the hotel. Young Jack's in a school play tomorrow. It's *Robin Hood* and Jack's playing the lead. Gladys has invited me along. That's if you don't mind, of course.'

'I don't mind at all. Emma, would you mind checking to see if there are any available flights?'

Emma retrieves her phone again and after a few minutes informs Dad that there are seats on a nine thirty flight later this evening.

'But you won't arrive home until after midnight,' I protest, feeling concerned at the thought of Dad having to hail a taxi home.

'I'll book a local taxi to be there waiting,' says Emma, sensing my concern.

I feel reassured as I sink back into the pillow and realise that no matter how independent Dad is, he is getting on in years. He needs me. As soon as I'm well enough I will have to head home. Even if I do feel torn about it.

Chapter Twenty-Two

Early in the afternoon, I leave hospital with Emma and Dad. I thank the hospital staff for looking after me and ask a nurse to donate the huge teddy bear to the children's ward. I'm pretty sure Gianni won't mind.

It's another beautiful day, with a cloudless sky, and it feels so good to be warmed by the sun again. Even so, my legs feel wobbly and I don't have much energy, so I walk slowly, with my arm through Dad's.

Emma puts my luggage into the boot of the Fiat, which is parked close by the hospital, and then we walk a short distance to a nearby café. The three of us spend the afternoon sipping *granitas* and relaxing under an umbrella at a quiet table in the back garden of the café. Later, we stroll to the station and Emma and I wave goodbye to my dad as he boards a train to the airport.

When we return to the car, I feel a twinge of excitement as Emma starts the drive back to the farmhouse. It's just after eight o'clock when we pull to a stop on the gravelled driveway. It feels strange knowing that this will be the last evening I'll spend in our apartment at Villa Marisa, looking out at the soft white moonlight from my bedroom window. Tomorrow will be the last time I'll hear the morning chirping of birds and watch Gianni's green tractor rumbling across the field, as the sun rises in a pink-streaked sky.

As I step from the car, Viola opens the front door of the farmhouse and welcomes me. She folds me in a lingering hug and plants a kiss on both cheeks, then holds me at arm's length and takes a good look at me. 'You look a little pale, Maisie, but thank goodness you are OK. Gianni was so worried about you. We all were.' She invites us in for some food but I very politely decline her kind offer as I just want to rest.

'OK, but maybe I will send some lamb stew over for you. It contains rosemary, which has very healing properties.'

§

Once inside our apartment, Emma gets busy packing her clothes, folding them neatly into her suitcase. I ask her why she isn't just tossing them all in as it's the end of the holiday. She laughs and tells me that she has washed and pressed them all here so that she won't have to do it when she gets home.

'Plus I can rest easy knowing that if my case is searched at the airport, for whatever reason, it will be full of clean underwear,' she tells me, nodding with satisfaction.

'Will Joe be home when you get back?' I ask her.

'He's due home tomorrow. He actually has four days off before he sets off again for France.'

'Maybe you should do something together. Try and rekindle a little romance?' I suggest.

'Well, if he wants to arrange something I suppose that would be nice,' says Emma, without much enthusiasm.

'Have you ever thought about going with him on one of his trips?'

'I did go with him once or twice in the early days. But it wasn't the romantic jaunt I'd anticipated. You spend hours on the road, or in warehouses waiting around for the truck to be unloaded, interspersed with stops at greasy spoon cafés. And I'm afraid sleeping in the cab and meeting hairy-arsed drivers on your way for a shower at the truck stops in the morning didn't really fill me with joy.'

'Suppose not.' I can't help laughing.

'Besides, I don't really have any more holidays left this year. School managers don't get as many holidays as the teachers. Maybe I should do a post-graduate certificate in education and become a teacher myself.'

'Would you consider doing that?'

'No thanks. It's one thing seeing the kids at the office window but I wouldn't fancy teaching a class full of teenagers. I take my hat off to those that do. Right, while I've still got the car, shall we drive down into the village for something to eat? I know you're not quite up to walking very far. Or if you don't fancy going out I could call Alfredo's and order a pizza to collect.'

'Actually, a pizza back here might be nice,' I say, not really feeling up to chatting to Alfredo or anyone else in the village. I just want to slip into my pyjamas and relax.

'Of course. I'll ask Alfredo to make up something nice.'

As Emma makes the call to the restaurant, I glance out of the lounge window at the swimming pool. It's been such a wonderful tonic being here and it's just a shame I can't stay in the apartment a little longer…

Thinking about what I want to do with my life back home has given me a bit of a headache of late, long before I sustained another one in the accident. Cheryl told me once that she decided to become a hairdresser at the age of five, when she would plait her older sister's hair. She never considered doing anything else. I think people who have a strong passion for a particular thing are very lucky…

Emma has phoned my boss at Tesco and told her about my accident. A lot of staff are saving for their summer holidays, so apparently there was no shortage of volunteers willing to cover my shifts.

'Twenty minutes for our pizza, but I think I'll drive down now and say goodbye to Alfredo,' Emma says, unhooking a white cardigan from a hanger in the hallway.

'Will you miss him?' I tease.

'Probably not. We've had some good conversations though. He's a really nice man.'

'I wonder if he's ever been married?'

'No. Apparently, he was engaged many years ago but when he and his fiancé split, she went to live in Florence. I think his restaurant is his life now. Right, I'll see you in a little bit,' she says, heading for the door.

I glance around the apartment. Emma has undoubtedly been busy, as the whole place is spick and span. I open the fridge, which is empty apart from two large bottles of water and some bread, cheese and cherry jam, which must be for breakfast tomorrow. There's some coffee left, so I make myself a mug and take it through into the comfortable lounge. I'm still a little stiff and sore, but thankfully the headache has all but disappeared.

I sip the delicious coffee and can almost feel myself drifting off, when there's a knock on the door.

'That was quick!' I say, opening the door and expecting to see Emma.

But it's Gianni. He's standing there, smiling. 'It seems you can unpack your bags, Maisie.'

'What do you mean?'

'Our new arrivals are a no show. Some sort of family emergency. The place is all yours for a while longer. If you still want it.'

A feeling of relief floods through me as I sit down and take in what Gianni has just told me. 'Oh, I can't tell you how grateful I am, Gianni. I feel sorry for the family with the emergency obviously, but I'm so happy to have the chance to stay here a little longer. I'm not sure I could have faced moving into another place.'

'You have been fortunate. All the apartments near the village were booked up as it's high season. You may have been forced to share my home, so perhaps you have had a lucky escape,' he says, raising an eyebrow.

I quickly thank Gianni for his kindness and explain that I just didn't want to be a burden. We chat for a while longer and soon enough Emma arrives back, clutching a carrier bag and a huge pizza in a box.

'Hi, Gianni. Would you like a slice of pizza?' she offers, as she shrugs off her cardigan. 'Gosh, it's still warm out there.'

'No, thank you, I have eaten with my parents this evening. When you eat with them you don't feel hungry for days afterwards.' He smiles. 'Right. I will leave you ladies to it and say good night to you both.'

As I tell Emma the good news I feel like leaping up into the air.

'Really? Oh my god, that's fantastic! You'd better start unpacking!'

'There's plenty of time for that,' I say, eyeing my suitcase in the corner.

'You're right. Unpacking can wait. You've had a brush with death. Stuff like that isn't important. And I've been thinking… When we get home you can always stay at our place, until you find a full-time job. If you can't afford the rent on your flat, that is.'

'Do you really mean that?'

'Why not? We've got the room. I'm rattling around in that house when Joe's away.'

'Thanks, Emma, you're a true friend.'

I think about what Emma has just said. She's right, I have had a brush with death. Maybe I should stop worrying about the future and let tomorrow take care of itself.

Chapter Twenty-Three

After sleeping like a baby, I wake the next morning to the smell of freshly brewed coffee. Emma is sitting at the breakfast table, where a pot of coffee and two mugs are waiting. There's also a basket of sliced bread and a pot of honey on a tray.

'Good morning,' Emma says. 'Come and have some breakfast. I'll be leaving in about two hours' time at around twelve o'clock. Before I leave, I want to nip down to the village store to get you a few essential items. I'm not sure what you'll do without a car though. I've arranged to drop the Fiat off at the airport.'

'I don't intend on going far,' I say, sitting down at the table and pouring myself a mug of steaming, fragrant coffee. 'I'm really staying here to rest and recover.' I take a slice of bread and spread it with honey. It tastes delicious. This is the first time since the accident that I've really felt like eating.

A glance at my phone, which shows a message from Dad saying he's arrived home safely. I quickly tap out a text to tell him I'll ring him later.

'I'd like to come with you, Emma, if you're taking the car down to the village. I fancy a nice cake for later from that little bakery. Plus, I'm almost out of shower gel.'

'Fine,' she says. 'Enjoy your breakfast first. Then, while you're having your shower, I'll write a shopping list.'

꙳

We've just parked up and are heading towards the small supermarket in the village when a moped pulls into the square. A man jumps off and removes his helmet, then strolls towards us. I can tell from the dark, curly hair and the broad smile that it's Luca.

'*Ciao*, Maisie. How are you? I hear you have an accident. You are feeling better now?' he asks in his charmingly accented English. He greets Emma and me with a kiss on both cheeks.

'News sure travels fast around here.'

'It's a small village.' Luca shrugs. 'People have asked Gianni how you are doing. Everyone here is very kind.'

Especially Gianni, I think to myself, *who is kind and heart-stoppingly handsome.*

'Well, thank you, Luca. As you can see, I'm fine, apart from feeling a little tired. Actually, I'm staying on for a week or two longer.'

'It will do you good. Maybe I can take you for coffee before you leave. As long as you don't bring any superglue.' He throws back his head and laughs, then turns on his heel and walks back to where his moped is parked.

We head into the supermarket and I find some jasmine shower gel. I'm just turning over various bottles of hair conditioner, when a shop assistant, who's been stacking some bottled water close by, approaches me.

'I see you looking at conditioners. May I recommend this one?' she says, picking up some olive-oil conditioner. I notice it's only two euros for a tub. 'Apply it to your hair and leave it in for five minutes. There is no better conditioner than olive oil.'

'Thank you,' I say, placing the conditioner into my basket. Emma says she's found most of the things on her shopping list so we both go to the till to pay for our items.

Walking round the square to the small bakery, we arrive to find it's busy with morning shoppers buying from a batch of freshly baked bread. I can't resist the smell and pick up a small loaf, then eye the cakes on offer and choose a honey and almond sponge. When it's my turn at the counter the young woman smiles at me in recognition and asks me how I am.

'I'm fine, thanks. I'm staying on at the farmhouse for a little while, but my friend here is leaving today. Our other friend has already gone home to England.'

'Well, I hope you enjoy the rest of your stay,' she says, putting the cake I have chosen into a white box and tying up the box with string. 'Here,' she says as she hands it to me. 'A gift from Lucia's Bakery. A little thank you for your custom and a good wish to feel better soon.'

'Oh wow, that's so kind. Thank you so much. I'm sure I'll soon be walking down here to collect my morning bread.'

We head back to the farmhouse and soon enough it's time for Emma to leave. She glances around the living room and sighs. 'I feel a bit sad leaving here. I'll miss this place. Tomorrow I'll be back to work, up to my ears in stuff no one has bothered to do in my absence.'

We have a long embrace in the driveway and Emma is waved off by Viola, Gianni and Maria. I'll miss her, but I know I'm not ready to return home yet.

As I walk across the gravel towards the apartment, Gianni follows me. 'What are you going to do with the rest of your day?' he asks.

'Well, I'm going to rest for an hour. I'm afraid I'm still not up to very much activity. I think I'll sit in the garden and read a book. Emma's left a couple behind for me.'

'If you feel up to a little drive later, I will be going into Greve in Chianti to deliver some hams to a customer. It's a very pretty place. Shall I call over around two o'clock to see how you feel?'

'That sounds really nice, actually,' I say, with a tingle of excitement. 'I love exploring new places. I might have to stop and rest though.'

'OK. I may even treat you to a *gelato*.'

'Why… *Grazie, signore. Sei molto gentile.*'

'*Molto buona!* I see you have been practising your Italian.'

'A little. Or should I say '*un po*'.

Gianni departs with a huge smile on his face and I head to the garden to read a few chapters. It's just after twelve and the sun is beginning to gain strength. After a few minutes I drag the umbrella fully over me and settle into the comfortable padded chair, and it isn't long before I am snoozing gently in the midday sun.

I awake after a half-hour snooze and head inside for another shower, enjoying the smell of my new jasmine shower gel as the foam cascades down my body. I massage my limbs with a shower mitt and smother my hair in the olive-oil conditioner, before grabbing a towelling robe and stepping out of the shower.

A short while later I am dressed in a knee-length floral sundress and I'm brushing my hair, which feels surprisingly sleek, when there's a knock at the door. It must be Gianni. I quickly glide on some pink lipstick, realising I have butterflies in my stomach as I go to let him in.

He stands in the doorway, looks me up and down, and then lets out a little wolf whistle. '*Molto bello.* I take it you are not dressed like that to hang around by the swimming pool?'

'I might be,' I say with a grin. 'Maybe I'm the type who wears fancy dresses and high heels to hang the washing out back home.'

'Somehow, I don't think you are,' he says, laughing.

'What are you trying to say?'

'What I'm trying to say is, would you like to come to Greve in Chianti with me?'

'We're going in that?' I ask, pointing to a white van that looks a bit like a builder's van.

'Yes. It is my refrigerated vehicle. The hams have just been taken from a low temperature, which has to be maintained.'

'So I'm travelling with the pigs today?'

'You are in very good company. They are of the highest quality. Fit for a king.'

I climb into the passenger seat and Gianni make his way down the driveway and turns towards Greve in Chianti.

'So, you keep the hams in the barn, do you?'

'Yes. I take the pigs to be slaughtered by a local butcher and then the flavourings are added.'

'What flavours do you add?'

'Juniper berries, rosemary and garlic are added to these particular hams, along with salt and pepper. When they have been prepared, I hang them in a special cool room until they are ready to be delivered.'

'How long does the process take?'

'It depends on the level of maturity you want the meat to have. Sometimes weeks, maybe months, depending on the strength of the flavour.'

'A bit like maturing wine in vats, I suppose.'

'Yes.' He turns towards me and smiles. 'Maybe a little like that.'

※

'Is that a castle?' I ask, as a fortress comes into view.

'It's a Medicean fortress commissioned in the sixteen hundreds on the orders of Lorenzo de Medici, but apart from the section you can see from here, it was never completed.'

I lean back to enjoy the rest of the drive, allowing my eyes to rest on several medieval hilltop churches and acres of vineyards and olive groves, before we arrive at the village of Greve. Gianni drives into a triangular-shaped market place, named Piazza Matteotti, and I feel as though I've entered a movie set, half expecting to see Audrey Hepburn seated at an outdoor café. Gianni tells me that over the years the village possibly grew up around this triangular piazza. There are large porticoes along the three sides, which protect shoppers from searing heat or from rain.

Gianni turns right, away from the piazza, and parks outside an ancient stone building that houses a butcher's shop on the ground floor. As the door of the shop is pushed open, the most incredible smell of cured meats and herbs hits my nostrils.

'*Ciao*, Gianni,' says a slightly balding man. Gianni introduces me to Paulo, the shop owner, who shakes me warmly by the hand.

While Gianni goes outside again to drive the van in through a side entrance, I stay in the shop to have a look round. I've never seen a shop like it and find myself mesmerised by the hanging prosciutto, salamis and ageing cheeses. The white walls are lined with shelves holding oils and balsamic vinegar of every colour, size and description.

While Gianni unloads his hams at the back, I go outside the front of the shop to look at the adjoining houses.

'It's beautiful here, huh?' Gianni says, as he comes to stand beside me.

'Absolutely stunning. These ancient buildings are just amazing. I would love to have a walk along there one day,' I say, pointing up at the ancient castle walls high above.

'Maybe when you have fully recovered we can fulfil that wish. But for the time being, now that my business is done, may I take you for something to eat?'

We stroll a short way until we find a small trattoria with blue wooden window frames set into the walls and pots of bright flowers alongside them. The restaurant is not too busy and we are soon shown to a table on the terrace. Our waitress disappears with our drinks order as we peruse the menu. We finally settle on a seafood risotto for me and a mushroom and aubergine tagliatelle for Gianni.

'You're not having meat?' I ask in surprise.

'In my job, some days all you want is some vegetables and pasta.'

The waitress brings our drinks and, as we wait for our food, we sip our wine and chat easily. While we talk, I study Gianni's face, which is just so handsome. I think back to Sophia's wedding, when someone remarked that every woman fancies him. How can they not? And how can I forget that kiss? It was brief, yet the kind of kiss that leaves you wanting more. I find myself wondering… Could I really be ready for more?

'So, tell me, Maisie, if you had never won this holiday in a competition, would you ever have thought of visiting Tuscany?' Gianni asks, his words cutting through my thoughts.

'Do you know, I'm not sure,' I answer honestly, as the smell of our food arriving hits my nostrils. 'I've been to Spain a couple of times and Greece, but I'd never really thought of Italy. Apart from Rome maybe. I've always fancied going there.'

'Well, I have to say that I feel very lucky that you won the prize and ended up visiting my village,' he says, his brown eyes twinkling.

'Me too,' I reply with a grin.

꧁꧂

We say little as we devour our tasty food, a comfortable silence falling between us. The rice in my risotto is smooth and creamy, paired brilliantly with salty seafood and topped with fresh dill and lemon. Gianni declares his pasta dish '*perfetto*'.

After our lunch, I ask Gianni if he knows of a nearby cash machine. He leads me away from the piazza and we approach a 'hole in the wall' alongside a shoe shop. I slot my card in the machine, but then my mind goes completely blank. After a few seconds, I key in what I believe to be my PIN number, but it isn't recognised. I try again, mildly panicked, fearful of the machine swallowing my card.

The number is wrong.

I can't remember it, I think in disbelief. *I've had the same number for years and I simply can't remember it.*

'Is everything alright?' asks Gianni, noting my anxiety.

'No, not really, I think we need to go,' I say, heading off in the direction of the car.

'Of course, if that is what you want,' he says, following me.

Once I'm in the passenger seat, I exhale deeply. 'When I put my card in the machine, I couldn't remember my PIN number… I still can't.'

'Try not to worry. Didn't the doctor say you have might have some short-term memory loss?'

'He did, but it scares the living daylights out of me.' I can feel myself shaking.

'Maisie, remember, this is only temporary. Come here.' He reaches over and envelops me in his strong arms. I'm trying not to cry. I must be strong. But it's no use, because when Gianni tells me that 'everything will be OK' I find myself bursting into tears.

Chapter Twenty-Four

Gianni drops me off at the farmhouse and I thank him for a lovely afternoon and apologise for getting teary, but he just smiles serenely and tells me not to worry about it. I'm going to go inside and give Dad a ring to find out how his day has been. Plus, he also has a copy of my PIN number in case of emergencies.

Dad answers on the third ring. 'Hello, love, how are you feeling today?'

'I'm fine. Thanks for texting me when you got home last night. How was your flight?'

'Really good. I sat next to a teenager who kept offering me jelly beans, which I'm a bit partial to, so that was a stroke of luck.' He chuckles and the sound is so reassuring. 'What have you been up to?'

'I've been to a place called Greve in Chianti today with Gianni. He had to deliver some hams to a butcher's there. It's a gorgeous old village. We had lunch on the terrace of a trattoria there. How did Jack's play go?'

'Oh, he was brilliant, a real natural. All the kids were a credit to the school and I really enjoyed it. I remember taking your mother to watch the remake of *Robin Hood* at the cinema. She loved that Kevin Costner.'

'Ah… Well, tell Jack well done from me next time you see him…
Actually, Dad, I had a bit of a forgetful moment in Greve. I couldn't for
the life of me remember the PIN number for my bank card. You've got
a copy of it, haven't you, in that blue notebook in a kitchen drawer?'

'Yes, I think I have. Hang on a minute. And don't you be worrying yourself, Maisie. The doctor said to expect such things. Back
in a second.'

When he retrieves the number and recites it to me I can't believe
I forgot it. The first two digits are twenty-eight, which is the number
of Dad's house and my old family home. I remember thinking it
quite a coincidence when the card arrived.

'What are you up to tonight then, Dad?'

'Not much, really. I'm a little tired, what with arriving home late
last night and going out today. Gladys gave me a Tupperware box
full of stew at the school today and I'm looking forward to having
some for dinner. Then I'll just put my feet up and watch one of
those Westerns from that box set of DVDs you bought me.'

'Sounds perfect. I'm a bit tired, too. I could just do with an
early night and a movie myself,' I say, thinking it a shame that the
television here doesn't have an English movie channel.

After saying goodbye to Dad, I have a quick shower, change into
a light cotton dress and take my book out into the garden area. It's
heading towards six o'clock, but the sun is still fairly strong. I read
a few pages, but find that I can't concentrate, barely able to take in
the words on the page. Maybe it's something to do with the bump
on the head.

I'm on my way back inside, when my mobile phone starts
ringing. It's Cheryl.

'Hi, Maisie, how are you doing?'

It's so wonderful to hear my friend's voice. 'Cheryl, hi, I'm OK, how are you?'

'I'm good. I've had three blokes having perms today. Would you believe perms've become a bit of a fashion thing for young men?'

'Really? Whatever next?' I tell her about my day with Gianni. I don't tell her about the memory lapse, though, because she will only worry.

'Sounds amazing. Gianni is just so gorgeous,' she says with a sigh.

'You know, the more I get to know him he seems like a really nice person too.'

'No one's that perfect. He must have a secret dark side.'

'Well, I'll let you know if I find one!'

'I'm just joking,' she says with a giggle. 'Anyway. I was ringing to give you some news. I was in The Corkscrew bar on Coronation Road last night and you'll never guess who I got talking to.'

'Jason Donovan?' I say, recalling the last time he appeared at the Empire Theatre in the city centre, where she managed to get a selfie with him at the stage door.

'No!' She laughs. 'Blake Smith.'

Blake is a well-known celebrity hairdresser who owns several salons in the North-West.

'I got chatting to him at the bar when I ordered a purple fizz cocktail and he pulled a face and asked me if I was actually going to drink it. I think the colour put him off. Anyway, I recognised him and asked him if he had any jobs going in one of his salons. He told me if he had a pound for every time someone asked him that he'd be able to retire. I even offered to cut his hair.'

'You never.'

'I did. I'm not being funny, but he could do with a different hairstyle. I could take years off him.'

'I bet you could.'

'Anyway, he wasn't biting until I told him I used to work for Jo Leyton and then his ears pricked up. Seems he knows her pretty well and really rates her as a hairdresser. So… *I've only gone and got a trial day at the flagship salon next Tuesday!*' she practically squeals down the phone.

'Oh, Cheryl, well done! That's fantastic. Best of luck with that.'

'I know, I can hardly believe it. Who knows, this winter I might not have to worry about my old car playing up, I might be getting the train straight into town.'

'What about cups of tea in old ladies' living rooms?'

'I've changed my mind. I think I'd rather have a latte in a luxury salon,' she says with a laugh.

We chat for a while longer before Cheryl ends the call, telling me she's going to pop to her mum's house for drinks as it's her brother Luke's birthday. 'Mum's baked him a cake, which is why I'm going. Her cakes are amazing. Luke's twenty-four today, but Mum fusses over him so much it's no wonder he won't leave home.'

It's almost a quarter to seven when our call ends and I realise I was chatting to Cheryl for almost an hour. Feeling a little peckish, I pull some cheese and grapes from the fridge, and crackers from a cupboard, and take it all outside.

The patio is still lit by a warm sun. It's so quiet here. There's the sound of cicadas and the occasional noise of a car or tractor, but that's it. I made the right decision in choosing to recuperate here.

I can't even imagine climbing the flight of metal stairs to my flat at the moment. But I can't stay here forever. *I'll have to go home at some point*, I think with a sinking heart.

Chapter Twenty-Five

I'm barely awake the next morning when I hear a gentle tap on the door. Grabbing my robe, I open it to find Gianni on my doorstep.

'Good morning. I just came to check that you are OK. Did you have a good night's sleep?'

'I did, thanks. I had a very early night and I think it's done me the world of good. I'm going to have some breakfast and then go for a short walk.'

'Sounds good. I called to see if you would like to join me for dinner tonight at Alfredo's? I have a very busy day today and won't have time to cook for myself. Or should I say, I won't want to.'

'Yes, I'd like that,' I reply, feeling a fizz of excitement in my stomach. 'What time were you thinking?'

'I will knock for you at seven thirty, if that's alright?'

'Sounds good to me. See you later then. I'll look forward to it.'

I eat a breakfast of creamy scrambled eggs on toast before I set off for my morning walk. I take a left turn out of the village and walk along the road that is becoming so familiar to me. The sun is massaging my shoulders and the hum of Gianni's tractor gently working the land is a comforting sound. It feels like a lifetime ago since we first arrived here in the taxi and Gianni braked suddenly in his tractor, causing the dramatic coffee spillage. If I'd known back then what would unfold between us – I don't think I would have believed it.

I walk gently for around half an hour, careful not to overdo things. Returning along the gravelled driveway to the farmhouse, I see Maria knocking on the door of my apartment and call out to her.

She turns from the door and a smile lights her face as she sees me. 'Oh, hello, Maisie. I just came to see how you are feeling. I brought you this,' she says, lifting up a jug of juice. 'It's peach juice. Freshly made from our own peaches.'

'How lovely, Maria. That sounds delicious. Actually, would you like to come in and have a glass with me now? I've got some cake in the fridge.'

'If you're sure, yes, that would be nice.'

Inside the kitchen, Maria pours two glasses of juice and takes the them out to the patio. I follow her with the honey and almond cake.

'How do you feel now that your friends have returned home?' Maria asks me, as I put the cake on the table and sit down beside her.

'Fine, to be honest. We've had lots of chats on the phone already.' I suddenly find myself telling Maria all about my life back home and my separation from Harry.

'It would seem a lot of men can't be trusted,' she says. 'It makes me wonder whether I should even bother going on this date this evening.'

'You've got a date?'

'Yes, it's someone I met at the wedding. He lives not far from Siena. I'm going out to dinner with him tonight and I have no idea what to wear.'

'I'm sure you'll look amazing, whatever you choose. What about wearing that lovely red dress you wore at the hen party? I really think red is your colour.'

'Thank you, maybe I will.'

'I suppose it must be quite difficult to meet someone in a small village like this,' I say, cutting two slices of the cake and taking a bite from one of them.

'Yes, you're right.' Maria sighs. 'I know everyone here and I treat most of the young men in the village like brothers. That is why an occasion such as a wedding generates such excitement. It's an opportunity to meet new people.'

I think of the moped guys and imagine it must be the same for them, given the attention they pay to holidaymakers and wedding guests.

'Do you ever see yourself leaving the village?' I ask Maria, trying to hold back from cutting another slice of the delicious cake. Maria has delicately nibbled at the small slice she insisted on.

'I don't know. I love living here. I help Mamma run the holiday lets and sometimes I help Gianni deliver the hams. It's very much a family business here.'

'So you really are a country girl?'

'I think so, but I have nothing much to compare it with, really, apart from places I have visited on holiday. When I go away, though, I find I'm always happy to return home. I even find Florence a bit overwhelming. So perhaps I am a country girl at heart.'

'Well, I hope your date takes you somewhere nice. Actually, your brother is taking me to Alfredo's tonight. You would be welcome to join us,' I say, before wondering why on earth the words just slipped out of my mouth. Maybe Gianni would not welcome the idea at all.

'Thanks, but I think Marco has somewhere in mind. Besides, I don't think my brother would want me cramping his style.'

I find myself blushing like a teenager.

❧

Once Maria has gone, I decide to spend the afternoon job searching. I keep worrying about what I'm going to do for work back home. There's a vacancy for a school-crossing patrol assistant, or a lollipop lady as they were called when I was at school. There are jobs for warehouse workers, production assistants and clerical workers, none of which I am qualified for. It seems that every single type of employment needs a specialised certificate of expertise these days. I suddenly realise how limited my choices are unless I retrain at something.

Just out of interest I google 'how to become a wine merchant', thinking of Frederico's suggestion. It seems that had I been a graduate I could have started work as a management trainee with a large retailer, and once again I regret not finishing my degree.

Giving up my search, I spend the rest of the day relaxing. Towards the evening, I have a long soak in a jasmine-scented bubble bath, and think about what I should wear for my date with Gianni. I've worn most of the clothes I packed, apart from a long black dress. I wonder whether black is a little too formal, although the material is a kind of cheesecloth, which is nice and casual. The dress is quite low cut, too, so I'll have to try it on and give it a whirl.

I get out of the bath and towel myself dry, then go to the wardrobe in my bedroom. Since deciding to stay on at the apartment for a few more days, I've unpacked my clothes again. I take the black dress off its hanger and try it on. Thankfully the dress looks fitted and elegant and the neckline isn't quite as low as I remembered. I smile and do a twirl in front of the long mirror in my bedroom, and reckon I can get away with it.

Chapter Twenty-Six

On the stroke of seven thirty there's a tap on the front door.

'I like a man who's punctual,' I say, inviting Gianni inside.

'Wow! *Bellissimo*,' he says, kissing me lightly on both cheeks. He's wearing that heady mix of woody, citrus aftershave that stirs my senses.

'You don't look too bad yourself,' I say, which is a bit of an understatement. He looks absolutely gorgeous in a charcoal suit with an open-necked white shirt. I can't help thinking he might be a tad overdressed for dining at Alfredo's, but I keep that thought to myself.

'So, would you like to drive down to the village in the car, or are you up to a little walk?'

'I'll be fine walking. I may have to stop a few times on the way home though. That hill's a bit of a killer.'

'I will carry you, if that's the case.' Gianni smiles softly, holding my gaze with his big brown eyes.

We cross the driveway just as Maria's date is arriving to collect her. She has opted for the red dress and looks absolutely stunning. We stop and introductions are made, Gianni shaking Maria's date warmly by the hand. 'My sister has an early start in the morning so don't keep her out too late,' he says, winking.

'I'm sorry, my brother is so embarrassing!' Maria swats Gianni with her handbag.

'Don't worry, I have an early start myself,' Marco replies. 'Good to meet you.'

'It must be nice having a big brother to look out for you. Or a big sister for that matter,' I say, as we stroll down towards the village.

'You have no brothers or sisters?'

'No, I'm an only child. I never felt lonely though. It just would have been nice to have an older sister to borrow clothes and make-up from.'

'I'm not sure I've ever felt the desire to do that,' Gianni says, chuckling.

A sense of humour too. I'm beginning to think that Cheryl might be right, there must be something wrong with him. Maybe he has smelly feet…

Strolling downhill we pass some residents sitting outside their shuttered houses. Several of them greet Gianni personally and smile warmly at me. As we arrive in the village two young women seated outside a restaurant raise their arms and shout, '*Ciao*, Gianni!' The same thing happens a few yards further on. Everyone seems to know him and, judging by the glances the women are giving him, I suspect he really is the most eligible bachelor in the village. Walking alongside him makes me feel rather proud.

Alfredo welcomes us warmly when we arrive and asks me how I am feeling. After assuring him that I am much better, to my surprise he does not show us to one of the outside tables, but leads us inside the restaurant. I feel slightly disappointed at the thought of dining inside, as it's a lovely evening and I would have loved to dine in the warm outdoors, watching the stars come out. Alfredo guides us to the rear of the restaurant and to a small door at the side of a staircase. When he opens it I let out a gasp.

It's a beautiful scene. On a small terrace, a table is set for two with a bottle of wine in a straw basket at the centre, alongside gently flickering tea lights. An olive tree on the left of the terrace has been strung with coloured fairy lights.

'Oh my goodness, is this for us?' I whisper.

'Well, it's not for us,' says Gianni, standing next to Alfredo and draping his arm around him.

'It's absolutely lovely, Alfredo. I didn't realise you had VIP dining areas.'

'I don't. This is a favour for my friend Gianni and his very lovely companion. It is so good to see you up and about.'

I can't believe Gianni has arranged all this especially for me. I understand the reason for him dressing up so smartly now and I'm glad I chose to wear my black dress. We step out onto the terrace and sit at our table, from where the view is one of farmland and rustic houses, in contrast to the busy scene of church, restaurants and bars seen from tables outside the front of the restaurant. The sun is casting shadows on the terracotta rooftop as dusk rolls in and I take it all in as Gianni opens the bottle of wine and pours us each a glass.

'To your very good health,' he says, chinking his glass against mine.

'Thank you. Yours too.' I take a sip of the wine, which is smooth and delicious, tasting of cherries and violets. I'm certain it's a Chianti Classico. 'Is there a menu for this evening?' I ask, looking around but unable to locate one.

'Actually, tonight Alfredo has organised a special dinner for two. I believe the first course will arrive shortly.'

Several minutes later a plate of mixed bruschetta arrives.

'Oh, I love bruschetta,' I say, eyeing the selection of tomato, anchovy and olive tapenade toppings on toasted bread. 'Do you like to cook?' I ask, wondering whether Gianni is not just expert at curing hams.

'Truthfully? Not really, although I have been told that I am a very good cook. I think I have to be in the mood and then I really do enjoy it. Most of the time I live on soups, cheeses and cold cuts of meat, as well as occasionally taking dinner with my parents. My mother would feed me every day of the week, if she had her way.'

Missing Mum all of a sudden, I think how lucky Gianni is to have both of his parents.

I'm trying to imagine what we will be served for our main course when Alfredo appears with two huge platters of food balanced on a tray.

'This is called *spaghetti alla trabaccolara*. My grandmother grew up near the port of Viareggio, were this recipe originated. I believe the fishermen created the sauce for this dish when they were on board their ship.'

He places the plates in front of us and I inhale the delicious aroma. Large chunks of fish, covered in a tomato sauce, are nestled in the spaghetti.

'How did you know I would like seafood, Gianni? A lot of people don't.'

'Ah well, I noticed you ate my mother's *cacciucco* seafood stew at Sophia's party before her wedding.'

'But you weren't there when we ate the meal.'

'When I carried the remains of the food back to the farmhouse for the poker game, I noticed that your plate was empty.'

'Blimey, have you ever thought about becoming a detective?' I joke, feeling flattered that Gianni has done his homework. He's certainly gone to a lot of effort for this evening.

I wrap some sauce and spaghetti around my fork and take a bite. The sauce is heavenly – tangy tomato paired with the saltiness of anchovies and the fragrance of garlic and parsley. 'There seem to be different types of fish in here,' I say, poking around the sauce with my fork.

'You have red mullet, hake and gurnard,' Gianni says knowledgeably.

'I've never heard of gurnard.'

'It is a bit of an ugly fish, almost prehistoric-looking, but chefs agree it's one of the tastiest you can eat.'

'Just shows you can't judge a book by its cover.' I take another huge forkful and close my eyes in delight, marvelling at how the simplest of ingredients are made to taste so extraordinary. I open my eyes again and glance across the terrace to the twinkling lights in the distance. 'It's just so beautiful here. I can't believe you have managed to arrange all this, Gianni. Alfredo should take bookings for this terrace for lovers who want intimate dinners. I'm sure it would be permanently booked up.' I suddenly wonder why I used the word 'lovers'. *That isn't what we are!*

Thankfully, Gianni doesn't comment on the remark other than to say, 'I think Alfredo prefers to have his customers dining at the front. This is a special favour to me.'

We finish our main course and sip the Chianti, as the light slowly begins to fade and the stars start to twinkle above us. When Alfredo reappears to refresh our drinks, Gianni orders a bottle of Prosecco. 'It's a celebration!' he says, when I look on in surprise.

Alfredo quickly returns with the Prosecco and champagne flutes. He is followed by a waiter bringing two plates of dessert on a tray. 'Now, this was difficult as there are so many amazing desserts to choose from,' Alfredo says, picking up the plates and placing them in front of us. 'I hope you are happy with my choice.'

It's a peach crème brûlée, which couldn't be more perfect, as it's sweet and creamy yet not too heavy. We finish the evening with a cappuccino for me and an espresso for Gianni, and I'm feeling pleasantly relaxed after my second glass of Prosecco.

'This has been such a lovely evening, Gianni, I can't thank you enough.' I can hardly believe my luck as I bask in the magic of this wonderful place with this handsome man in front of me.

'It is my pleasure. You deserve it after what you have been through.' He reaches across the table and gently places his hand on top of mine and a bolt of electricity shoots through my body. 'I was worried about you, Maisie. I was just beginning to get to know you when you had the accident. I am happy I have been given the chance to maybe get to know you a little better now.'

'I'm happy about that too.'

Gianni leans across the table and kisses me softly on the lips. 'I was hoping you would say that.'

My senses are reeling as I excuse myself and nip to the ladies', feeling dizzy from Gianni's kiss. I pass Alfredo in the corridor, who stops me to ask how Emma is.

'She's very well. Missing the sunshine here, I think, it's pouring down back home.'

'Well, next time you speak to her, please give her my regards.'

In the ladies' I rinse my hands under cool water as I seem to have come over all hot and flustered. And I don't think it's all down to the sultry summer weather.

At the end of the evening, Gianni and I say our good nights to Alfredo, embracing him in a hug and thanking him for the wonderful food, before heading outside into the village square. The bars and restaurants are busy with tourists and locals, and moped guy Luca is sitting outside a bar with a young woman. It seems his luck may have changed. He raises his hand and shouts, '*Ciao!*'

Walking back to the farmhouse, Gianni recalls the earring incident with Luca at the party after the wedding and we both laugh.

'Luca and his friends are nice enough young men,' Gianni says. 'I remember them when they were young boys riding their bicycles along the country lanes, although these days it's mopeds. Luca is very down to earth, despite his father being quite wealthy. His father owns most of the shops in the square.'

'Do many young people leave the village?'

'Some do. Unless you are a farm worker there is little employment other than in the shops and bars. Some return in later life to inherit their family homes. There is a certain magic about this place that draws you back.'

As we ascend the hill towards the farmhouse, my steps slow a little as I begin to feel tired.

'Are you alright? There is still that offer to carry you, if you like.' Gianni jokingly flexes his muscles.

'No, I just need to walk a little slower, and maybe do this,' I say, as I loop my arm through his and feel my pulse rate quicken.

It's as if darkness has suddenly fallen when we reach the top of the hill and the stars are shining brightly in an indigo sky.

'Thank you for a wonderful evening, Gianni.'

Wordlessly, he wraps his arms around me and kisses me, and I lean in to him, finding myself kissing him back, my body melting into his. Our lingering, passionate kiss feels just wonderful and I want to stand at the top of this hill forever, safe in Gianni's strong embrace.

Chapter Twenty-Seven

I have the mildest of headaches the following morning – last night was so worth it though After a tumbler of water and a couple of paracetamol, I'm just heading out of the apartment for my morning walk when I see Maria walking towards me carrying a bundle of fluffy fresh towels.

'Good morning, Maria,' I say, as she comes closer. 'How was your date?'

'Oh, it was lovely, thank you. Marco was the perfect gentleman. He's taking me to an open-air concert in Siena this weekend. How was your date with my brother?'

'Really nice, thanks.' I hope I'm not blushing at the thought of that kiss last night, which gives me goosebumps whenever I think about it… and I haven't been able to stop thinking about it all morning. 'We had a really lovely meal at Alfredo's.'

'I'm glad you had a nice time. But I should get on,' she says, letting herself into the apartment next door. 'We have some new arrivals. They're over there, unpacking their car. They're an English couple with a young son.'

Leaving Maria to get on with her chores, I stroll across to say hello to my new neighbours, who introduce themselves as Mike and Amy. Their son, Josh, who I'm told is six years old, is already waiting by the pool, calling for his parents to come and swim.

'It's a little early for me. I'm sure that the water in the pool can't be warm enough yet,' Amy says, but Mike scrabbles around in the luggage to find towels and swimming kit and runs off to join his son.

I'm still thinking about how magical last night was when I hear the familiar rumble of Gianni's tractor making its way across the field towards the farmhouse. I turn and go back into the apartment, walking through to the garden down towards the fence. As Gianni brings the tractor to a stop and turns the engine off and I feel a heat rising in my chest.

'*Buongiorno!* How are you this morning?' He has a broad smile on his face.

'I'm good, thanks. You?'

'Really good. I had the sweetest dream that I was kissing a beautiful English girl. Or maybe it wasn't a dream? Maybe I really did kiss a beautiful girl last night.'

I realise I haven't been called beautiful in a long time and I rather like it.

He jumps down from his tractor and steps through the gate towards me. He's wearing jeans and a white T-shirt that shows off his olive skin perfectly. 'Are you going for your morning walk? Or can I persuade you to join me for a coffee?'

'Tempting, but maybe I will join you later. I want to press on with a little exercise,' I say, realising that my morning ritual is doing me the world of good.

'Of course. I will look forward to it.' He leans over and kisses me gently on the cheek, leaving me blushing furiously.

The lady who lives in the terracotta-tiled house with the goat in the garden says, '*Buongiorno,*' as I walk past. The goat still comes to the fence every day, hoping in vain to be given something to eat. An elderly man, who is watering his garden further along, also nods and says, '*Ciao!*'. I suppose the locals are becoming accustomed to seeing me now. It's a strange thought that I'll be returning home soon.

It's a glorious day again today. The sun is bright but not as fierce as it has been of late, so it's the perfect day for walking or sightseeing. Strolling along, I'm finding it difficult to stop myself thinking of that heart-stopping kiss with Gianni. If I close my eyes I can almost feel the spark of desire that took me completely by surprise.

Some time later, as I head back towards the farmhouse, I spot him up ahead in his tractor. He slows down as I approach. 'Are you ready for that coffee? If so, why don't you hop in?'

I get onto the seat and squeeze up beside him and for the first time in my life wonder whether I could possibly cut it as a farmer's wife.

'I still can't thank you enough for last night, Gianni, it was absolutely perfect.'

'I thought it might cheer you up after spending time in the hospital. Plus, your friends had left. I didn't want you feeling down.'

Oh, don't worry, you really cheered me up, I think to myself. 'Well, it was very thoughtful of you. Maybe I can cook you dinner this evening in return?'

'You would like to cook for me?' He looks a little surprised.

'Why not? Nothing fancy. In fact I'm not sure what I'll make. It will be a surprise.'

Gianni helps me down from the tractor and I sit at a table in the garden, while he goes inside to make coffee. After a while, he brings a tray with two mugs outside and joins me at the table. As we sip the steaming liquid, I ask him if he has taken a holiday this year.

'I took a coastal break earlier in the year with a friend of mine whose relationship had recently ended. It wasn't too long after my own break-up either. We hired a boat and went fishing during the day and sat around drinking beer in the evening, vowing to stay single for a while. I imagine women do the same sort of thing when they break up with someone.'

'What? Go fishing and drink beer?'

'Well, what do they do?' he asks, a look of mock intrigue on his face.

'Ah, that would be telling. But there's usually a lot of shopping involved and copious amounts of wine. Oh, and maybe a voodoo doll if things were really bad.'

'Wow! I'm sorry I asked!'

We finish our coffee and Gianni returns to work, while I make my way across the driveway. Suddenly a car appears and pulls up on the gravel. To my surprise it's Frederico.

'Hi, Frederico, what brings you here?' I ask, as he gets out of the sports car.

'I called to see you.' To my surprise, he pulls a bunch of flowers from the passenger seat and hands them to me. 'How are you feeling now?'

'Oh, thank you so much! These flowers are beautiful. And I'm feeling a lot better now. I'm enjoying going for regular walks. I want to get back to normal fitness as soon as possible.' I pause. 'I haven't had a chance until now to thank you for coming to visit me in hospital. My dad told me you'd been in. It was really kind of you, but how did you hear about the accident?' I ask. 'The winery must be twenty miles away from Pisa. 'Actually, would you like a cold drink or something?' I ask gesturing, towards the apartment.

Frederico nods and follows me inside. I pour us each a glass of lemonade from the fridge.

'Alfredo told me about the accident,' he says, taking a sip of lemonade. 'He is a customer of ours. Shortly after I saw you with your girlfriends that day in Pisa, he came to the winery to select some new wines for his restaurant. He was friendly with one of your friends... Emma? She had told him you were in hospital after being hurt in a road accident. Naturally I wanted to find out how you were. So... yesterday I spoke to Alfredo and he told me you were still here at the farmhouse. Are you planning to stay on for a while?'

'I would if I could. Believe me, I love it here. If it wasn't for my dad back home, well, who knows?'

I find myself telling Frederico about walking out of one of my jobs and how I live in a little flat. 'So you see, I haven't exactly got anything to really rush home for.'

Frederico is quiet for a moment. 'Then maybe I should come clean about the real reason for my visit here. Obviously, I wanted to deliver my good wishes and the flowers, but I was wondering... if you were to stay here, would you give some serious thought to working at the winery? You could work through to the end of the season. It doesn't go quiet until around the beginning of November. I mean, you could start when you feel up to it, of course.'

'So you *were* serious when you asked me before... Are you still short-staffed?'

'I'm afraid so, yes. We hired two guys from Finland who had experience working in wineries. Things seemed to be going well, when they suddenly decided to move on. They were travelling in Europe, which I knew from the start, but they'd told me they would stay in Tuscany for three months, rather than three weeks. It's so hard to find reliable seasonal staff.'

A tingle of excitement builds inside me as I consider Frederico's offer. The problem is, I don't think I could afford the weekly rent here at the farmhouse.

'Can I give it some thought?' I say. 'I don't think I'm quite ready to work yet, though. My recovery may take another week or so.'

'You'll think about it? That's enough for me.' Frederico smiles and his green eyes light up with delight.

As I wave him off, I wonder whether or not I'm going crazy. Have I been seduced by the summer sun and the thought of spending time with Gianni? If I stay on here I will lose my job at Tesco and most certainly my flat. On the other hand, I'm certain I'll be able to find some sort of job when I get back to Liverpool. And didn't Emma say I could stay at her place until I got myself sorted?

A summer job. I dreamed of doing something like this when I was younger, but never thought I would be considering such a thing at the age of almost thirty. I wonder what Dad would think of the idea... I decide I'll sleep on it tonight and give him a ring in the morning. I might even have changed my mind by then.

Chapter Twenty-Eight

I go into the kitchen to put Frederico's flowers into a sink of water to soak, then head down into the village. In the supermarket, I buy minced pork, tarragon and garlic to make meatballs. I have plenty of spaghetti and Parmesan back at the apartment, as well as salt, pepper and some mixed herbs. I also have some tinned tomatoes, but decide to buy some plump, fresh tomatoes to make a homemade sauce. I add breadsticks and a bottle of local red wine to my basket, and after paying for everything at the till, I then pop to Lucia's bakery for some chocolate profiteroles.

Local residents greet me as I walk back to the farmhouse, smiling broadly. Climbing up the hill feels easier today and I'm happy that I seem to be regaining my fitness.

Back in the kitchen I set to work adding all the fresh ingredients into a bowl and mixing them together with my hands, before placing the mixture in the fridge. I boil and skin the tomatoes, before simmering them gently over a low heat to make a sauce. *The beautiful mauves and creams of Frederico's bouquet will make a nice centrepiece for the table tonight*, I think, as I place the flowers in a vase of fresh water.

Preparations for this evening done, I'm about to take a coffee onto the patio area when my phone rings. It's Emma.

'Emma, hi! How are you?'

'I'm OK, how are you?' she asks. I've known her long enough to know that she doesn't sound like her usual self.

'I'm doing so much better,' I tell her. 'I knew it would do me good to stay on for a while longer. It's another glorious day here.'

'I wish you could send some of that sun over here. It's been miserable since we got back here. I really miss that weather.'

'I know, the people who live here don't realise how lucky they are. So, what have you been up to? How was your first day back at work?'

'Pretty much as I expected. There was a bit of a backlog, although not as bad as I imagined. Actually, I've applied for another job. I've got an interview for Head of Student Services at the university on Wednesday. The money is really good.'

'Oh, that sounds great, Emma! Good luck with that. Do you know Cheryl has a training day tomorrow at Smith's on Renshaw Street?'

'I do. That's really exciting, isn't it? She deserves to go far, she's a fabulous hairdresser. So… what's new with you?'

'Gianni took me for dinner last night to Alfredo's. We had a wonderful evening. Alfredo asked after you.'

'Did he really?'

'Yeah, I think he is a little bit taken with you.'

I can hear Emma exhale and suddenly she begins to cry.

'Emma? Emma, are you alright?'

She takes a deep breath. 'Me and Joe have split up.'

'Oh, Emma, I'm so sorry. Are you OK?'

'Yeah, missing you. Sorry, that sounds selfish. I've been at my mum's overnight. I've just nipped home for a few things. She's insisting I go back later for Sunday lunch, but I don't think I could eat a thing.'

'Oh, I do wish I was there to give you a big hug. What happened?'

'Joe came home for four days in between driving jobs and just sat there on the sofa playing racing games on his Xbox the whole time. By day three I'd had enough and we had a blazing row. He tried to say he "deserved to have some downtime" as life on the road in a lorry is stressful. When I asked him what was the point of us even being together any more he went all quiet. Anyway, we ended up sitting up all night talking. It's definitely over between us,' Emma says, stifling a sob. 'We both agree it's time to move on. We'll end up destroying each other if we stay together. It's just going to take a bit of getting used to being single again, I suppose. The thought of being alone is scary.'

'Oh, I'm so sorry. I really am. I felt exactly the same after Harry and I broke up. Where will Joe go?'

'His mum's house. There's plenty of room there. I suspect it won't be long until he gets a place of his own though.'

'You won't have to sell the house, will you?'

'Hopefully not. With a better salary, I will probably be able to afford to buy him out and pay the mortgage myself. Fingers crossed my interview goes well… Say hi to Alfredo for me. You can give him my e-mail address, if you like. I wouldn't mind getting the recipe for that delicious Tuscan casserole they serve at the restaurant.'

'Will do. Please ring me any time you like, day or night. And let me know how you get on at the interview,' I say, hanging up.

Poor Emma. It can't have been easy trying to maintain the relationship. I can imagine she must have felt pretty lonely with Joe being away for so long at a time.

I spend the rest of the afternoon continuing my job search on the Internet, while considering Frederico's offer of work at the winery. Would it really be possible to spend the rest of the summer here? My heart sinks when I think about the practicalities of such a notion. Apart from the cost of accommodation, how would I get to and from the winery every day, as I don't have a car?

My mind overrun by worries, I add some seasoning to the tomato sauce and shape the mince mixture into meatballs, before heading into the bathroom for a shower. As I rub shampoo into my hair, I'm reminded of the days back home when Cheryl would call round and wash my hair in the small kitchen sink. Perhaps that's where my life really belongs and I should put this fantasy of a new life firmly out of my mind.

It's a little before seven o'clock when Gianni knocks at the front door. He's carrying a huge bunch of flowers and a bottle of limoncello. He looks drop-dead gorgeous in a pair of smart navy shorts and a white polo shirt. He greets me with a kiss and walks into the kitchen, where he notices the vase of flowers on the table.

'I see someone has beaten me to it,' he says.

I could let him think I had purchased the flowers for myself, but I tell him that they are from Frederico.

'I see I am not your only admirer.' Gianni's expression is hard to read as his gaze meets mine.

'Frederico just called round to see how I was doing,' I say, as I pour him a glass of red wine. 'Well, that's what he said at first. In reality, he came to offer me a job at the winery.'

'The winery?' he says in surprise.

I tell Gianni about the day Emma, Cheryl and I went on the wine tour and how I seem to have impressed Frederico with my knowledge of wine. 'But I really don't know all that much. In fact, I could do with asking him about the value of some wine I seem to have acquired accidentally.'

Gianni's brow creases into a frown. 'Accidentally?'

I find myself telling him all about the bag mix-up at the airport.

'Well, I'm afraid I know nothing about the value of wine, so I can't offer any advice. If it tastes good, I like it! Frederico should certainly know the worth of the wine, though.' He pauses for a moment. 'Maybe you should consider his job offer. That is, if you don't mind being around someone who considers all women a possible conquest.'

'I have no interest in Frederico. And I know what he's like, Gianni. Maria told me all about him. I was just excited by the thought of working here over the summer holidays, I suppose. It's a non-starter though. I would have to drive to and from the winery and I don't have a car. I certainly can't afford to buy one.'

'Maybe I could help you with that, if you are seriously considering the job.'

'Really?'

'Yes. I have a car that I barely use. When I'm working, I use the van. Other than that, I always walk into the village.'

'You'd really let me use your car?' I can hardly believe what I am hearing.

'Why not? Unless there's something I should know. Are you a crazy driver?' He raises his eyebrows.

'No, of course not. Ten years no claims bonus, me.'

'Well, then, I don't see a problem. I would encourage anything that would keep you here in Tuscany a little longer.' Standing up, he wraps his arms around my waist and draws me closer. 'As long as I don't have any competition.' He kisses me deeply and I go weak at the knees.

'I don't think there's any danger of that…' I whisper faintly.

Chapter Twenty-Nine

'You are sure you are not Italian?' asks Gianni, as he tucks into the meatballs and spaghetti and declares it '*magnifico*'. 'This sauce is delicious. As good as my mother's.'

'Now I know you're joking. You went a bit far with that last comment.'

'OK, well, maybe *almost* as good. Did your mother teach you how to cook?'

'Not really. She was a wonderful cook, but it was usually English dishes.'

'Was?'

'My mother passed away almost two years ago,' I reply, feeling a lump in my throat.

'I'm so sorry,' says Gianni, placing his fork on his plate. 'I hope I haven't upset you?'

'Of course you haven't, how would you have known? Anyway, my knowledge of Italian cuisine comes from an Italian cookbook written by an English chef called Jamie Oliver. Someone bought it for me as a Secret Santa present and I pretty much worked my way through it. My attempts at home-made pasta weren't so great though.'

'Ah, pasta takes a long time to perfect. Especially egg pasta.'

I tell Gianni all about my mother and he listens intently, an expression of sympathy in his eyes. I like talking about Mum. If I didn't talk about her, I fear that her memory would fade into the distance somehow. It's a relief to find I can finally talk about her without being overcome with emotion.

'Right, come on, Gianni, eat up,' I say, changing the subject. 'I went to a lot of trouble to make this. Obviously not as much trouble as you went to last night, but of course I did actually cook this myself!'

Gianni holds his hands up. 'Fair enough. And I think this dish is good enough to be served in Alfredo's restaurant,' he says, dabbing his mouth with a napkin having cleared his plate.

'The meal's not over yet. Would you like some dessert?'

'Thank you, but I'm not really one for dessert, although I did enjoy Alfredo's choice at the restaurant last night. But you go ahead. I like a woman with a good appetite.' He stares at me and I can feel myself blush.

He tops up our drinks with a glass of local wine as I take a small portion of the profiteroles out of the fridge.

'You made this too?' he asks in a surprised tone.

'Of course I did!' My fingers are crossed behind my back.

Like everything else from Lucia's bakery, the profiteroles are amazing. Gianni is watching me the whole time I'm eating and I suddenly feel a little self-conscious. Especially when I bite into one of the little chocolate-covered choux balls and a blob of cream escapes and drips down my chin. Not the look I was going for.

Gianni laughs. 'You are never ordering these in a restaurant next time I take you to dinner.'

I feel thrilled at the thought of there being a 'next time'.

I'm about to make some coffee, when Gianni points to the bottle of limoncello on the kitchen counter. 'What about this? You must finish a meal with a shot of limoncello.'

I retrieve two small glasses from a cupboard and we sit down on the sofa. Gianni opens the bottle and pours a small amount of the yellow, translucent liquid into each glass. '*Salute*,' he says, chinking his small glass against mine, before we both down the contents in one. It tastes of zingy lemons and something vaguely herbal. It's like sunshine in a bottle, but for some reason it reminds me that I'm short of cash.

'Oh, Gianni, I forgot to ask you where I could find a cash machine. I need some cash,' I tell him. I also need to pay this week's rent.

'Tomorrow I will take you to find one. For now, let's just enjoy this evening. Relax.' He takes the glass from my hand and places it on the coffee table before leaning in for a kiss. I can taste the lemon on his tongue as I kiss him back, my head spinning. A few minutes later, Gianni stands up and leads me slowly by the hand to my bedroom. He opens the door, and then kicks it closed as he gently nudges my legs towards the edge of the bed, holding my gaze the whole time. It's as if I am trapped under a hypnotic spell as he kisses me deeply, sending shivers all over my body. Lying together on the bed, he undresses me slowly, covering every part of me in soft, gentle kisses. As my body arches slowly into his, and his large brown eyes seem to look into the depths of my soul, I feel as if I'm going to explode.

Chapter Thirty

I lie in the following morning and smile lazily as I remember the night before, grabbing the pillow next to me and curling into it. It still smells of Gianni's intoxicating aftershave, but he must have gone to work hours ago…

I remember falling asleep as the dawn arrived, and Gianni telling me playfully that I was insatiable, and I smile contentedly. I think I'm going to need the whole day in bed to recover. Maybe on this occasion I'll give my morning walk a miss… Then, as I'm about to doze off again, I remember that something important is happening today.

It's the day of Cheryl's training at the salon and I send her a quick message to wish her good luck. Not that she'll need it, but I want her to know I'm thinking about her. I'm sure she'll be a style director in no time, once her talent has been recognised. Emma also has her job interview at the university tomorrow. It would seem that all three of us are at a crossroads. Thinking about the job that Frederico has offered me, I realise I will need to make up my mind as the offer won't be around forever. But first I need to talk to Dad.

Reluctantly, I get out of bed and shower, and I'm just putting some coffee into a cup, when there's a knock on the front door.

It's Gianni. He looks shattered. 'Good morning, beautiful,' he says, moving in for a kiss. 'I hope you had a good sleep.'

'I haven't been awake for long, to be honest. Fancy a coffee?'

'Coffee is the only thing keeping me awake today, although I'm not complaining. Actually, I have to deliver some hams to a shop in Poggibonsi later on. Would you like to come with me?'

'Great. Just give me ten minutes,' I say, nipping to the bedroom to grab some clothes. But Gianni is following me…

'Out,' I say, jokingly, pushing him off as he puts his arms around me and playfully nuzzles my neck, 'otherwise I'll get far too distracted. Go and help yourself to coffee in the kitchen.'

'OK, but only if you agree to let me see you again this evening.'

❧

It's only a fifteen-minute drive to Poggibonsi and we are soon parked up. It's a busy town with pretty buildings dotted around.

While Gianni delivers the hams, I pop into a little delicatessen to purchase a few things. I've eaten two huge meals the past two nights, so some cheese and crackers will be enough for me later.

It's another glorious day, the sun shining high in a bright, unbroken blue sky. When Gianni has finished his business, we take a stroll, hand in hand, along the riverbank. We pass shops that are housed inside ancient buildings, and coffee shops with faded wooden fronts are bustling with customers. There's a sudden quacking from the river as a duck swims past us, followed by four cute, brown-feathered ducklings. A sunbeam casts flecks of light onto the slow-flowing water, giving it a glorious feeling of peace and tranquillity. I feel well and truly content. The combination of my prescribed tablets and sunshine seem to be working wonders for my well-being. But walking hand in hand with my gorgeous Italian lover is probably doing me more good than anything else. Since the passion and tenderness of our love-making last night, I feel that I've become a different person. Gianni has changed me, and it's definitely for the better. I feel good about myself again and so much stronger today. Now I really can see my future here in Italy, perhaps with him, perhaps working at Frederico's winery… and these positive thoughts fill me with happiness.

A thrill passes through my body, and I stop walking and turn to Gianni to kiss his cheek, my free hand stretching up to stroke his thick, black hair. But we end up kissing one another deeply, unconcerned about passers-by, just lost in one another's arms. Finally, shaken but smiling, we pull apart and continue to walk the perimeter of the town, stopping for pistachio *gelato* before heading back towards Gianni's van. As I step into it, I realise I have completed the walk with relative ease, so it seems my fitness really is improving.

'What are you doing for the rest of the day then?' I ask Gianni on the drive home.

'I have a bit of paperwork to do then some young men from the village are coming over to harvest some olives.'

'You don't do it yourself?'

'I don't have the time now, there are so many trees. The workers will cash the olives in as payment and give us lots of bottled olive oil. What about you? How are you going to spend the rest of your day?'

'I think I'm going to have a swim and then read for a while. I'm halfway through a brilliant book about a Russian immigrant who is trying to make a new life for himself in London.'

'I think maybe I should read more. Although I must confess I'd rather watch a movie than read a book. Maybe you would like to watch one with me this evening?'

'In Italian?'

'There will be subtitles,' says Gianni, as we pull into the farmhouse, where I notice a silver car parked in the driveway. 'And wine. Oh, and nibbles,' he says, as he leans over and nibbles my ear, before kissing me deeply again.

'Mmm… that sounds like an offer I can't refuse.'

Gianni lets me out of the van as Viola appears in the driveway. 'Maisie, you have a visitor,' she says, as a familiar figure follows her out of the farmhouse, taking my breath away.

I can hardly believe who is walking towards me.

'Harry! What the hell are you doing here?'

Chapter Thirty-One

'Hello, Maisie. How are you doing?'

Gianni makes a gesture that he'll ring me later, before he jumps back into his van and heads off towards the barn.

'I can't believe you're here, Harry,' I say, unable to take it in. 'Why have you come?'

'Can we at least go inside?'

I lead the way into the apartment and ask him if he'd like a cup of coffee. Harry looks refreshed and lightly tanned. He's wearing a white linen shirt, smart tan-coloured shorts, and a pair of Ray-Bans.

I make us each a coffee and we take our mugs outside onto the patio area, taking in the view of the green and yellow hills in the distance.

'I came to see how you were, but I can see that you look fine. In fact, you look really good.' His remark takes me by surprise as I can't recall the last time he paid me a compliment.

'You look well, too. It's nice to know that you care about my welfare, but why would you come all this way? You could have just phoned me to see how I was doing.' I'm completely thrown by his presence. He looks handsome and so familiar sitting here having a coffee with me just as he might have done in the old days.

'I wanted to see you in the flesh. I thought this was just a holiday, but Emma and Cheryl have long gone home. I thought you might have gone home with your dad, but my mum told me you were staying on here for a while.'

'I wasn't quite ready to go home and Dad gave me his full blessing. He wants what's best for me. The sunshine here is doing me the world of good. Talking of sunshine, you look tanned. Have you been away?'

'Lads' weekend in Barcelona. The hotel was near the beach so I slept there during the day.'

Sleeping off the previous nights' excesses, I think to myself. I wonder if Harry will ever grow up. He's forty years old in a couple of months but still goes on endless lads' weekends.

'Harry, please tell me why you've come all this way to see me,' I say, confusion rippling through me.

He takes a deep breath. 'I miss you, Maisie,' he says simply. 'I walked past our old house the other day and a load of memories came flooding into my head. We had some good times there didn't we, babe?'

'I suppose we did. I loved living there.'

Why did he have to mention our old house? He knows I loved it.

'Remember that house-warming barbecue we had and you gave the new neighbours food poisoning?' Harry says.

'Excuse me, but I beg to differ! It was you who was in charge of the chicken, as I recall. That was the thing most likely to have caused it.'

'If you say so. I don't suppose it could have been your cremated burgers, could it?' He grins. 'And remember the time you shovelled up a load of snails from our garden and threw them over the fence into next door's garden? The bloke next door watched the whole thing from his bedroom window.'

I'm laughing loudly at that particular memory, which cost us a bottle of good wine as an apology. Just like that, we are back to joking around and bantering like the old days.

He's looking at me with his startling blue eyes and I can barely meet his gaze. Why did he have to come here and unearth memories that I'm trying my very best to bury?

'We had some fun together, didn't we? I loved taking Jack for days out too. Remember that chimp at Chester Zoo that picked up a load of poo and hurled it at you? Jack still talks about that. He misses you, you know.'

'That's not fair,' I reply, trying to summon my inner strength. 'I still see him when I can, but as I'm not with you any more it's bound to be less frequent. I'll always cherish those times we spent together, but that was in the past. Too much water has gone under the bridge now. Things change. I'm trying to look ahead to the future.'

I'm also trying to stop tears from spilling over. Those memories of taking Jack out will remain with me forever. Harry and I never really discussed having children, which was something I was relieved about at the time. I wasn't sure I could cope with looking after a baby on my own, with Harry spending long hours building the business. But we had Jack to enjoy, and I miss him so much.

'I'm trying to look to the future too. I wasn't the best of husbands to you, was I? I'm not sure I ever did apologise for my behaviour.'

'You didn't.'

'Well, I'm apologising now. I'm sorry I hurt you, Maisie. I was vain and foolish. I think having quite a lot of money at the time went to my head. Pathetic, I know, but what can I say? I'm sorry. I really screwed up.'

'You certainly did. And talking of screwing, finding you with someone else in the storeroom of the shop… well, that was a real low point. You hurt me a lot.'

Harry has covered his face with his hands, then slowly looks up at me. 'I suppose I got what I deserved then, didn't I? Losing you and the shops. I just can't seem to meet anyone who can hold a candle to you.'

'I'm sure that in time you'll meet someone who's good for you.'

'Well, that's the thing. I don't want to meet anyone else. I want to try again with you.'

I can't believe my ears. Suddenly my newly relaxed state has evaporated, and I feel the beginnings of a headache. Why the hell did Harry have to come here? Why now, as I'm beginning to get close to Gianni? I must be strong and not view him through rose-tinted glasses.

'The thing is, I'm back in business,' Harry continues, with a huge grin on his face. 'I did a pop-up shop in town and I sold out of everything in half a day. I did the same the following week with a load of household items that I got from a warehouse. It was fire-damaged stock and I got pallets of goods for next to nothing. I've got a contact now so it's something I'm going to continue doing. People were literally falling over themselves for the bargains. It was like Black Friday on a Monday afternoon in July. Plus the market stall is still raking it in.'

'I'm glad things are going well for you, Harry, really I am. But I'm not sure I want to go back to that life.'

'But I've made a ton of money, Maisie. You can have anything you want. You don't even have to work if you don't want to, although I could use a bit of help on the market stall, if I'm honest. I'm going to rent one of those swish apartments at the Albert Dock, overlooking the river. Loads of premiership footballers have got places there. The view from those balconies in the evening is something else. And you're only five minutes away from all the nightlife.'

As Harry rambles on about all the things I could have back home, it's as if he has just lifted a veil from my eyes. I wonder whether he ever really knew me at all. I realise that he hasn't changed a bit. With a heavy heart, I wonder if he ever will.

'Harry,' I say gently. 'I don't desire any of those things. I'm not about fancy houses and expensive nights out.'

'But you liked the house in Crosby, didn't you?'

'I liked it because it was on the most beautiful tree-lined road and five minutes' walk from a park. I liked the original period features in the house, such as the cast-iron fireplaces and the high ceilings. I liked the little coffee shop on the corner of Moor Lane, where I would have a latte and a slice of cake with Emma. What I didn't like were the evenings I spent alone, while you were out gallivanting until the early hours of the morning.'

'But that was all in the past. I'm different now,' he says, shifting slightly in his seat.

I get an image in my mind of the lads' weekend in Barcelona that he has just returned from. Somehow, I find it difficult to imagine him strolling along, soaking up the works of Gaudí and the stunning history of the place. I don't suppose he's changed at all.

'I don't know what you want me to say.' I sigh. 'You turn up here, bringing up memories and expecting me to make a decision about my future just like that? It's not fair.'

'Will you at least think about it though? We could go on dates and stuff when we get home, if you don't want to rush things. We can start over. Don't you think we owe it to each other to give our marriage another try?'

I have an images of us moving in together: a riverside apartment; no more shoebox flat; no more working at Tesco… But then I have a reality check. I would be lonely, unhappy, because Harry would hardly be there. There is no starting over for us. *There is no us.*

I clear my throat. 'I'm sorry, Harry, but I don't think it will ever work between us. We're just too different. We don't want the same things in life and the sad thing is, you don't seem to be able to see it. If you really loved me you would consider my needs as well as your own. I think we need to press on with the divorce proceedings.' I collect the coffee mugs and take them inside to wash up, when there is a knock at the door.

It's Frederico. 'Hello, Maisie. Have you been able to give any more thought to the job offer?' he asks. 'My latest temporary worker has the brains of an oak wine vat.'

Harry has followed me into the kitchen.

I introduce Frederico to Harry, whose gaze flicks between us both. 'Oh, I get it,' Harry says, a slow smile spreading across his face. 'No wonder you don't want to come back to Liverpool. Not while you're sleeping with some smooth-talking Italian, hey?'

'Don't be so ridiculous!'

'This is not the case,' says Frederico. 'I came here to see if Maisie has made her mind up about working for me. I am sorry if I misunderstood, but I thought you were no longer together in any case.'

'Well, maybe I've come out here so see if I can't change her mind about that,' Harry replies, standing toe to toe with Frederico.

'Perhaps this is a bad time, Maisie,' Frederico says, moving to the front door. 'I'll ring you tomorrow. I may need to know your answer by then though.'

'Not a problem,' I say, ushering him out of the door, only to find Gianni standing on the other side. I think of the old joke about men being like buses and three turning up at once.

'What do *you* want then?' asks Harry, somewhat rudely, as Gianni steps inside. 'Maybe it's you who's the big attraction around here, unless you've come to offer her a job as well?'

I'm trying not to blush and give the game away, while wondering why I should even give a toss. Harry was the one who cheated after all. This could be a taste of his own medicine.

'I have come to see if you are alright,' Gianni says to me, completely ignoring Harry.

'Why the hell wouldn't she be? And what's it got to do with you anyway?'

I can see Gianni's jaw twitch. 'Maybe Maisie and I have become friends. I always show concern for my friends,' he replies, just managing to keep his tone even. He is taller than Harry and around ten years younger, so I wouldn't fancy Harry's chances if things got a bit nasty, which I'm hoping to goodness they won't.

'Maisie, can we get rid of this clown and finish our chat?'

'I don't think there's anything left to chat about, Harry. I think we've said all we need to say.'

Harry stares at me searchingly, before turning on his heels to leave. 'Well, I'll be waiting for you when you come to your senses and stop living in a dream world over here. Please think about what I've said. I'll be in touch,' he says, before stepping forward and kissing me lightly on the cheek. His smell is so familiar and reminds me of…

The front door closes and Gianni steps towards me. 'Are you alright?'

'I think so. Would you mind giving me a little space? I think I need some time to get my head around what's just happened.' My heart is whirling like crazy.

'Of course. I will see you when you are ready. You know where I am.'

As I mull over the conversation with Harry and all the things he was offering for the future, I wonder why he chose to come and see me now. Perhaps his latest relationship has floundered. Or maybe he really does miss me and thinks we can have a future together now that he's back on his feet financially. I felt a stab of something I can't explain when he walked away. Sadness maybe? Harry stirred up memories of happier times as we reminisced about our life in the old house but you can't stay together out of sentiment.

I pour myself a glass of wine and take it outside to the garden area, realising that because of all the drama, I have yet again missed an opportunity to ask Frederico about the wine in the wardrobe.

My watch tells me that it will be almost five o'clock in the UK so I imagine Cheryl's training day will be winding up soon. I do hope she's had a good day. I tap out a quick text to tell her I'll give her a ring later.

I finish my drink before heading over to the farmhouse to pay Viola for this week's accommodation, hoping she has a card machine.

'*Ciao*, Maisie, please come in,' she says, ushering me inside.

There's a pot of something simmering away on the top of the oven that smells wonderful – a delicious herby aroma hangs in the air.

'Would you like a drink?'

'No, thank you. I just came over to pay for my extended holiday.'

Viola frowns slightly, before telling me that it has 'already been taken care of'.

'Oh, please, I don't expect any favours, it's your livelihood,' I say, retrieving my bank card from my small shoulder bag.

'No, no, I mean the rent has already been paid for this week,' she says, smiling brightly.

'What do you mean? Who paid it?' *I can't have Dad paying out all this money*, I think.

'It was Gianni.'

'*Gianni?*' I say, hardly able to believe my ears.

'Yes. I think my son wanted it to be one less thing you would have to worry about as you recuperate. Don't worry about it. Gianni has plenty of money and no one to spend it on. Well, not until recently!' She winks, before lifting the lid from the saucepan, dipping a wooden spoon into the contents and tasting it.

'Mmm… maybe a little more salt and a touch of parsley. You can never have too much parsley in a fish soup.'

I'm overwhelmed with gratitude to Gianni for paying this week's rent, but I can't expect him to continue doing so. With sudden realisation I see that, like it or not, I will be forced to head home soon anyway. The wages for my job at the winery won't even my cover my rent here during high season. Perhaps Harry was right. I have been living in a dream world and maybe my dream of staying here is over.

Chapter Thirty-Two

I'm crossing the driveway, when my phone rings.

'Maisie! Hi! It's Cheryl. Are you OK to talk?'

'Of course. How did your training day go?'

'Brilliant. I totally nailed it. I start full-time from next Monday.'

'Fantastic! I knew you'd nail it. Well done you! I hope you're still going to give me mates' rates for a haircut though.'

'Yes, of course, although I may have to come to your place under the cover of dark. Don't want to be caught moonlighting.'

'Ha! Fair enough. Do you think your old clients will come to the salon now for their hairstyling?'

Cheryl exhales deeply. 'I'm not sure they will, you know. I don't think a lot of them will be able to afford the salon prices. Especially the older people. I have to think about my future career, though, and I know a few mobile stylists that I can recommend. I hope they'll all be OK with that.'

'I'm sure they'll understand. And, as you say, it's your career you need to focus on. Was Blake Smith in the salon today?'

'He popped in for a little while just after lunch, but I was mainly observed by the salon manager, Sam, who's really lovely. I've done all kinds today, which have really tested my skills, but Sam was more than satisfied. She was thrilled that I'd kept up-to-date with current trends, as being mobile means you can often be out of the loop. It seems subscribing to an online hair magazine and never being off YouTube has paid off! I'm out celebrating tonight, Maisie. It's just a shame you can't be here to join me. Anyway, enough about me, how are you feeling now?'

'I'm feeling good, thanks. Almost back to normal really, apart from the odd lapse of memory.'

'I'm so glad you're better. Have you decided how long you're staying for?'

I let out a long sigh. 'Not exactly. Frederico has offered me a job at the winery for the rest of the summer season. I would absolutely love to do it but I can't afford to stay on here.'

'Couldn't Gianni Salami help you out there? Doesn't he have a two-bedroomed place? Or maybe you wouldn't have any use for two rooms…' I can picture her raising her eyebrows.

'Well, actually, that may be a possibility. I just don't want to rush things. Oh… you'll never guess who turned up here today.'

'Go on.'

'Harry.'

'Harry your ex? Are you kidding? What did he want?'

'He wanted to know when I was going home. He started pulling at my heartstrings, talking about our old life together, especially at the old house. He knows how much I loved that place. He even tried to tell me that Jack was missing me.'

'That's a low blow.'

'I know. Anyway, he went on about how much money he'd made just recently and talked of renting an apartment on the Albert Dock. The upshot is he wants us to try again.'

Cheryl is quiet on the other end of the phone, which isn't the reaction I was expecting.

'Everything OK?'

'Yeah, I think I know why he might be sniffing around again though. Hairdressers hear everything, remember.'

'What do you mean?'

'Well, I was doing a customer's hair recently and we got chatting about holidays, as you do. I told her all about going on holiday to Tuscany and how you had won the holiday in a competition. She told me she'd heard about that from her friend, who, would you believe, was Harry's mum Gladys. She then went on to tell me how annoyed Gladys was with Harry moving back home after his recent break-up with a fitness instructor from the Body Beautiful gym in Seaforth. Apparently the girl kicked him out after discovering he was cheating.'

He probably cheated on that lads' holiday to Barcelona, I think to myself. I knew he hadn't changed. I was right to trust my instincts.

'Sorry, hope you're OK,' Cheryl says anxiously.

'I'm absolutely fine,' I reply honestly. I am fine, I realise – I'm more than fine. 'Thanks, Cheryl. Anyway, you enjoy your celebration this evening, my super-talented friend!'

'Thanks, I will. What are you up to this evening then?'

'Well, I was going to watch a movie this evening with Gianni, but I don't know if I'm in the mood now. I think I might just get on with the book I'm reading and have another early night. I am supposed to be taking things easy.'

'I know,' Cheryl says gently. 'But don't you be thinking about Harry. You'd have nothing but heartache if you got back with him. Do what makes *you* happy.'

She couldn't be more right, I think, as I hang up.

❦

After my phone conversation with Cheryl, I cross the courtyard towards the pool area and run into Gianni. 'Oh, Gianni, do you mind if I give this evening a miss? I'm exhausted. It must be all the drama of today.'

Gianni has a serious expression on his face. 'You mean I have to watch *Pretty Woman* on my own? It took me hours scouring the TV channels to find that.'

A slow smile across his face as I start apologising and saying maybe we could watch it another time.

'I'm teasing. Of course, I completely understand.'

His hair is slightly messy and his black T-shirt is now dusty from his work in the fields. He's smiling at me with his gorgeous, deep brown eyes and I'm thinking to myself that I must be crazy to turn down his offer. Yet, for once in my life, I want to be fully in control of my emotions. My heart has always ruled my head but look where that got me…

'You were prepared to watch a romantic comedy with me?' I ask, narrowing my eyes suspiciously.

'Of course. If it makes you happy it makes me happy.'

'But who said I like romantic comedies? If you must know, I prefer a good action film. I'd rather watch Jason Statham than Julia Roberts.'

'I wouldn't.'

'Ah, so that's why you wouldn't have minded watching *Pretty Woman*... to perv at Julia Roberts in the bath?'

'Actually, I find the piano scene far more seductive.'

We both laugh.

Gianni steps towards me and wraps me in a hug. Releasing me, he kisses me softly on the lips. 'Sorry about the dust,' he says, eyeing my white T-shirt, which is now the colour of cement. 'Go and rest. Tomorrow I actually have a day off work. If you are feeling up to it, would you like to accompany me to Siena?'

'That sounds wonderful. I'll very much look forward to that.'

'*Fantastico*. We will leave at nine thirty. You have a good evening. Tonight I suppose I'll have to make do with Julia Roberts.'

Chapter Thirty-Three

Clouds have rolled in overnight and for the first time since the beginning of my holiday, the sun is not shining. I barely slept last night, tossing and turning as I went over my conversation with Harry. I know in my heart that we are not meant to be together any more, but his presence here yesterday has shaken me.

I've given it a lot of thought and have decided that the best thing I can do, for my own sanity, is to stay on here for a while longer. I need to do something for me, Maisie, for once. I've also thought a lot about working in the winery. I've hardly got a healthy bank balance, so it seems like a perfect solution.

The first thing I do when I get out of bed is to give Frederico a call. When he picks up the phone, I say brightly, 'Good morning, Frederico. Would tomorrow be too soon for me to start work?'

'Maisie! Do you mean it? That would be perfect. My current workers saved me the trouble of firing them as they didn't show up for work this morning. They should have been here an hour ago.'

'Does that mean you're short-staffed today?'

'We can manage. There's enough of us here to do the tours, we're just a bit short at the bar. I'll have to pitch in there today. If you could arrive here tomorrow at around nine o'clock, I'll show you what's what.'

'Of course. I'll look forward to it. See you tomorrow,' I say, hanging up, feeling a thrill of excitement. *Me, possibly on the career path to becoming a wine merchant. Who would have thought it?*

I shower and dress, then eat my breakfast of toast, honey and fresh peach juice. Afterwards, I open the front door and stand outside it on the driveway. Even on a dull, cloudy day, the place looks picturesque. I can imagine that waking up to the views around the farmhouse every morning throughout the year must be a joy. As I stand there, I remember that Emma has her interview at the university this morning and make a mental note to ring her later on.

I'm about to walk back inside when the family next door appear. Josh runs excitedly across to their car, as his dad, Mike, locks the front door of their apartment.

'Good morning. Weather's changed a bit, hasn't it?' says Amy. 'We've found a little dinosaur museum up in the hills and we thought we'd head off there today. Josh is dinosaur mad.' They drive off in their silver hire car and little Josh waves to me through the back window as they disappear round the corner.

I turn round to the sound of my name being called, as Gianni strolls towards me across the gravel driveway. As usual he looks breathtakingly handsome, wearing dark-coloured jeans and a pale yellow shirt. 'You are keen! Are you ready to leave?' he says, jangling his car keys.

'I just stepped out to admire the view, actually, although, yes, I am almost ready. I can't believe how even on a grey morning this place still looks spectacular. I don't think I'd ever get tired of the views,' I say. 'Right, I'll just nip inside and get a jacket.'

'I wouldn't bother, the clouds will soon pass over. The sun will be out by lunchtime. I'll get the car and bring it round.'

'I think maybe I'll just get something light,' I say, heading inside and pulling a colourful cotton kimono from the wardrobe to go over my black vest and white trousers.

We begin our drive to Siena and I tell Gianni about starting work at the winery tomorrow. 'Assuming it's still OK to use your car, that is?'

'Of course. You can drive us home today, if you like. Familiarise yourself with it.'

'You mean you would like to have a couple of Moretti beers with your lunch?'

'Well, I hadn't thought about that, but if you insist,' Gianni says, grinning.

I'm watching his tanned arms on the steering wheel, admiring his easy, laid-back demeanour, and I can't deny how alluring I find him. I'm not sure Gianni even realises the effect he has on women. There is nothing vain about him, despite his obvious appeal. Once again I feel very lucky.

'You know, this is the first proper day off I have had in months. There is always something to be done around the farm so I usually just take a break for dinner in the village. Most recently with a beautiful woman.'

'Oh, really, should I be jealous?'

His face creases into a broad smile, crinkling his eyes at the corner. 'You make me smile. It would be hard for me to find anybody around here more beautiful than you. Maybe you just don't realise it.'

It's funny that I was just thinking exactly the same thing about him.

'Anyway, today I thought I would take a full day off without any distractions. Maybe my ex-girlfriend was right about me giving all of my attention to my work. I don't want to make the same mistake again.' He turns to glance at me and my stomach does a little flip.

Our journey passes quickly as we engage in comfortable chat, telling each other about our lives and our friends. Gianni has two good friends in the village, one being the guy he took the fishing trip with, following their mutual break-ups. He tells me they meet up some evenings for drinks.

I tell him about my close-knit friendship group at home. 'Before the break-up with Harry, I used to have a lot more friends, but they kind of fell by the wayside when I was low. I often turned down invitations from them when I was in a bad place and eventually they stopped asking me. I realised who my true friends were. I could count them on one hand.'

'Why run with a large herd if you know you can't keep up? Some people are happier with one or two reliable friends. Being true to yourself is what makes you happy,' Gianni says.

That one sentence says it all really, I think. *Being true to yourself is what makes you happy.* 'I know what you mean,' I tell him. 'And I'm lucky to have a couple of close friends who understand me.'

'You should go with your instinct. I believe the phrase is "go with the flow". As you say, real friends will understand your moods. As for everyone else, who cares what they think?'

'Wow. You make everything sound so simple.'

'That's because it is. People spend half their lives worrying about what other people think of them, when in truth those people are far too preoccupied with their own problems.'

'Have you ever thought about becoming a counsellor?'

'Never. I could not cope with people bemoaning the problems they create for themselves. For example I know a woman in the village who constantly complains about her lazy good-for-nothing son. I tell her to throw him out, he is twenty-eight years of age but she won't hear of it, preferring to be a martyr, fussing over him. As well as making excuses for his bad behaviour.'

'Maybe he would have nowhere to go?'

'Then he should find somewhere. Or treat his mother right. He's a grown man. Sometimes a man needs a shock in order to sort himself out.'

'Are you talking from experience?' I ask, half jokingly.

'Maybe,' he replies quietly.

'Your parents threw you out?'

'They did and it was the making of me. When I was young I wasn't such a nice person to know. I was vain and selfish. My father gave me a generous allowance for college and I spent most of the money on alcohol and girlfriends. I dropped out, came home and spent my days drinking in the village and doing nothing. In the end my father threw me out. It was probably the best decision he ever made. It was the making of me.'

'Thank goodness for that. I was beginning to think you were irritatingly perfect. Where did you go?'

'Travelling around Europe. In Italy at first, bartending, working as a courier for pizza places, that type of thing. Anything that earned money. I shared low-rent places with other guys, coasting along in life. My luck changed when I was working in a café at the Bay of Naples and caught the eye of a rich widow. I went to work for her on her yacht.'

'As what?' I ask, raising an eyebrow.

'Whatever she needed me for. Chauffeuring, mixing drinks for her friends, a general handyman, I suppose you might call it. She paid me well. Anyway, a year later I had travelled around Europe and made a fair amount of money. I had also grown up a lot. I returned home and vowed to help my father out. I became a pig farmer a couple of years later.'

'And you've never regretted coming back home?'

'Never. How long can you drift around? I always felt the pull of home even on the deck of a luxurious yacht in the moonlight. Maybe even more so then. My mother prepared a fattened calf to celebrate my return. Well, actually it was a pig, but you know what I mean.'

'I can understand why you could feel the pull of home,' I say, glancing around at the awe-inspiring surroundings.

Suddenly I have a vision of an orange sun setting over Crosby beach back home and I think of Dad. They say home is where the heart is. The trouble is, at this moment in time, my heart seems to belong in two places.

If I thought Florence was something, as we approach Siena the sight takes my breath away as tall, imposing medieval buildings zoom into view. Gianni parks the car and we head for the Piazza del Campo, the main square. A stunning Gothic building awaits us, which Gianni informs me is the town hall, and a tall tower that appears to have a white crown at its peak.

'That is the Torre del Mangia,' Gianni says. 'It was built in the fourteenth century, I believe. There are four hundred steps to the summit and the view of the city is quite spectacular. Fancy a little run up to the top?'

'Maybe I'll save that for another day,' I joke, thinking it a shame that such ancient buildings don't have lifts. I would have loved to have seen the view of the city from the top of the tower, but I don't think I'm up to climbing all those steps.

'Did you know the James Bond movie *Quantum of Solace* was filmed right here in Siena?' asks Gianni as we stroll along.

'Really? No, I didn't.'

'The film opens with Bond chasing a villain down these very streets and across the rooftops, having raced through medieval aqueducts in his Aston Martin.'

'Yes, I remember that.' I glance at the jumble of stone houses, some with lines of washing strung between them, and picture Daniel Craig scaling walls and racing across rooftops here. It's easy to see why both Siena and Florence have both been chosen as film locations.

The square is a shell-shaped space of pastel-coloured marble flanked by terracotta buildings. There's a uniqueness about this place that makes it utterly mesmerising. 'This square has such an unusual shape,' I say to Gianni. 'It's not the usual town square.'

'It was originally a marketplace and meeting point for three hillside communities in the twelfth century. It was built on the intersection of three roads,' he explains.

I picture a bustling marketplace, with chickens squawking in cages and villagers dressed in long robes shuffling over the worn cobbles. My eyes move on to a red-brick building with arch-shaped windows and high turrets, which looks like something straight out of a fairy tale.

I point to the building. 'Was that some sort of castle?'

'It was a palace. The Palazzo Pubblico. It was originally built for the heads of government. Would you believe it is the present-day town hall?'

'Wow, imagine working in one of these buildings. It would be so much nicer than working in some soulless office on a busy high street or on an industrial estate.'

'We'll go inside later, if you like. There are some amazing frescoes on the ceilings, as there are in many of the buildings around here. Shall we have a coffee first? Then you can decide what you would like to see next.'

'Perfect. I'd love a cappuccino.'

I'm staggered by the beauty of the buildings in Siena. It has an almost magical feel to it and the cobbled, medieval streets make me believe that round the next corner I could quite possibly come face to face with a knight on a white horse.

We find a tiny café with a doorway so low Gianni has to bend down as we enter. The café is painted yellow inside and I have to avert my eyes from a selection of tempting-looking cakes and pastries at the counter.

'I don't know how some Italian women stay so slim,' I say, glancing across at two slender women in floral dresses who are tucking into coffee-and-chocolate marble cake.

'Ah, but the secret is to have cake at breakfast time. That way you work the calories off throughout the day. A little of what you fancy does you good.' Gianni winks.

We order two cappuccinos and sit down at a small table, close to a window that looks out onto the square. When the coffee arrives it is deliciously hot and creamy, and we both sit in silence while we enjoy the drink.

'So, we can go inside the palace buildings now, if you like?' Gianni suggests, when we've finished. 'Or maybe you would like to take a walk down the cobbled side streets? You could almost lose yourself there. There are eleven streets that meet in the middle.'

'Sounds good. Maybe we could return to this square later as it's closer to where the car is parked,' I suggest.

'OK. And let me know when you feel tired. I don't want to wear you out.'

I have a flashback to the glorious night we spent together... He certainly tired me out then. It was so good to feel the warmth of his body next to mine and the intimacy between us was so spontaneous. I was feeling very happy, until Harry appeared, briefly throwing my emotions into turmoil as he resurrected old memories. But I've realised once and for all that he's just no good for me. Gianni, on the other hand...

'Are you looking forward to going to work tomorrow?' Gianni's voice breaks into my thoughts. 'Are you sure you are ready for it?' he asks, as we stroll along occasionally stopping to peer through shop windows.

'I feel fine. And my job at the winery will be mostly behind the bar anyway.'

We stop at an ancient building that sells gifts and jewellery and I look at the window display. Above the doorway is a black and white plaque, which seems to appear on all of the buildings.

'What's the story with the black and white?'

'It is a reminder of the days gone by and the history of the horses in the town.'

'Horses?'

'A memory of the races that took place here in the sixth century with the black and white horses. The very first settlers arrived here on horseback, and the horses are held in very high regard.'

'Thank you for bringing me here today, Gianni, I think it's exactly what I needed,' I say as we pause for a few minutes and sit on a bench facing a small fountain. A couple are eating sandwiches on the adjacent bench, a brown dog looking at them expectantly for scraps of food.

'I am glad to hear it. I thought it might do you good following that meeting with your husband yesterday. I take it you didn't know he was coming to see you?'

'Ex-husband. And no, I had absolutely no idea. I thought it was a bit strange really, although following a conversation I had with Cheryl last night, it all kind of makes sense.'

I tell Gianni all about Harry cheating on his girlfriend and once again finding himself living back at his mother's house.

'That must have been a difficult thing for you to hear.'

'No, not really, if I'm honest. There may have been a little sentiment on his part, though, because he could have just gone into town and met someone new rather than coming all the way to Italy. He's never had any trouble attracting female attention.'

'Do you still find him attractive?' Gianni looks into my eyes, as we stand up again and walk on.

'No, I don't feel that way about him any more. I just meant that he always had a certain charm around women.'

An overpowering smell of rosemary drifts towards me as we stroll past a market stall that's nestled in alongside several others down a narrow side street. Dozens of dried herbs are overflowing in baskets and an old lady in a shawl beckons me over to smell them. Bottles of olive oil, limoncello and violet soaps tied with string are also on display. I purchase some soap and a small muslin bag filled with fresh lavender, which the old lady assures me will aid restful sleep. Gianni has disappeared to an adjacent stall and is being handed a package wrapped in tissue paper when I catch up with him. He slips it into his pocket without saying a word.

'Would you like to take a short walk across to the Piazza del Duomo and take a look at the cathedral? It has the most beautiful Renaissance art inside. Maybe after that it will be time for a little lunch.'

'Sounds good to me.'

'Thank goodness for that. I took the liberty of booking us tickets for the cathedral online.'

'You cheeky thing!' I reply, feeling well and truly spoilt.

Stopping at a fairly busy road, as we head in the direction of the cathedral, I feel my body stiffen suddenly. As if sensing my anxiety, Gianni takes my hand and curls it tightly inside of his. We cross the road with a throng of people and he doesn't let go of my hand until we reach the other side.

'Are you alright?'

'Yes, I'm fine. Thank you for looking after me. For a split second there I was standing on the pavement in Florence before... well, before I ended up in hospital.'

'Don't worry,' he replies. 'You have me now.'

The narrow side streets leading towards the cathedral are crammed with shops and stalls selling religious artefacts and statues of the Virgin Mary. Gift shops and cafés with outdoor tables nestle side by side in the atmospheric ancient buildings. As we approach the Piazza del Duomo, the Gothic cathedral looms into view. The exterior stone has stripes of the familiar red and greenish-black marble, and grey stone columns.

Stepping inside, my eye is immediately drawn to the ornate mosaic floor of blues, greys and gold. The place is so beautiful I'm not sure where to look next, but soon find myself gazing upwards at the dome in the centre of the building, where the bronze lantern glints in the sunlight. Gianni tells me there are some works here by Renaissance masters Michelangelo and Donatello in the cathedral, so we set off in search of them.

As I walk beside him in this magnificent building, I think of Gianni's kindness following my accident and how he would make the trip to the hospital even though he knew I would be asleep when he arrived. The smile of delight on his face when he entered the ward carrying that huge teddy bear, and found that I had woken, was so genuine.

I'm admiring a stunning marble sculpture by Michelangelo, when I feel my phone vibrate in my pocket. It's a text from Emma.

Hi Maisie

Hope you're feeling ok. I think the job interview went well. Fingers crossed!!

Give us a ring when you get the chance

Emma x

There's a ladies' nearby so I ask Gianni to wait a minute, and nip inside to give Emma a quick ring.

'Sorry, Em, I forgot about the time difference I was thinking you would still be in there. So how did it go?'

'As I say, I think it went well. There were some really tough questions, but I think I answered them all OK. I was interviewed by a panel of three people so that wasn't intimidating at all! Two of them were very pleasant, but one was a right poker-faced sort who kept writing notes and barely made eye contact with me.'

'There's always one. Let me know how you did as soon as you find out.'

'Will do. Where are you by the way? Sounds a bit echoey.'

'In the toilets of Siena Cathedral, would you believe? I've come for a day out with Gianni. And you're right, it's absolutely beautiful here. Even the toilets are a work of art. Anyway, enough about me, how are you bearing up?'

'Ah, yes, I really loved Siena. And don't worry about me, I'm doing OK – better than I thought, actually.'

'Brilliant. Have a good day, Emma. Speak soon.'

'Will you miss your friends if you stay here for the rest of the summer?' Gianni asks, when I meet up with him again outside.

'A little, but you never feel too far away from friends these days with social media. I've got video calling on my phone so I can at least see their faces if I'm missing them too much.'

Gianni and I explore the rest of the cathedral, stopping to admire the richly adorned altars and stunning stained-glass windows. Angelic statues and scenes of the Stations of the Cross stare down at us from above. We find a bronze statue of St John the Baptist by Donatello and marvel at its beauty before we head for the exit.

Walking back into the square outside, I squint in the bright sunshine before quickly putting on my sunglasses. 'Ah, this is just gorgeous. The sun makes me feel so much better. I wonder if I even need my antidepressants any more.' *There aren't many of them left*, I think to myself. *I may need to see a local doctor.*

'Maybe you should arrange to see a doctor,' Gianni says, somehow reading my thoughts. 'Dr Tomaselli visits the village on Tuesdays and Thursdays in a small surgery next door to the bakery. No need for an appointment, just turn up.'

How much simpler things are here. It's virtually impossible to get a doctor's appointment quickly back home.

Gianni stops and pulls me towards him, planting a gentle kiss on my lips. 'Maybe being here with me is exactly what you need, Maisie.' There's a seriousness in his voice that thrills me.

We stroll a little further, before finding another small café for lunch. In the quiet garden at the back, under the shade of an umbrella, I choose a delicious, rich lasagne and Gianni orders spaghetti vongole, made with fresh clams. After we have eaten, I suddenly feel tired and stifle a yawn.

'Maybe that's enough walking for one day,' Gianni says, as we step outside into the blazing sunshine once more.

'I know, I mustn't forget I have to go to work tomorrow,' I say, feeling a mixture of excitement and nerves.

'Then perhaps an early night is in order. If we can manage it…'

Chapter Thirty-Four

Early the next morning I'm about to step into the shower when my phone rings.

It's Emma. 'Hi, Maisie. I won't keep you long. Just to let you know I've just had a phone call from the uni. I didn't get the job.'

'I'm so sorry to hear that, Emma. Gosh, they were quick to let you know. Will you still be able to afford the mortgage payments?'

'I think they probably had someone in mind for the job. And regarding the mortgage, as luck would have it, we've had a temp called Natalie in the school office this week who's been looking for a room to rent. She's going to rent one of my bedrooms, so that will keep me going for the near future at least.'

I suddenly wonder if Emma's offer of a room for me still stands, now that she's taken on a lodger.

'Anyway, just wanted to wish you good luck on your first day at the winery, Maisie. Who'd have thought it, aye? Working a summer season! I wish I could do that again.' Emma had a job at Camp America over one summer when she was nineteen; she had a ball.

We finish our chat with a promise to speak again soon. I shower quickly before getting dressed in a pink cotton blouse and black linen trousers. Gianni kept his word about not wearing me out last night. We dined on pizza and a couple of beers, before we snuggled together on the couch, sharing some passionate kisses but nothing more. Maybe my constant yawning was a bit of a passion killer.

I step into Gianni's car rather nervously, but soon settle into the journey, listening to the soothing tones of the satnav lady as I navigate the glorious, winding country lanes. I'm not sure that I could have done this without the reassurance of the virtual guide leading me to my destination. As I ease into the driveway of Variso Winery, Frederico is there to greet me. I can hardly believe my eyes when I see what he is wearing. He's dressed in a short-sleeved pink shirt and long black shorts, so that we appear, once again, to have matching outfits.

He lets out a laugh when I step out of the car. 'Maisie! Good morning! Excellent choice of outfit, I see.' He smiles as he glances at his watch. 'And I see that you are very punctual. I like that. Come inside and I will introduce you to everyone. We have five English tours today. You will serve them drinks at the bar, oh, and try to sell the wine as a souvenir of their trip. There will be restocking of shelves in between and keeping the general areas tidy. Does this sound OK?'

'Of course!' I reply, jittering with excitement.

I am shown inside and introduced to Nicole, a bubbly French girl, who greets me with a beaming smile, and Hera, an Italian girl, who acknowledges me with a vague air of disinterest.

'So, Maisie, are you here for the rest of the summer?' Nicole asks in her adorable French accent.

'Yes, hopefully. What about you?'

'For sure. I will go home mid October to start university in Lyon.'

We chat for a while longer, placing drinks mats along the polished oak bar, and soon a number of tourists begin to filter up the metal staircase into the room. The rest of the day passes in a blur. A young couple sample some wine first, the woman thoroughly enjoying it, but the bloke, who had clearly been dragged here, declaring, 'All red wine tastes like vinegar to me!' They don't purchase anything, despite me trying my very best.

Next up are a trio of middle-aged English women, who enjoy all the wine samples as well as the cheese and salami snacks. They each buy a bottle of a popular dry white wine called Trebbiano, as well as a dessert wine in a glass bottle shaped like Tuscany. I also manage to sell a vintage bottle of Sangiovese red wine that costs one hundred euros a bottle.

'Oh, go on, then. It's my dad's seventieth birthday next month. He loves a good red wine,' says a jovial blonde woman who's wearing enough gold jewellery to open her own shop. Hera gives me a surly sideways glance as I ring up a 180 euro sale on the till.

Before I know it, the day is over. 'Well, it's good to have your help, Maisie,' Nicole says, as we tidy the bar areas and get ready to finish up for the day. Hera just gives a half-smile as she collects her coat.

'Congratulations on the sales,' Frederico says, as he walks me across the car park. 'You did well on your first day. Maybe sales is your thing?'

'It must be my honest face,' I say, fluttering my eyelashes.

'Perhaps! Anyway, Maisie, have a good evening. Maybe tomorrow you can stay and have a little drink with me?' He grins, fixing me with those seductive green eyes.

'Maybe,' I say as I depart. 'But I'm not so sure I should mix business with pleasure,' I say over my shoulder as I head to my car.

Arriving at the farmhouse just after six thirty, I am greeted by the most glorious aroma wafting towards me from my apartment, and I wonder whether Viola has left me some food. Opening the kitchen door, I'm surprised to find Gianni wearing a striped apron and stirring a pot of something on the stove.

'Gianni, what are you doing here?' I ask in surprise.

'It's only a chicken casserole. I thought you might appreciate some home cooking after your first day at work.' He has a taste of the casserole from a wooden spoon.

'Too right I do.' My stomach gives a little growl as I realise that I have eaten just a few slices of salami and cheese, and that was a few hours ago.

Gianni guides me to a seat at the table, which is set for two with a bottle of red wine left open to breathe, before bringing the casserole over and spooning a good-sized portion onto my plate. He spoons the same amount onto a second plate and then sits down opposite me.

'Ooh, I could get used to this. Thank you.' I take a forkful of the chicken and vegetables as Gianni pours us each a glass of wine.

'This is to celebrate your first day at work and your return to good health. So… how was your first day?'

'I really enjoyed it. I even managed to flog some good vintage wine. It's made me think about learning another language, too. All the staff there are multilingual.'

'Nearly everyone speaks English,' Gianni says, with a shrug.

'Yes, but that's hardly the point. Maybe I'll start with listening to an Italian language CD on my way to work in the morning…' I stop talking to eat the melt-in-the-mouth chicken, which is steeped in a tangy and fragrant sauce. When the last traces have gone, I put down my knife and fork and sit back with a contented sigh. 'That casserole was utterly delicious, Gianni. Was it your mother's recipe?'

'All my own work. In fact I think it is better than my mother's, but I would never tell her that.'

'Ah, but I might!' I stand up from the table.

Gianni gets up and grabs a tea towel from a hook on the wall, flicking it in my direction. 'I dare you to say that again.'

'I said, I might tell your mother that you think you are a much better cook than she is.'

I turn my back as Gianni flicks the tea towel again, only this time it sounds like the crack of a whip as it lands squarely on my backside.

'Ow! That hurt.'

A laughing Gianni scoops me into his arms, kissing me on the forehead and apologising. 'I'm sorry, I didn't mean to be so heavy-handed. Here, let me rub it better…' He puts me down again and as he rubs my buttocks, his breath is hot against my neck. 'I'm thinking now that you are a working girl you will be needing an early night,' he says in a strangely hoarse voice.

'It's only just after seven o'clock.'

'So you should be asleep before midnight,' he breathes, nuzzling my ear.

'I need to get changed, I haven't even showered yet.'

Gianni silences me with a kiss on my mouth, before scooping me up again with his strong arms and carrying me into the bedroom.

Gianni is sleeping soundly just after ten thirty. As it's two hours behind in the UK I decide to give Cheryl a call. I pull on my robe and tiptoe out to the living room, shutting the bedroom door quietly behind me.

Cheryl is full of enthusiasm for her new job at Blake Smith's salon and tells me that two soap actors from *Hollyoaks* had been in today. It seems the thought of collecting more tips in a week than she could earn in a month as a mobile hairdresser has further ignited her passion for working in a salon. She asks me about my work at the winery and I tell her all about it and how Frederico was pleased with my sales.

'Lucky you. Eye candy when you go to work and the same when you get home, huh? Anyway, I was just wondering, are you definitely staying over there for the whole of the summer?'

'It looks that way, yes.'

'How long will that be?'

'Until the end of October, why?'

'That's what I thought. The thing is, I was just wondering, how do you fancy subletting your flat while you're away? Our Daisy's desperate to get out of our family madhouse. She's been looking for a cheap, one-bedroomed flat, but there's nothing going around here.'

It doesn't take me long to give Cheryl an answer. 'I think it's a brilliant idea. Dad offered to cover the rent on the flat while I'm away, but this is a better solution. Daisy can move in whenever she likes. You've got the spare key.'

As I settle back into bed, Gianni wraps his arms around me sleepily. A sense of contentment washes over me as another little problem seems to have resolved itself. Everything seems to be finally working out.

Chapter Thirty-Five

It's just after eight o'clock the next morning, when I spot Maria walking across the courtyard carrying a grey bucket filled with cleaning tools. She has a spring in her step, which may be something to do with her blossoming relationship with Marco, her new boyfriend.

'*Buongiorno*, Maisie. I hope you have a good day at work. You will have some new neighbours later today.' She smiles.

'Oh, that will be nice. You have a good day too.'

It's the middle of August now and a strong sun continues to beat down even at this time in the morning, casting a magical morning glow over the green landscape.

Business is booming today at the winery, with Frederico and his brother Angelo zipping in and out of the bar areas, checking everything is ready for the tours, before welcoming the customers who are disembarking from the coaches. The day passes in another blur, with me achieving more successful sales at the bar and more snotty glares from Hera. There was a brief moment of panic today when a six-year-old boy wandered off alone among the grape vines. I discovered him safe and sound, seemingly unperturbed, playing with the family dog.

Leaving work later in the day, I bump into Frederico, who asks me if I would like to join him in a glass of wine. I point to the car and remind him that I'm driving. The last thing I want to do is be on the wrong side of the law, especially as it's Gianni's car. Frederico eyes me curiously, with a lop-sided grin.

'Do you always do the right thing, Maisie?'

I consider his question carefully. 'Most of the time, yes, I suppose I do. Life is much less complicated that way, which is how I like it.'

'Well, at least come and have a coffee. I will show you the good wines that are locked away in a vault.'

My interest in the wines is piqued and I find myself following him down several steps at the rear of the property. We enter the cool, dark interior and he unlocks a heavy wooden door. There's a faint musty smell inside and a thin layer of dust is covering rows of bottles.

'This was a fine vintage,' says Frederico, pulling a bottle from a rack. 'A nineteen forty-six Chianti Classico. It's worth several hundred euros a bottle.'

I recognise the vintage at once.

'And this one is really special. A Variso Classic Reserve, aged for over sixty years. This is a rare vintage and would auction at around three thousand euros.'

I think I recognise that one too.

'Wow, I didn't realise wine could be so valuable. I certainly have a lot to learn.'

'That is not a lot of money to a wine collector. Rare wines can fetch tens of thousands. Even vintage champagne can be valuable. A woman recently had six bottles of vintage Krug languishing in her cellar from her wedding in nineteen fifty-six. Turns out it was an excellent year. They sold for almost sixteen thousand euros at auction. This is probably our most expensive vintage,' says Frederico, pulling a dust-covered bottle encased in a fine gold netting from a rack. 'A rare Sangiovese Merlot hybrid from nineteen seventy, which was an excellent year. It's worth in excess of ten thousand euros now. We had two of these, but one of our workers, who left in a hurry, stole three bottles of wine including one of these precious ones.'

There's no mistaking it. *I have the missing bottles back in the safe.* Well, two bottles of it anyway. With a sigh of relief I realise that we actually drank the least expensive one, worth just a few hundred euros, rather than thousands.

'Frederico, I think I may have something that belongs to you. Although I will not be able to return all that you had stolen.'

Frederico's mouth gapes open, and his green eyes glow, as I tell him about the wine sitting in the back of the safe at my apartment at the farmhouse.

'I'll bring it in to the winery tomorrow,' I say, thinking that I'd better handle it with kid gloves.

'You must have a reward, Maisie. We never thought we would see that wine again. I can hardly believe it.'

'I think the delicious lunch at that swanky restaurant was enough, thanks,' I say, recalling the eye-wateringly expensive menu.

'No, no, I insist. I will add a little bonus to your wages.' He kisses me on both cheeks. 'Thank you, Maisie. My father will be over the moon when he hears about this. He grew the grapes for these wines with his own hands as a young man. He was saddened at the thought of someone not appreciating its value. I can't wait to tell him the good news.'

We say our goodbyes, with Frederico still shaking his head in disbelief, and I'm soon winding my way along the dusty roads, marvelling at my increasing confidence. The sun is low in the sky and I grab my sunglasses from the seat beside me to stop the glare. *Who knew a commute to and from work could be so relaxing*, I think to myself, as I pass olive trees and sandstone farmhouses, with the ever-familiar cypress trees standing tall and proud in the background.

As my car scrunches into the gravel driveway of the farmhouse, I am surprised to see Gianni awaiting my arrival. He greets me with a kiss, which sends a thrill through me.

'Hi, Gianni, you haven't been cooking for me again, have you?'

'No, but I do have another surprise for you. But first you must put this on. No peeking.'

To my surprise he hands me a blindfold. I'm hoping this isn't some weird kind of *Fifty Shades* thing, although I suppose it's unlikely with his mother Viola gazing out of the kitchen window. He guides me slowly by the hand and a feeling of excited anticipation creeps over me. When we finally stop, I wonder what I am about to witness.

'OK, you can open your eyes now. Say hello to your new neighbours!'

My hand flies to my mouth as I take in the scene before me. Sitting on two chairs around the pool area are my dad and Harry's mum, Gladys. Jack is splashing about in the pool, playing with a beach ball.

'Auntie Maisie!' he squeals as he lifts himself out of the pool and races towards me, his sky-blue shorts dripping water on the pool tiles. He envelops me in a long, soggy hug.

'Jack, I can't believe it! Dad, Gladys, what are you all doing here?' I ask, glancing from one to another. I can barely take it all in.

Viola is standing by the table, which is set with cheeses, meats and her delicious home-made olive bread. She winks at me as I walk towards her. 'I hope you like your surprise.'

Gianni is casting a loving glance in my direction.

'Did you arrange all this, Gianni?'

'Guilty as charged,' he says, raising his hands. 'Your father told me at the hospital that next time he visited Italy, he would like it to be a proper holiday. I suggested he came over before the end of the summer. Bringing Jack along is giving his mother a break, too, I believe.'

Not for the first time, I feel a sudden rush of affection for Gianni as I think of the trouble he has taken to arrange everything. I'm so happy to see everyone. I'm so lucky.

We enjoy the delightful supper provided by Viola, feasting on tender herby chicken, tangy cheeses and soft olive bread. Gianni hands us each a shot of limoncello, including a fresh lemonade shot for Jack, and proposes a toast.

'To family and friends. And to always being true to yourself.' He casts a glance in my direction. '*Salute!*'

Gladys eventually drags Jack from the pool and takes him off to bed, as the sun is gently setting over the horizon, leaving Dad and me alone to talk. I resist the urge to overwhelm him with affectionate hugs, knowing that he would good-naturedly shrug them off.

Suddenly Dad clears his throat and looks me in the eye. 'Maisie, I've got something to tell you. I don't know why, but I feel a little nervous about it.'

My first thought is that he might be ill and I feel my heart sinking, scared to hear the worst.

'I've been doing a lot of thinking lately and the thing is' – he hesitates for a moment – 'I think it's time I sold up.'

'Sell up?' I don't understand what he's saying.

'The house. I think it's time for me to find something smaller.'

'You're selling the family home?' I'm almost too stunned to speak.

'Hardly a family home any more, without you and your mother,' he says, a sadness behind his eyes. 'It's a big house, love, far too big for me now. It takes a lot of looking after too. I think it's time I moved on. Anyway, I've been to view a cracking one-bedroomed apartment in Coronation Court. It's only up the road and it faces the park.'

'Yes, I know where it is.' The words come out of my mouth a little more sharply than I intend.

'Gladys has already got her name down for an apartment and put her house on the market. There's a new phase of one-bedroomed flats being built, but I'll have to act quickly if I want one. They'll be snapped up.'

'Gladys seems to have had quite an effect on you.' I hate how I feel a sudden surge of jealousy at the thought of her somehow replacing Mum in my dad's affections.

'She's a practical woman is Gladys. And she's a good friend. It's nice to have a decent friend. It can feel a bit lonely at times.'

I feel a pang of guilt as I think about how I have upped sticks for a summer in Tuscany.

'I understand that, Dad,' I say gently. 'And if this apartment is really what you want, then I'm happy for you.' I squeeze his hand and he smiles at me.

'The flats look really smart, Maisie. Brand new and with white goods included, although there's a separate laundry room too. There's a community lounge with a drinks machine and a library. I think I'd be happy there, love, although there's no doubt I'd miss my garden. I might put my name down for one of those allotments near the beach.'

'That's a good idea. I know how much you enjoy growing things. You'd probably miss that.'

'And just so you know,' says Dad, 'no one could ever replace your mother in my eyes.'

'Oh, I know that, and what you want does make sense. I want you to be happy.'

'There'll be quite a bit of money left after the house sale goes through and I want you to have it. I've already paid for the rental on this place until the season ends.'

'Oh, Dad... You've done *what?*'

'I don't want to hear another word about it. Gianni's parents gave me a really good price for a long-term let.'

Although I'm ever so slightly mad at Dad for wasting his money on me, a huge feeling of relief washes over me, knowing I can have the apartment for a while longer.

Despite all the excitement, sleep doesn't come easily to me tonight. As the moon bathes my bedroom here in Tuscany in a gentle glow, and I cuddle into Gianni, I find myself thinking about the house I grew up in and wishing it could have stayed in my family forever. I wonder who will have my bedroom? – I hope they'll appreciate the south-facing room and how it is often bathed in beautiful soft light early in the morning. I think of my dream catcher and the little flecks of dust caught in the shafts of sunlight. Whoever buys the house, I hope they'll love it. Perhaps it will be bought by a young couple who will rip out Dad's garden, making way for outdoor furniture and modern living…

I'm not going to think about that. Everything changes. Maybe it's time for me to go with the flow.

Chapter Thirty-Six

I have an afternoon shift at the winery today, so this morning I am heading into the village for an appointment with Dr Tomaselli. Entering the surgery, I find a small, grey-painted waiting room with a dozen or so dark wooden chairs. There are already four people waiting, two of them elderly, and a woman in her thirties with a young child. The child is coughing somewhat violently.

Before too long, a white-haired doctor with a weathered complexion appears from a side door and asks for the next patient. Two more people have since entered the surgery and all eyes seem to be on me, so it must be my turn. I follow the doctor back to his room.

'Good morning. How can I help you?' he asks, lacing his fingers together as he faces me across a small, pine-coloured table.

I tell him about my medication and how much better I have been feeling of late. Especially since I have been here in Tuscany. 'So the thing is,' I say. 'I wonder if I really need to be taking the antidepressants any more?'

The doctor chews the end of a pencil thoughtfully. 'Being on holiday, away from everything, can certainly lift the spirits. But I would not recommend you stop taking the anti- depressants yet. You have only been taking them for a couple of months. Barely time to feel their full benefit. I will give you a repeat prescription and I suggest you come back to see me in another month, when we will review the situation. If you feel strongly then that you would like to stop the pills, we will reduce the dosage. All in all, you seem to be doing very well.'

'I am,' I agree, unable to stifle a smile.

He writes a prescription from an old-fashioned pad, before ripping it off and handing it to me. Collecting my tablets from the village pharmacy, I just can't imagine the smiling pharmacist, in the clinical white coat, discussing my business with anyone else.

As I walk back up the hill to the farmhouse, I give Emma a quick call. I tell her about my surprise guests, but of course it turns out that both she and Cheryl knew all about Gianni's surprise. He had let them into his secret.

Emma tells me that having Natalie, from her school office, as a lodger has really lifted her spirits because 'she's an absolute hoot'. She's also had had a couple of e-mails from Alfredo and will be trying out his chicken casserole recipe for supper tomorrow night… 'I might pop over for a few days at the end of September, if I can get a flight,' she finishes.

'That would be just fantastic, Emma. I'd love to see you.'

�☙

There's a bit of a party atmosphere at Villa Marisa tonight. Viola and Gianni have pooled their culinary skills and laid on a fabulous barbecue. Fresh local fish, marinated in ginger and lime, is emanating delicious smells over the burning coals, and lamb and pork steaks lie infusing in garlic, parsley and rosemary. Bowls of salad, together with sautéed potatoes, fresh bread and homemade dips, are dotted around the table. Gianni has even made pork burgers specially for Jack.

'Well, this is lovely, isn't it?' says Gladys, tucking into some fish and sautéed potatoes. 'No wonder you want to stay here, Maisie. It's absolutely bloody gorgeous in Tuscany. I didn't think I was really one for the heat, but I think I might have changed my mind.' Gladys tells me what a fool her son Harry is, yet again, and concedes that he is no good for me. 'But I know someone who is,' she says, nodding in Gianni's direction. 'It's obvious he adores you.'

Dad's right about Gladys; she's a good sort, who sees straight to the heart of things. I think she'll be a really good friend for him. *Or more*, I think with a smile. Whatever the future holds, I will support them.

Watching Gianni laughing and playing football with Jack, and showing him some skills, I feel another, sudden rush of affection for him. I wonder, briefly, what kind of a father he would make, before shaking away the thought. *What's got into me?*

A successful evening comes to a close as Jack is yawning, yet refusing to admit he is tired.

'It's almost eleven o'clock,' says Gladys. 'Your mother would have a fit if she knew I was letting you stay up until this time.'

'He's on holiday,' Dad chuckles. 'Although I won't tell your mum if you don't, eh, Jack? Come on, lad, we'd better get you to bed.'

⚓

Eventually, everyone has made their way to bed, and soon it's just Gianni and me, sitting together in the moonlight.

'I still can't believe you arranged for Dad to come over. That was such a nice thing to do. I don't even know how to thank you, Gianni.' I lean over and stroke his cheek.

'I think maybe I would do anything for you, Maisie.' Gianni bends his head towards me and kisses me deeply. 'You have stolen my heart,' he says, breathlessly, when eventually he raises his head again. 'I may even be losing a little interest in the pigs.'

'You must never do that! It's your livelihood.'

'Perhaps I just need someone to help me with everything. When your summer job ends at the winery, you could, perhaps, stay on and help me here, Maisie? How would you feel about being a farmer's wife?'

The words hang heavily in the air between us.

'It's a figure of speech,' Gianni says hastily. Of course I mean a "farm worker"… whatever you prefer to call it,' he says, looking flustered. 'Unless of course you *would* like to be a farmer's wife…?' His eyes look beseechingly at me.

I place my finger shakily over his lips, my heart melting. 'Why don't we just see how thing turn out?' I say, almost calmly, although my stomach is doing happy little somersaults.

'Oh, here, I almost forgot. I have something for you.' Gianni hands me a tiny parcel, wrapped in lilac tissue paper. I open it to find a colourful, plaited-rope bracelet with a tiny dream catcher hanging from it. I think this must be the gift that he bought at the market in Siena, when I noticed him purchase something and then slip it into his pocket.

'Oh, Gianni. It's just beautiful,' I tell him. 'How thoughtful, how delightful. Thank you so much.'

'Well, I'm hoping you will have nothing but sweet dreams from now on. But it's there for emergencies.' He smiles, as he wraps his arms around my waist and pulls me close to him.

'So what were you saying about me being a farm worker? As a matter of fact, I would love to stay here after my summer job ends.'

'Do you mean it?'

'Yes, but I'd rather not make any plans. Just take things one day at a time.'

'You mean: let's make a plan to not have any plans? Let's go with the flow?'

'That's exactly what I mean. Sometimes things work out better that way. If it's meant to be, it will be. I'd be happy to give it a go, if you are?'

'That,' says Gianni before he kisses me passionately on the lips, 'sounds like a plan.'

Epilogue

'What about Alessio?'

'That's quite nice. Yes, I think I could go with that. And for a girl?'

'I think it has to be Isabella. As that's the only name we seem able to agree on.'

'Bella,' I say firmly.

'Izzy,' Gianni says.

'Or maybe we'll just stick with Isabella,' I reply with a smile, stroking my tiny baby bump.

I never imagined making my life here in Tuscany, although it seemed Fate had other ideas. I finished my summer job at the winery and stayed on here with Gianni, learning all about his work on the farm and giving him a helping hand here and there. Frederico's father gave me 1,000 euros as a reward for returning the vintage wines, which I've put into a trust fund for our new arrival. I've even had a go at making fresh pasta, which wasn't so successful in the beginning but it's pretty good now – if I say so myself. Well, I have had two years in which to practise...

Living here has done wonders for my well-being, too. Don't get me wrong, it isn't perfect and I had a little wobble last year when I was on medication for a short while, but on the whole it's an *almost* perfect life. I couldn't be happier.

Gianni was so thoughtful and kind during my last (thankfully brief) time of darkness. He would fill the house with fresh flowers, place fresh lavender underneath my pillow and give me soothing massages when I felt a little troubled. My love for him has grown so much over these last couple of years. I feel I can get through anything when he is by my side.

Dad's settled in to his retirement flat and regales me with stories of the comings and goings of Coronation Court. He's been over here for two more holidays with Gladys, and Jack came too. Emma and Cheryl have visited for long weekends and are planning a longer trip this summer. And Harry? I last heard he was dating an air stewardess he met on a flight home from another lads' weekend to Amsterdam. Good luck to him, I say.

Emma's getting on with her life without Joe and has a new job in a school where she's started dating a teacher called Alex. Things seem to be going well and she's hoping to bring him over in the May holidays so we can meet him. It seems there was never any likelihood of a romance with Alfredo over here but he made her think about what she wanted from a relationship. And she regularly cooks up the Tuscan chicken casserole he gave her the recipe for. She'll be able to meet our new arrival when she visits too. Cheryl's career continues to go from strength to strength and she's recently won a regional hairdressing competition. She's happy to be footloose and fancy-free at the moment, despite having no shortage of hopeful admirers.

Our baby, our happy surprise, is due in April, which is the month of Gianni's birthday.

'Perhaps we should call the baby April,' Gianni suggests out of the blue.

'April and May?' I giggle.

'I never thought of that,' he says with a laugh. 'Although no one ever calls you May, it's always Maisie.' He wraps his arms around me and pulls me towards him. 'You will make a wonderful mother.'

'Only because I have you,' I say, nuzzling into him. We enjoy such a simple life together in this beautiful place, and I realise that this was exactly what I needed to find. I feel so lucky. And to think it all began when I entered a competition and won a free holiday!

As for not making any plans? Well, that seems to have gone out of the window as we're getting married in the autumn, which has always been my favourite season. We're having the wedding here at the villa and Viola is already excitedly making plans.

I glance out across the green landscape and think how lucky our child will be, being raised in such beautiful surroundings with a doting aunt and grandparents to hand.

I'm looking forward to the changing colours of the landscape in the coming months and the sound of Gianni's tractor gathering the harvest. Autumn was Mum's favourite season too and I know she'll be watching over me on my wedding day – she'll be there with me, I'm certain of it. Life has taken a turn in a direction I could never have imagined but I know she would approve. This summer of love and limoncello might just have been my happiest summer ever!

A Letter from Sue Roberts

I want to say a huge thank you for choosing to read *You, Me and Italy*. If you did enjoy it, and want to keep up-to-date with all my latest releases, just sign up at the following link. Your email address will never be shared and you can unsubscribe at any time.

www.bookouture.com/sue-roberts

I hope you loved *You, Me and Italy* and if you did I would be very grateful if you could write a review. It's been such a joy revisiting the Tuscan landscape through this book and maybe I have even inspired you to visit the area! Who wouldn't love culture, Italian food and of course a shot or two of limoncello?

I'd love to hear what you think, and it makes such a difference helping new readers to discover one of my books for the first time.

I love hearing from my readers – you can get in touch on my Facebook page or through Twitter.

Thanks,
Sue

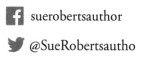

suerobertsauthor

@SueRobertsautho

Acknowledgements

With many thanks to…

As ever I would like to thank my publishers, Bookouture, and my editor, Christina Demosthenous, for her invaluable advice and guidance. A special mention and huge thanks to all the book bloggers and readers who have read and appraised the book.

To the design team for their glorious book cover and to Kim Nash and Noelle Holton for their tireless publicity and promotion.

A special mention goes to my wine-buyer friend Liz for her insight into the wonderful world of wine!

Thanks to my family, friends and colleagues for their constant support and encouragement. It means a lot.